WHISPERS IN
THE DARK

Also by Eleanor Taylor Bland

WHISPERS IN
THE DARK

ELEANOR TAYLOR BLAND

ST. MARTIN'S MINOTAUR........NEW YORK

www.minotaurbooks.com

ISBN 0-312-20379-9

First Edition: November 2001

10 9 8 7 6 5 4 3 2 1

In memory of the sister of my heart, Retta MaudeBland Gilliam,
my dear friend Elliott Dunn, Jim Harrington, artist;
Mary Robinson, who was always more than a librarian;
Hugh Holton, who was always there for us all;
Nora DeLoach, thank you for "Mama";
and Willaida Jernigan, super fan.
May flights of angels lead you on your way.

A C K N O W L E D G M E N T S

In appreciation for my continued good health, this book is dedicated to Dr. Jack Pickleman, MD, FACS, Professor of Surgery, Chief, Division of General Surgery, Dr. Claudine Siegert, Dr. James Bergin, and the surgical, physical therapy, and nursing staff at Loyola University Chicago Medical Center; Stritch School of Medicine, Maywood, Illinois. To Charles V. Holmberg, MD, Everett Kirch, MD, Nilish D. Mehta, MD, and Y. Mehta, MD, and the staff at Victory Memorial Hospital, Waukegan, Illinois; to Robert S. Baker, MD.

Special thanks to my family, for all you have given: Kevin, Todd, Melissa, Anthony, LaTaja, Todd Jr., and AntoNia; Sandra, Lela Jo, Cindy, Peggy, Doris, Brenda; Julia, Carl, Ora, Walter; and the family of my heart, Eunice, Althea, George; Louise, Georgina, Johnny; Janice and Alex; Dolores, Joanne, Jack; Fred. I will always remember.

To my agent, Ted Chichak, who is always there and always much more than a friend.
To my editor, Kelley Ragland, whose objectivity and belief in Marti I rely on.

To my friend Margaret Kaiser, one hundred years old.
To the members of my writer's group, the Red Herrings.
To Fred Hunter, David Walker, Michael Allan Dymmoch, Hugh Holton and Adele, Bill Spurgeon, Libby Heilman, Mary Harris, and Judy Duhl, Scotland Yard Bookstore.

Many thanks to special friends: Torrie Flink, Ann Zubre, Patricia Jones, Ann Howell, Charlotte Rush, Tracy Clark, Katie Rinehart, Anne Marie Stohl, Patricia Schaller, Sandra Branker, Bea Lombre, Cindy and Tom Hansen, and Barbara and Jake Wallace.

For technical assistance: W. Elliot Dunn, attorney-at-law; Jean Pederson, artist; Sharon Laughlin, art historian; Debbie Hoffman, Warren-Newport Township Library; Sandy Sherwood, Waukegan Public Library; Lucy Rahn, artist.

WHISPERS IN
THE DARK

SEPTEMBER 13

A fine rain was falling as Det. Marti MacAlister made her way through the tall grass to the wooded area where the arm had been found. It was cool for early September, and the rain, little more than a mist, felt cold. She shivered as she reached the shelter of a stand of red oaks. Ahead, she could see a small cluster of men, perhaps half a dozen, all but one in uniform. Plastic yellow tape banded around a cluster of tree trunks identified the crime scene, and she could see the bent figure of the pathologist squatting near the remains. A photographer was taking pictures. Marti had her camera, too. Behind her, wood snapped as her partner, Matthew "Vik" Jessenovik, caught up with her.

"It's just ahead," she said.

"Whoopee!" Vik had been catching up on his paperwork when the call came in. He was the only cop she knew who enjoyed filling out forms, and he had not been pleased with the interruption. Vik was four inches taller than her five-ten. He had lost a little weight recently while his wife was sick. His height and thinness, combined with a craggy face, prominent eyebrows, and a beak nose, skewed by a break, gave him what she called his vulture look.

As they approached the group of men, one of the uniforms came toward them.

"As far as we can tell, there's nothing else here," he said. "Just the arm."

"What, no head?" Vik asked.

"No, sir."

"Too bad. Is it the left hand?"

"No, sir."

"Jeez, struck out again. It won't match that hand without arm that we found last summer." He turned to Marti. "What the hell is this, the dumping ground for miscellaneous body parts? The winter before last we had all those female bits and pieces turning up. Now this. I know our missing parts inventory doesn't match up to what they've got in Cook County, but nobody has found any heads. What do they do with those, drop them off in Wisconsin, maybe, or Indiana?"

Marti wished she hadn't left her umbrella in the car. "Maybe they throw the heads in the lake." It was only a few miles away.

She assumed the man wearing jeans and a yellow rain poncho was the one who had found the arm. At least it was an adult. She hated it when kids found something like this. She looked around for the dog who'd unearthed it—that was the usual scenario—but didn't see one. The man looked a little younger than she was—late thirties maybe. A pair of binoculars hung suspended from his neck.

"What were you doing here?" she asked.

"I'm a birder," he said. "I was just having a look around. I kicked the log—wasn't watching where I was going—then I saw the two fingers and got on my cell phone."

"How often do you come here?"

"This is a first. I've been doing a lot of bird watching along the Des Plaines River, wanted to see what was in the local wooded areas away from the water."

"How long were you here before you found it?"

"Since just before daybreak. But not here." He cupped his hand over his eyes and looked around. "That way." He pointed north. "I started walking about a mile from here."

"Was there anyone else around?"

He shook his head. "Just me, a yellow warbler, and an in-

2

teresting variety of sparrows. I was looking for a gray catbird, but I haven't spotted one yet."

Marti was careful not to smile as Vik gave the man a look that suggested he thought he was at best a bit odd. She walked over to the yellow-ribboned barrier. The area was sheltered by wide tree branches. She could see that a log had been disturbed. The slender, feminine hand protruded from a pile of dry, brown leaves. A measuring tape traced its length to where it was severed just below the elbow. The rest of the arm was unexposed.

"Gordon, hold it a minute," the photographer said. "I've got to reload."

She recognized the doctor examining the arm. Gordon McIntosh was young and rotund, with short, red hair and a scattering of freckles. She liked him, but he wasn't Dr. Cyprian, their pathologist of choice. She took her camera out of the case. As she watched and snapped photos, Gordon uncovered the length of the arm.

"No dirt," he said. "It wasn't buried. Female. I can't see where any animals got at it. There is some insect activity, but nothing extensive. It hasn't been here long. And, most interestingly, it's been frozen. It's just thawing out."

"Frozen?" Marti asked.

"Frozen," Vik echoed.

Gordon agreed. "That is a bit odd, isn't it?"

Marti looked at Vik and shrugged. This was a new one on her. "Anything else?" she asked.

Gordon McIntosh turned and looked at her. "What more do you want, a name and address?" He grinned. "We have to leave something for you to detect, don't we?"

"Thanks, Gordon."

"You two tell me who this is, and I want to know by tomorrow morning."

"Sure thing," Vik said. "If you can come up with the head by then."

Marti stared at the hand. The fingers were curled in a beckoning gesture. It was probably just a death spasm. For a moment she wondered how the arm came to be here and why. She stopped short of asking herself what had happened to the owner of the arm, how and when she had died. Those were questions she might never be able to answer. She checked the number of remaining exposures and shot the rest of the roll of film. By the time the arm was removed and they walked back to the car, it was raining steadily.

Within an hour, the coroner, Janet Petrovski, called. "I've got a few more arms in the freezer, Marti. Gordon McIntosh is checking to see if any of them might have been severed with the same implement."

"Gordon tends to get a little overenthusiastic sometimes."

"I know, but I'm having the records pulled on the other dismemberments so you can go over them. It's worth checking out while we've got the time."

"I suppose," Marti said. The homicide rate in Lincoln Prairie had declined by 6.3 percent within the past year. Janet, along with Marti's boss, Lieutenant Dirkowitz, had been looking at unsolved cases. This would be the first time since she'd been on the force that she might have the time to take on something cold that did not impinge on a case that was current.

"Pull the paperwork, Janet, and send it over," she said. "I hope this one is different; the only one we've found that was frozen when we got to it."

"Scary, isn't it?" Janet agreed.

Marti knew they were both thinking "weirdo" and were both reluctant to say it aloud. "I don't know much about frozen body parts, Janet; but if Gordon thinks he's got something, we can look at it in the morning after the postmortem."

As soon as she hung up, Vik said, "Look at what?"

"A few more severed arms."

He leaned back in his chair. At least a minute ticked by before he spoke. "More arms?"

"In Janet's spare parts inventory."

"We have more arms."

"She's sending over the paperwork."

Vik got up and walked over to the window, coffee cup in hand. "Did she say how many arms?"

"A few."

"Were any of the others frozen before disposal?"

"I don't know."

"Well then, whether they have anything in common or not, I suppose the next question is, where are the bodies they go with?" He dumped the dregs of his coffee into the hanging planter and snapped off a couple of sprouts dangling from the spider plant. "Miscellaneous body parts. Damn! I joined the department to keep the peace, not the pieces."

When the reports arrived from Janet's office, Marti made a copy for Vik and settled in for some light afternoon reading, while he avoided looking at his copies by going through his in-basket again. Rain tapped in a steady patter against the window. It was cool enough for the air-conditioning to be off but too soon for the heat to be turned on. The room temperature was as close as it would come to being just right, which meant she did not need her jacket. Marti put her feet on her desk. There were three other arms with hands attached. She searched for references to freezing or thawing and found none.

"Well, it looks like the Coroner's Office was the first to freeze the others."

"Thank God. I think."

"Two female, one male," she said. The first was found in 1979. "Fingerprints but no match. Tattoo of a lily just above the juncture of thumb and index finger. Guess what they called her at the morgue?"

"If there's going to be a quiz, don't make it too difficult, MacAlister."

"Jane Doe Lily Day. The next arm was found just over a year later," she went on. "Another tattoo. A rose just above the wrist. And fingerprints but no match."

"So what did they name her?" Vik asked. "Rose Red?"

"It was a him, John Doe number seventeen. And since there were no prints on file, they either hadn't done anything illegal or hadn't got caught."

She read through the reports. "Both were under twenty-one. The next arm wasn't found until nineteen-ninety-four."

"Long time between number two and number three," Vik said.

"And the arm found in ninety-four was that of an older woman. It might not have anything to do with the other two. We're probably talking about three separate incidents. Maybe McIntosh will come up with something."

"It'll have to be something distinctive. Sears has a lot of sales on hatchets and hunting knives. And one arm does not a corpse make. Where are the rest of their bodies?"

"Maybe the cadaver dog they brought in will find something on today's arm."

The reports on the prior cases were scanty. The first two arms had been found in the fall. Miss 1994 had been found in the spring but had been dead for eight to nine months.

"Miss Nineteen-ninety-four was found off Route Forty-one." She checked one of the city maps that hung on the wall. "They couldn't find one person to question, and that whole area is industrialized."

"It wasn't like that in ninety-four," Vik said. "There wasn't anything there then but trees."

"So checking out the place now isn't likely to tell us much of anything. Maybe I can locate the developer. They take aerial shots. Maybe they kept the before photos."

"Why bother? This is a total waste of time."

"Maybe to us it is, but the dead have rights, too." It bothered her that these people were not only unidentified, but there wasn't even a missing persons report to check out. "Maybe we should talk with the lieutenant. The case is cold. This is going to be time-consuming. Some of it goes back twenty years."

Vik agreed. "Good idea. If we're lucky, he'll agree that this is a complete waste of time."

The lieutenant's office was in another wing of the building. He had a window facing east and a limited view of the lake. Today the blues were in layers, the sky sort of slate, the water a clear blue farther out but murky and almost gray near the shore. Although restricted, it was a view Marti could get used to. Dirkowitz had been a linebacker with the University of Southern Illinois Salukis. In his mid-thirties, he still wore his blonde hair close-cropped, and he still stayed in shape.

Vik explained what they had so far.

Dirkowitz leaned back, steepled his hands, and touched his fingertips to his chin as he listened. "I didn't realize we had so many unidentified body parts," he said, when Vik stopped talking. "And this most recent part was frozen before it was disposed of, which means we're not going to be able to determine time of death."

"That's it exactly, sir," Vik said. There was a hint of optimism in his voice.

"If we don't find additional parts, something that allows us to make an identification, we just say the hell with it."

"Oh no," Vik said, "nothing like that. It's just that it's damned near impossible to figure out who one hand, or arm, belongs to."

The lieutenant nodded. He picked up an apple-shaped grenade that he kept on his desk. Marti knew it wasn't a souvenir of the Vietnam War but a reminder of his brother who had died there.

"Is this a significant part of our backlog?"

"No, not at all," Vik said. "Right now we've got eight cases that have been open for quite a while."

"All with bodies."

"Yes."

Marti suppressed a smile. Vik was trying to remain neutral, but she knew he would rather take on any of the open cases with bodies than a cold one that involved an arm with hand.

"What do you think, MacAlister?" the lieutenant asked.

"I think the odds of resolving a case with more to go on are greater than finding out anything when we only have a body part."

Vik looked at her and raised his eyebrows just a tad. She could tell he had expected her to champion the cause of the missing parts.

The lieutenant weighed the grenade. "So, Jessenovik, you would rather take on a case with more substance."

Vik hesitated. "There is something about the arm, sir," he admitted.

It was Marti's turn to be surprised.

"But," he went on, "I really think it would be futile, and we need to go with a case where it's more likely that we'll get some results."

"MacAlister."

"I can't argue with that, sir. But Vik is right. The arm is definitely a challenge."

Dirkowitz held the grenade by the stem. "Well, it seems to me that since there isn't any fun associated with this job, we should at least allow ourselves a challenge every now and then. Give this arm with hand a week, unless something immediate comes up. Consider it a semivacation. You've earned it. If you don't get anywhere in a week's time, come see me."

He dropped the grenade on his desk, adding another dent to scarred wood, a signal that the meeting was over.

By the time Marti tracked down the developer, it was after five and nobody answered the phone. She left a message on voice mail.

"Three right arms, one left," Vik said. From the tone of his voice, his attitude hadn't changed; but he was scanning his copies of the coroner's reports. "All found in wooded areas, but not forest preserves. Lily Day and John Doe weren't found anywhere near each other, but Miss Nineteen-ninety-four was found in the same general area as Lily Day. Arm number four wasn't found anywhere near where the others were. Dumb." He shook his head. "Real dumb. Stupid perps, that's the problem, Marti. If whoever did it had the brains to wrap up the pieces and throw them in a Dumpster, they'd be in a landfill somewhere and we wouldn't have to bother with any of this. I don't know where people's heads are anymore."

"Especially not these four," Marti replied. He did have a point. The rest of the remains had been disposed of without anyone finding them. "Maybe someone wanted the arms to be found."

"Oh, come on, MacAlister. What do you think we've got here? A ritual killer? A mass murderer? Every time we get a case that's the least bit unusual, you come up with the big city cop ideas. All we've got is four arms found over at least twenty years. Whoever offed Lily Day is probably dead by now."

"But this one was frozen first, Vik. If, for example, the victim died during the summer, when it was hot, it would have decomposed quickly. Maybe the killer didn't want that. Maybe whoever did it wanted us to find it."

"Something like that would take a real nutcase. How often do we have a killer around here who is also an exhibitionist?"

"What other explanation is there?"

"Who knows? People do strange things for strange reasons. What do you want to bet we've got someone here who thinks he's Einstein and figured that freezing the arm first was clever."

Marti decided not to argue the point. Odds were that Vik was right. "If they can pin down when number four was left there, we might be able to locate a few people to question."

"Don't hold your breath." He did a Groucho Marx imitation with his eyebrows. "We could have this all wrong, MacAlister. It's probably one of those executive types. Look at how cold-blooded they are, the way they send hundreds of people home without jobs and call it downsizing."

"Long day, huh, Jessenovik?" As she labeled file folders for the reports, she thought of the curved, pasty white fingers that seemed to call to her from their bed of leaves. "I've never worked a case like this before."

"Nobody works a case like this. You wait and see if enough parts show up to make an identification and take it from there."

"Maybe," Marti said. She wasn't looking forward to bedtime. Those fingers would probably show up tonight in some distorted dream.

She stopped at the fire station after she left the precinct. One of the minuses of being married to a fireman/paramedic was the constant schedule conflicts. Ben worked a forty-eight-hour shift and was off for seventy-two hours. When she was on a case, she didn't work a shift. Her schedule was dependent upon the stage of an investigation. The ambulance bay was empty. Ben was out on a call. Disappointed, she went home.

When she got there, the alarm system was off and the house was quiet—too quiet. Bigfoot padded over and nudged her hand. He was a mongrel the size of a Saint Bernard; and from the day they'd brought him home from the pound, her ten-year-old son Theo's dog.

"Where's Theo?" she asked.

Bigfoot wagged his tail and gave her an expectant look.

"I don't know. That's why I'm asking you."

She checked the message board. Nothing. There weren't any telephone messages either. According to the calendar thumbtacked to the kitchen door, Joanna, her fifteen-year-old daughter, was at the "Y" exercising and her closest friend, Lisa, was with her. Ben was on duty. Momma, Theo, and Ben's ten-year-old, Mike, should be at home. She sniffed. Bay leaf and garlic. A cabbage had been halved on a cutting board, and the oven was on and occupied by a roast, slow baking. Momma wouldn't go anywhere and leave food cooking. She took two deep breaths. There was a logical reason for this. Nothing was wrong. The boys were next door at Patrick and Peter's house, and Momma . . . no. They would have left a message on the board.

She stood still, listening. There was a low hum from the refrigerator, nothing else. Her gut feeling was that the house was empty, but why? Gun drawn, she went to the basement and began a methodical search. By the time she reached the family room on the second level, her heart was beating so fast she could feel it pumping in her chest. Her mouth was dry and she could smell her own sweat. The light from the windows seemed bright and harsh. She smelled something citrus, and looked for the source. An orange, peeled and half-eaten. A soft, irregular whir and tick stopped her. The clock, just the wall clock. It ran on a battery.

She inhaled deeply and exhaled fast. Nothing. At least not in here. There was just the usual clutter. A jigsaw puzzle still incomplete, Joanna's tennis shoes, Momma's crocheting. Nothing unusual. Nothing out of place. If they had forgotten to leave a note on the message board . . . no, they wouldn't.

Her beeper went off just as she headed for the third level. She ran to the phone in the hallway. Momma answered on the first ring.

"Marti, everything is fine."

Just hearing Momma say that made her stomach lurch. "What is it? Where are you?"

"Mike hurt his arm. We're at the emergency room. This is the first chance I've had to call."

Marti's hand shook as she turned off the oven and left a note on the message board for Joanna. She took a deep breath and headed for the car.

Marti glanced about the waiting room. Not only was it crowded, but at least three young children were crying. When she didn't see Momma, she flashed her badge and went through the double doors to the treatment area. She found them in the third room. Mike was on a gurney. Momma was standing beside him. Theo was huddled in a chair.

"Mike! Are you okay?" She rushed over to him.

"My arm," he said. Tears spilled on splotches of dirt and ran down his cheeks.

"They think it's broken," Momma said. Her voice sounded matter-of-fact except for one slight tremor. "We're waiting for X rays."

"We were playing mud baseball," Theo said in a small voice.

"And all I did was slide into third," Mike said.

Marti found a box of Kleenex and dabbed at his face. She touched his soft, kinky hair and kissed him on the forehead. "You'll be okay. You'll be just fine." Thank God it was just a broken bone. She wanted to take him in her arms and hug him real tight but didn't dare risk hurting him. She kissed him again.

Momma fussed with his pillow. Her face, in profile, had the strong, generous features that had been passed on to Marti then Joanna. Large, almond-shaped eyes, full lips. "You'd think that with all of that mud . . ."

Mike was wearing a hospital gown, but Momma was right; mud was drying on Mike's arms and Theo needed to stand under a hose. She wanted to take Theo home to get cleaned up, but there would be no separating the boys until they knew Mike was all right.

Metal scraped against metal as an orderly pulled back the curtain. "Ready to go for a ride, Mike?"

Theo sat huddled in his chair as they wheeled Mike out. His bronze face was all angles, widow's peak, cleft chin, just like his father's, and like Johnny who had seldom smiled, his expression was solemn.

"Are you okay?" Marti asked. Theo had a tendency to blame himself when bad things happened.

"We were just playing ball."

She hugged him. He seemed so fragile as he trembled in her arms. "Scary, isn't it, when you can do something as ordinary as that and someone gets hurt."

"I know."

"You okay?"

Theo nodded. "Mike didn't pass out or bleed or throw up or anything. It just hurt when he tried to move his arm."

She called Ben while Mike was in X ray.

"Holmgren Park? I saw the call on dispatch, but it wasn't for us. I started to call home." He sounded calmer than she felt, but he kept clearing his throat. "Mike's never been to the emergency room. I bet he's scared."

"A little. But he's doing okay."

"How's Theo?"

"Shaky, but okay."

"I'll be there as soon as I get someone to come in and cover for me."

Mike was in the cast room when Ben got there. Ben checked on him, sent Momma and Theo to the cafeteria, then sat in the small examining room with Marti.

"Theo doesn't think this was his fault, does he?" Ben asked.

"It doesn't sound that way. Not yet, anyway."

He squeezed her hand. "Scary, isn't it?"

She thought of coming home to that silent house and shuddered.

Ben was a large man, lean and muscular, but big. His hands, his touch, were always gentle, as if he was aware of his size and his strength. He put his arm around her. "You okay?"

She nodded. Unlike her first husband, Johnny, Ben didn't expect her always to be strong. "The house was so . . . quiet . . . I . . . um . . . I could tell nobody was there, but what if . . . I checked anyway. God, I was scared."

He squeezed her shoulder. "Bad enough when you don't have our mental checklist of possibilities."

"And the graphics, like instant replays, in your mind. Funny isn't it, one minute everything is okay, the next, bingo."

It would stay with her for days, for weeks maybe, that feeling when she walked into that empty house. This was how it had been for their children; except for them, it had been as bad as it gets. Permanently bad, forever. Mike had had a

13

mother one minute, the next there was a car accident and he didn't. Johnny was here one minute; then he was gone, killed in the line of duty.

"They really do handle things well, don't they?" she asked.

"I think they've survived a lot more intact than we would have if we were children when it happened."

She worried a lot—because Theo was so quiet, because Joanna needed to feel in control, because Mike still tended to overeat. Tonight, she just felt grateful.

"Do you have to go back to work?"

"No. I thought you might need me. I'm covered until morning."

Marti leaned against him, felt his arms around her, and was glad once again that she was no longer alone.

When they got home, Joanna was watching from the upstairs window. She did not come down. As soon as Mike was settled in the den, Marti went up to her. Joanna was still standing by the window, hugging herself as if she was cold. When Marti got close, she could see that Joanna had been crying. Although she knew Joanna was close to Mike, he was still her stepbrother, just as Ben was still her stepfather. She hadn't expected Joanna to be this upset.

"Everything's all right now," she said. As she explained what had happened, Joanna began trembling.

"Cold?" she asked, rubbing Joanna's bare arms. Joanna's teeth began to chatter.

Marti hadn't seen her this upset since Johnny died, but that had been four years ago.

"Come on, I'm getting you into bed."

Joanna let her lead her upstairs, where she stepped over a pile of sweats and slumped down on her bed. Marti disentangled the comforter from the jumble of sheets and blankets, and Joanna, still hugging herself and shivering, curled up beneath it.

"What is it?" Marti asked. She tossed several pairs of socks

14

into an empty clothes hamper and sat beside her.

Joanna shook her head.

"I'm sorry no one was here when you got home." Marti stroked Joanna's soft, auburn hair. When that didn't sooth her, she lay down beside her and gathered Joanna into her arms.

"It could have been you," Joanna whispered.

Marti didn't have an answer for that.

"What would we do if something happened to you?"

She didn't know, and she couldn't even think of a good lie. All anyone had was right now. She couldn't tell Joanna that; it would sound too scary. Instead, she held her until the trembling stopped. Then she went down to the kitchen and made them each a cup of tea.

2

Sharon ducked her head as rain pelted her face. Her rain scarf would keep her hair dry; an umbrella would only attract attention. The West Side of Chicago was no place to be at this time of night. The street was dark and deserted except for a pack of dogs about half a block ahead of her. She paced herself to avoid catching up with them and tried to avoid the puddles where the sidewalk sloped. She kept to the middle, away from the street, where a passing car might stop and its occupants attempt to accost her, away from the doorways and dirt and gravel paths, where rats lurked, human and animal. It was hard to believe that this was the street where she'd grown up. It had been a poor neighborhood then, but at least the sidewalks had been swept clean and the garbage cans kept covered and potholes and rats kept at bay by an alderman whom everyone knew. In those days they knew the cops, too. It had been safe here then.

A car turned the corner and she moved closer to the nearest building. It wasn't a drive-by; the headlights were on. The driver didn't look her way as he passed. She leaned against the wet brick until rain began trickling down her neck and under her collar. Rayveena didn't have to live here anymore. When she'd become eligible for senior housing, she'd refused to admit to her age. Now that she was eligible for hospice care, she wouldn't admit she was that sick. What had *she* done in some previous incarnation that was punishable by being born to that woman?

When Sharon reached the small house with the old asbestos-filled, pinkish gray shingles wedged between two brick apartment buildings, she hesitated. If it wasn't raining, she would have walked away. The rain made her grab the iron railing, which swayed away from her grip. The rain made her ascend the chipped concrete steps. The rain made her push the bell to warn Rayveena that someone was there before she pushed open the door that hung unbalanced from one hinge. The lock didn't work anymore. She wasn't sure why the bell did.

She had run up and down these stairs so many times she didn't need a light to find her way. Good thing it wasn't working either. The door to the second-floor apartment was ajar; the light inside was dim. Rayveena must be having a bad day. She didn't want anyone to get a good look at her. Sharon remembered when the lights were bright and men came and there was dancing and laughter and cheap wine. Honky-tonk singers would belt out the blues from a scratchy seventy-eight, describing her mother, "Put on your red dress, Momma" or, "Got me a high-yellow woman" or, "Got a woman like an angel, every night she spreads her wings."

Rayveena's hair was long then, straightened with a hot comb, black with dye and glossy with Bergamot. It hung down her back almost to her waist. She would toss her head and it would fan out, then settle long and straight again. Whenever Rayveena's laughter, deep and just a little husky, greeted her while she was still in the hall, she would know that there was a man there and turn and go back outside.

There was no music tonight, no laughter, just the sweet smell of marijuana as she went inside. Rayveena had the back of her chair to the door. There was a wispy layer of smoke above the chair that implied she was sitting there looking out the window. The couch was gone. Must have gotten infested with mice, or maybe the arm that was broken had finally fallen off. She could replace it, but Rayveena just sold off anything that was worth a few dollars. It wasn't like her to hold onto anything for any length of time unless it wasn't worth much to begin with. She could find something at a secondhand store maybe or the Salvation Army.

Sharon gripped the doorknob, unwilling to go into the room. Rayveena had had a neighbor call, so she wanted her for something. She didn't want to know what it was this time, didn't want to see this woman ever again.

"That you, girl?" Rayveena asked. Her voice was thready and so soft that Sharon strained to hear her even though she didn't want to hear anything Rayveena said. There was a green oxygen tank beside the chair that hadn't been there a few months ago.

"Yes, ma'am."

"No need for you to stay. I just need a couple of dollars."

This wasn't about a couple of dollars. Rayveena could have had the neighbor tell her to wire that to the currency exchange. She looked at the bureau that had been pushed into the living room. How many bottles of medication were there? Twenty? Thirty? She didn't know. She didn't think Rayveena could keep track of it well enough to take them as prescribed, but she didn't want to know that either. AIDS. The twentieth-century black plague. For all the times she had wished Rayveena dead, she had assumed it would be quick, a withdrawal-induced seizure, or her heart, not this slow leeching away.

"I can't get up from here tonight, girl." Rayveena coughed, a soft, phlegm-filled rumble that became gasping spasms. "Might need to go into the hospital for a few days." She stopped talking, took a few harshly drawn breaths, then said, "Need a little something to tide me over. Something for transportation back home."

"Should I call an ambulance?"

"No, girl. I ain't going nowhere tonight. Tomorrow be soon enough."

For a moment Sharon felt her throat constrict, felt a tightness in her chest. Was Rayveena dying? Should she get help?

"Maybe you should go tonight. Let me get an ambulance for you."

One bony hand rested on the arm of the chair. Even in this dim light Sharon could see the dry, flaking skin and a scaly rash from wrist to elbow. She remembered that arm smooth and tan and wrapped around some man's neck. Her hands shook as she reached under her raincoat for her purse.

"Just leave it on the dresser, girl."

She should walk over to the chair, hand it to her. Instead, she did as she was told.

"Good-bye, Rayveena. Have them call me when you go to the hospital."

"No need for you to see me there, girl."

Rayveena had not had that woman call so she could hand deliver some money. Hands clenched at her sides, Sharon walked to the chair. She had seen Rayveena toward the end of July, but what she saw now was much worse. She wasn't wearing her turban tonight. Her hair was short and completely white and had fallen out in patches so that there were places where she was bald. Every bone in her face could be seen beneath thin, translucent skin. The marijuana joint had been snuffed out, and she was breathing oxygen through tubing attached to her nose. There was a shunt in her arm that she kept in her lap. Repulsed, Sharon stepped back behind the chair where she couldn't see Rayveena's face.

"Are you sure you shouldn't be in the hospital now?"

"Not tonight." Short patches of white hair moved as Rayveena shook her head. "Be plenty time enough for me to go there."

"You can go to a hospice."

"No. There's no place for me there. I belong here."

"Where you can get that damned marijuana," Sharon said. "You can't even give up that shit now, can you?"

"You just leave that money, girl, and take your narrow ass on out of here."

"Yes, ma'am."

She turned away. *Never should have come here,* she thought as she ran down the stairs. *Never should have come here. Should have just sent the damned money.* She ran out the front door, slipped on the second step from the bottom, and landed on her butt in a puddle at the foot of the steps.

"Goddammit!" she shouted. "Goddammit!" She looked up. The light in the second-floor window went out. DeVonte was right. She needed to get away for a while. As she got to her feet, two men who were standing across the street began to walk toward her. "Oh, shit." Key in hand, she ran to her car. Behind her, she could hear the men laughing.

3

The rain cleared up the following day, but it was still overcast and cool as Marti and Vik walked to the Coroner's Office for the postmortem on the "arm with hand," as Vik liked to call it. It sounded like the title of a still life. Despite the dry weather in July, extreme heat in August, and today's fall-like weather, petunias and impatiens were thriving in the concrete pots on the sidewalk alongside the county building. Traffic was brisk on the one-way street, and all of the diagonal parking spaces nearest the courthouse were filled.

"Too bad we're not working on a real case," Vik said, "one we had some chance of solving."

"Maybe we'll get lucky. Fingerprints that match some that we've got on file." She had dreamed of hands last night. Ghostly white hands with elongated fingers tapering to white vapor as they beckoned to her. Mike's hand, extending from the cast, his brown skin mud-flecked and one finger pointing. And another hand that she didn't identify until after she had awakened and realized that the long, tan fingers with gaudy glass-stone rings and bright red fingernails were Rayveena's, her best friend Sharon's mother. Rayveena had been sick for some time, cancer, according to Sharon, and Marti wondered if the dream meant that she had died. When she called this morning, so early that she woke Sharon up, Sharon had said no, that Rayveena was in remission and doing just fine. Now, as Marti looked at the flowers again, they looked funereal. Her mood was as bleak as the sky. She was still upset about Mike, about not being there when it happened. No, she was upset because it could have been worse, because there were too many things in life that just happened, things she could not prevent.

The postmortem medical examination was brief and uneventful until there was a loud pop.

"Just the epiphial junction," Gordon McIntosh said. "This one was under twenty—the bone was still growing."

Gordon could not determine when the appendage had been severed. It was still partially frozen. There were no identifying characteristics. He had lifted prints the night before. They were not on file.

Afterward, they met in Gordon's office. It was the kind of room that made Marti uneasy. Everything in its place. Magazines stacked on a table, skull aligned next to the lamp, coasters for errant coffee cups near the edge of his desk. Marti thought about taking one and placing it under her coffee cup, but did not. She wasn't convinced that being this neat was good for one's physical or mental well-being. She placed the cup on Gordon's desk and watched for a reaction, glad when he didn't hand her a coaster or even seem to notice.

"Where is Cyprian?" Vik asked.

"He's still on vacation." Gordon gave them a good-natured grin. "You're stuck with me. At least for the next week and a half anyway. And if you're not happy about that, tough. I am. I've waited a long time to work with you two, and this is a great beginning."

Vik gave the cup he was holding a skeptical look. "You make this?"

"No. Secretary."

Vik tasted it. "Could be worse. Look, kid, I hate to tell you this, but this is one of those dead-end cases that will probably never be solved. There's nothing open locally right now that could match up; and if she's not from around here, it could be damned near impossible to get an ID unless other body parts show up. And face it, if they haven't started turning up by now, what are the odds? If we can't make an identification, we're sure not going to find out how she died or why." .

"Oh, but that's only the half of it," Gordon said.

"And the rest?" Vik asked.

"What she can tell us."

Vik took another sip of his coffee. "You've been watching those *Quincy* reruns on cable television, haven't you?" His wiry salt-and-pepper eyebrows almost met in a frown. "I hate to sound pessimistic, Gordon, but this is the real world. So far, she's told us damned little, and I don't think she's going to tell us anything more."

"I'm running more tests, Jessenovik, taking tissue samples from all of the arms with hands, making comparisons. Who knows. Everything they did with the first two was just perfunctory. I took another look at the reports. Victim A, nineteen-seventy-nine—one fleck of blue paint the size of a pinhead under the fingernail. Victim B, nineteen-eighty— traces of metallic silver on two of the fingers."

"And?" Marti asked.

"The paint is cerulean blue and acrylic, something that could be used by an artist. And the silver is used to develop black-and-white negatives. I think these two were artists."

Vik's scowl deepened. "Let me get this right, McIntosh. You think that a *fleck* of paint and *traces* of silver on two fingers connect the two victims."

Gordon grinned. "Maybe not, but it's not a bad piece of detective work, is it?"

Vik slammed down his cup. Coffee sloshed over the rim. Marti waited, but Gordon didn't wipe it up. Maybe he was just neat and not compulsive.

Marti took a cautious sip from her cup. It was almost as strong as precinct brew. "What's so special about this metallic silver?" she asked.

"It's sort of a by-product when you develop film. You begin

with silver salt, add a few chemicals, end up with metallic silver."

"Could you end up with that if you did something else, used other chemicals?"

"I'd have to research that."

"So," Vik said, "you're telling us that because you found those two things, we should assume we've got a couple of artists on our hands. All you have to base it on is a fleck and a speck."

"Well, I can't think of any other explanation for sky blue acrylic paint."

"That must be used for more than one thing."

"Perhaps, but the tests on the paint fleck don't indicate anything else."

Vik raised his cup as if he wanted to throw it. "Just how much can a speck of paint tell us, McIntosh?"

"Well, we know it wasn't affixed to anything, such as wood, and also that it was a compound used for painting, as in fine arts, the kind that comes in tubes, that you squeeze onto a palette."

Vik leaned back, temporarily appeased. Marti agreed. At least they had something definitive on the paint fleck. The metallic silver connection was still tentative at best. Before they left, they went through the photographs that had been taken at each scene of crime. There wasn't anything there to link the four arms other than being found in the woods. Marti gave Gordon's office a final look around before she left but could not find one trace of dust on the bookshelves or any dust bunnies under the chairs. Maybe someone that meticulous could come up with something, even though he hadn't given them much so far. It was early on.

It was beginning to look like the sun might put in an appearance when they went outside. As they walked to the precinct, Vik said, "Just what we need around here, an amateur telling us how to do our job. And we've got a week and a half to put up with him."

"Gordon's got you hooked too, hasn't he?"

Vik grunted and shoved his hands in his pockets.

Did they have the remains of an artist and a photographer? Arms with hands. A still life. Maybe that was a good metaphor.

Sharon sat behind the wheel of her car and watched as children boarded the buses that would take them home. She hated teaching. She had loved it once but not anymore. Working with middle-school children used to be a challenge. When did that change? She had taught language arts until most of the sixth-grade requirements became seventh-grade requirements. She had minored in biology, and now she was teaching science, sort of. The textbook assigned to her sixth- and seventh-grade classes was little more than a survey. Today, a student who had just transferred in from another district had asked a question that wasn't covered in the text. She had felt that old excitement of teaching someone who wanted to learn; and then, while she answered his question, one of her other students got bored and started a fight. She didn't know what she was doing wrong. No, she did know. She was teaching to the middle, the 70 percent who *might* learn. Those at either end of the spectrum, who were either slow and disruptive or smart and bored, weren't being reached at all. Worse, she was teaching to the tests that were now mandated by the state—not just subject matter, but formats—so that her students wouldn't be confused by the way the test questions were asked. It had become more important that they score well than that they learn the material. Somewhere, in all of this, she had become what she hated most, a bad teacher.

DeVonte was offering her a way out. He wanted to marry her. If she said yes, he would take care of her and she wouldn't have to work anymore. She wouldn't have to hate getting up in the morning or dread walking into the classroom. She could go back to school if she wanted to, learn other skills, become a CPA maybe, and find a niche in a corporation where they would give her a cubicle and a computer and she could deal with numbers all day and not have to bother with people at all. DeVonte had a condo in the Bahamas and he was going to relocate to California in the next year or two. She would be able to leave this place, leave these memories, leave . . . she wanted to get away from here; no, she *had* to get away. Away from everything. Away from Rayveena. She had to.

When Marti got back to the office, there was a message from the company that had developed the land where the third arm with hand had been found. There were no aerial photos in their files, but they would check with the architectural firm. Marti passed that on to Vik then checked the coffeepot. Morning coffee by Cowboy was in serious jeopardy, at least temporarily. Slim and Cowboy had pulled off a major raid where not just prostitution but drugs were involved. They would be testifying before the grand jury for at least the rest of the week.

Today Marti and Vik were in luck. There was almost a full pot. "Maybe we should get one of those big pots, Vik, one that holds thirty cups." Assuming that Cowboy did make it in before court, twelve cups once a day were not going to be enough.

"Meeting," she said, as soon as Vik had stirred in cream and sugar. "How much of a commitment are we going to make to finding out what happened to these arms with hands? Either we make a serious effort to solve at least the most recent case, if not all four, or we do a cursory investigation and file it."

Vik leaned back in his chair and put his coffee close enough to his nose to inhale the aroma while he was waiting for it to cool. "Are there any statistics on how many of these missing parts cases get solved without any additional parts turning up? Any stats on their identities being determined through missing persons reports?"

"How would I know?"

"Just asking." He took another deep breath and exhaled slowly. "Damn!"

She wanted some kind of verbal commitment before they got started. This was not one of their typical cases. No matter how much Vik wanted to identify the victims and the perps, if it required more than a minimal amount of patience, he was going to gripe and complain and get testy.

Vik put down his cup. "It bothers me," he said. "Some SOB out there has gotten away with murder—unless we find him. Not having enough evidence just doesn't seem like a good enough reason not to try."

"No," she agreed, "so we go for it."

"We go for it," Vik said. He seemed more resigned than eager.

"Then what we need is a plan."

"A plan?"

"Vik, this isn't your typical case. We have no ID, no witnesses, no motive, no cause of death, no weapon, nothing."

"I'd settle for a head."

"Well, Jessenovik, we don't have that either. So why would someone kill somebody, dispose of the body, but leave the arm where someone could find it?"

"Which arm?"

Marti slapped the top of her desk with the flat of her hand. "Jessenovik, get serious."

"A message," he said. "It's some kind of message. Are we assuming that all four arms with hands are connected?"

"I don't think we can, but we do have to keep that possibility in mind." She took out a legal pad and began making notes. "So, a message. What? And why?"

They tossed that around for a few minutes without coming up with anything.

"Well then," Marti said, "what about motive?"

"Are we assuming the first two victims had something to do with art?"

"I don't know." They either had two clues, or the paint fleck and traces of silver were coincidental. She tried to avoid dealing with coincidences without ruling them out. "I think we have to go with what we've got."

"Damned little."

"And the whole art thing might be a dead end. If nothing else, we eliminate the artist/art angle. Agreed?"

"Agreed."

They talked awhile longer, but neither of them knew enough about art, artists, or any local artistic activity to come up with anything else.

Marti put in a call to Nan Conser, who did volunteer work at the Lincoln Prairie Historic Society, and arranged to meet with her in an hour.

"Thin," Vik said, when she hung up. "Technically, we've got nothing."

"Thin," Marti repeated. She was not optimistic about solving any of this either, but at least they agreed that they had to try.

Lincoln Prairie's Historic Society was located in a large Victorian that had been renovated recently. Furnished with antiques, it was like entering a home at the turn of the century. Most of the artifacts were displayed as if someone still lived there, with only a small card that dated and explained them. Nan was on the second floor in a room used for storage. She was sitting on the hardwood floor, clad in jeans and a loose-fitting silk shirt with the sleeves rolled up to her elbows, wearing white gloves. There was a box beside her filled with yellowing letters tied with faded blue ribbons. Her dark hair, flecked with gray, was short and curly. She brushed at it as she looked up.

"Hi, Marti. How's it going?"

Marti sat in a chair with a cane back and seat. She was leery of sitting in anything that seemed old and fragile, but the bamboo frame looked sturdy enough to support her weight. After they spent a few minutes catching up, Marti said, "I need to get some information that might help identify a couple of still lifes that we've got lying around at the morgue."

Nan laughed. "Do I want to know what you mean by that?"

"Not really."

Nan put down the letter she had been reading, returning it to the untied bundle of envelopes that was on the floor. "Has it got anything to do with the body parts that were found in the woods yesterday?" She pulled off the cotton gloves.

"It's in the *News-Times* already?" Marti hadn't had a chance to read yesterday's or today's newspapers.

"Today's early edition. So does this have something to do with that?"

Marti was loath to give out any information, however trivial. As the first sergeant she had worked under years ago had warned her, "It's your job to gather information, determine the facts, and not to tell anything to anybody but me and your partner. On my shift, you will keep your mouth shut." The fact that the sergeant was telling her that because she was a female officer and therefore, in his opinion, genetically disposed to gossiping didn't cancel the validity of what he was saying. Instead of answering Nan's question, she asked, "Have we got any artists around here?"

"Sure, lots of them."

"Did we have any back in nineteen-seventy-nine?"

"Of course."

"Is there anyone around now who was around then who knows anything about local art?"

"Lucy Carlisle," Nan said.

"Oh?"

"Lucy is one of our local blue bloods. She's a well-known artist in this neck of the woods, and she's lived here all her life. She studied abroad for a while, so I'm not sure where she was in nineteen-seventy-nine, but she's one of those people who dabbles in everything from watercolors to oils. If nothing else, she can give you a crash course just by showing you her own work. Lucy's mother was an artist, too. Unfortunately, Lucy didn't inherit her talent, but she's competent—and knowledgeable."

Marti took out her notebook and jotted down the name

and address. Assuming that Lily Day and John Doe #17 had something to do with painting and photography, she needed to get a feel for the time when they died as well as some notion of how they could have lived here or even passed through without someone noticing. That would seem to indicate that they had lived someplace else and were dumped here. How would she ever find out? She fought back an almost overwhelming sense of frustration.

"Nan, what else can you tell me about local artists in the late seventies, early eighties?"

"In general, the Lincoln Prairie Arts Guild has been in existence for close to seventy years. I can find the membership lists that cover the period of time you're interested in if you need them. I'm not sure what you want to know, but if you want to tell me just a little bit more about these body parts . . ."

Marti smiled, but said nothing.

"Well then, the members of the guild, at that time in particular, were an insular, elite group. My mother, Lord rest her soul, was a wonderful artist, but we lived too close to the ravines and not close enough to the bluffs to be considered for membership. We were also what was known as 'shanty,' or poor Irish. There were several minority artists who were invited to exhibit at their annual show, but they were never invited to become members."

"Who, for instance?"

"Jimmy Binslow for one, although he's a photographer. Borderline, but he's also a Potawatomi Indian and added to the local color. They're going to have a permanent exhibit of some of his work at the Lake County Museum."

"Does he develop his own film?"

"He has to be getting up in years, and I don't think he does much photography now, but I'm sure he had his own dark room."

"And except for this annual exhibit, he was excluded."

"Yes."

Exclusion. That was an interesting angle, one that she had not considered.

"Then there's Carrie Pinkham, another minority. Sort of our local Grandma Moses."

Marti took down that information also. "What exactly did the guild do?"

"About the same things they do now: promote the arts, bring in artists to lecture and teach, exhibit local artists, and have fund-raisers, of course. Arlene Johns was the president during the time you're referring to. She's a potter now, not as good in other media, although I'm sure she thinks so."

Nan didn't know Arlene Johns's address, but she did know which strip mall her pottery studio was in.

"Now come on, Marti, don't be mysterious. Did your comment about still lifes have anything to do with what was found in the woods yesterday? When was it, last winter or the winter before, when they kept finding bits and pieces of that poor woman who was killed and dismembered somewhere west of here?"

"You missed your vocation, Nan. You should have been a cop."

"I am, an art cop. I find, identify, rescue, and restore things of lasting value. Now would you mind telling me why you're asking so many questions about what happened at least thirty years ago if you're working on something that was discovered yesterday. The News-Sun did not say skeletal remains."

"Nan, what do you know about metallic silver?"

Nan shook her head. "Mirrors, maybe? I think that's what's on the back. Or it may be a by-product of some kind of metal processing."

"Who can I talk to about art supplies?"

"Go to that hobby and art supply store on Grant Street. It's family owned. I think the old man is in Florida now, but his sons still run the place."

"Thanks, Nan, this is really a big help."

"How about a quick cup of tea," Nan asked, as Marti

reached for her purse. "No more questions, I promise. Especially since I'm not getting any answers."

"Sounds good." She was glad she came. She felt a bit less foolish about her only clues and a little less hopeless about getting somewhere. And she decided to invite Vik along to talk with Lucy Carlisle. A crash course in fine arts might be a good idea for both of them.

Lucy Carlisle lived on an east-west street on the far northeast side of town, Sunnydale Avenue, that was zoned for commercial as well as residential use. Although the block where Carlisle lived was still residential, all four corners at the intersection of Sunnydale and Clark, as well as other areas along Clark, were rapidly being developed commercially. Carlisle's was the first house from the intersection. The building on her corner housed a real estate agency and provided offices for an attorney and an insurance agent.

Carlisle's single-level ranch had been expanded vertically with a dormer and sat back from the street. A border of sedum and hostia grew on either side of a winding path that led to the front door. Crimson burning bushes created a tall hedge along the side of the house facing Clark Street, extending as far as a wooden shed right at the rear corner of the lot. The hedge buffered the property from most of the street noises. A triangle of black locust trees secured the opposite side of the lot. Birdhouses sat atop poles scattered about the lot. Marti took a second look at them and recognized a church, school, general store, and post office, along with little cottages with rose trellises painted on them. It was a village for birds. And occupied. Sparrows poked their heads out of the doors and windows and flew in and out. By the time she reached the heavy oak door with the brass knocker, she could almost pretend this was real country living.

Behind her, Vik said, "This is going to be an odd visit if we don't have an explanation for why we're here."

"We want her to tell us a little about art."

"But why? If we run across one of the perps while we're interviewing these people, or if the focus of our investigation gets back to them, we're going to tip them off. If that happens, and there is any evidence anywhere, it's going to disappear fast."

Marti considered that. Although she made it a point not to divulge information about a case, in this instance it might be the only way to get to the killer, or killers. "If a perp does find out, it doesn't have to be such a bad idea. Whoever did this has to be complacent by now. We might be able to flush them out."

"Or have our evidence and our case flushed down the toilet."

"I don't think we have much choice."

As Marti reached for the bell, Vik said, "I hope Lucy doesn't remember me. She was ahead of me in high school. Everything was hushed up when her mother committed suicide, but my father was a cop, so I knew. Not that I ever said anything. But it was just before Lucy graduated, and she didn't even show up to get her diploma. After that she pretty much kept to herself. Every so often there's something in the *News-Times* about Lucy showing her work, or her mother's; but aside from that, I think she's still hiding."

A short, plump woman who looked to be in her mid-fifties opened the door. She was wearing a smock smeared with dried paint splotches. Light brown hair with just a few gray strands hung just below her ears in a neat, simple cut. Makeup had been lightly applied. When they identified themselves, Ms. Carlisle looked up at them and said, "Why, come right in. I can't remember the last time a police officer has come to my door."

Marti exchanged a look with Vik, and he gave her the slightest nod. If they had found a lonely lady in search of someone to talk with, this could be a long afternoon.

The door opened directly into the living room. A cat with fluffy white fur sat at one side of a fireplace. Another cat, sleek

33

gray except for a smidgen of white on its front paws, sat in matching elegance on the other side. The white cat's ear twitched. The gray cat did not move.

For a moment Marti felt like she was entering a museum but one filled with light and color. Red-, blue-, and maroon-braided rugs were scattered on the hardwood floor. Brightly painted Indian pottery was carefully placed on the mantel above the fireplace. Maple shelving on one wall held a collection of papier-mâché animals that looked like miniature piñatas. Masks were arranged on another wall. There was a carousel horse in one corner, and a dollhouse about three feet high in another.

"Do sit down," Lucy Carlisle invited. "I was just about to have tea. Let me fix some for you, too."

Vik frowned and shook his head. He had vowed never to eat or drink anything with strangers after accepting tea from a woman who turned out to be a white witch. Marti accepted and noted the carnival glass vases on the tables with fresh-cut flowers.

Tea was served by the Mad Hatter himself or at least in a teapot shaped like his face. Scenes from *Alice* were in raised relief on each of the cups. After Lucy Carlisle had passed the cream and sugar, she looked at Marti expectantly.

"I'm afraid our reason for being here is somewhat vague," Marti told her. "We think a young woman might have traveled through Lincoln Prairie in the late seventies who worked with or was somehow involved with acrylic paints. We also think a young man might have been passing through who was a photographer or worked with someone who was."

"My, my," Ms. Carlisle said, "that is vague. The arts have always thrived in Lake County, although not a lot of people took notice, especially not back then. I wasn't recognized until the late eighties."

"What did you do?" Vik asked.

"I'm working in pastels now. I have worked in acrylics and

also with tempera. I tried oils recently, but I really don't like them."

"How long have you been . . ."

"Painting. I paint. If you'll come upstairs, I'll show you."

Canvases lined the walls leading to the second floor.

"Are these yours?" Marti asked.

"Most of them are my mother's. A few are by other local artists." She didn't point out which were which. Upstairs was one big room with a sloping ceiling. There were shelves of art supplies, a refrigerator, bookcases with books and magazines stacked helter-skelter, and an easel by a wide, curtainless window with a northern exposure. From the looks of what was on the canvas, Ms. Carlisle was beginning to work on a landscape.

Carlisle walked over to four abstracts that hung box-shaped on one wall. "This was my acrylic period." The paintings seemed moody and weighted to Marti. Grays and blacks and browns with flashes of white, green, and yellow.

"Then I tried portraits for a while." The people were a totally different experience. The canvases had to be at least a foot and a half by three feet. A bullfighter with a bull so alive that it was almost like freezing a frame from a movie. And Marti almost touched the nude, a kneeling woman with her arms outstretched and her face up, eyes closed. Since Marti's artistic ability began and ended with stick figures, she was impressed. She turned to look at Vik and could see that he was impressed, too. She didn't expect him to admit it.

Ms. Carlisle gave a short laugh. "That didn't last long. Portraits were in vogue then, but they weren't something I particularly enjoyed. So I began experimenting with sound."

By that she had to mean the next group of six paintings, which were nine by twelve. Marti wasn't sure what they were: one in pastels—mauve, teal, and lavender—was all short, curved brushstrokes; another had long, flat, black, green, and purple lines, some thick, some thin, with spikes at varying intervals. It made Marti think of an EKG reading. One almost jumped off the wall: circles, squares, and triangles, superimposed over one another and all in primary colors.

"I'm working on local landscapes now. Back to oils, but I don't like them that well."

So far, there were three.

"The ravines," Vik said, "and the bluffs along Lake Michigan. And this is that barn off of Route Forty-three."

"Oh, those are my mother's," Lucy Carlisle said. Marti thought she caught a hint of disparagement in her voice. Could mother and daughter still be competing, at least in Ms. Carlisle's mind?

Marti liked the senior Carlisle's landscapes the best. They were different from the other work, with thick layers of oil paint. She took a step closer and realized that the composition, along with how thin or how thick the paint was applied, gave the scenes depth and dimension. She liked being able to recognize something that was familiar. She glanced at the easel. The landscape this Carlisle was working on seemed flat and lifeless. That must change as the picture was completed.

"I'm afraid I can't answer your questions. In fact, I'm not even sure what the question is. There could have been any number of people working with acrylics. As for photography, no one comes to mind. I think they did more of that on the coasts than here. At least I never heard much about it."

Marti wondered why she didn't mention Jimmy Binslow but didn't ask. Another thought came to mind. She remembered the seventies as a time of cults and alternative lifestyles and people protesting the war and dropping out of society. "Was there any kind of artists' colony here back then?"

"In the late seventies? No, not in Lincoln Prairie. There were those of us who painted, but we were a very loosely connected group of people. This is an isolated vocation. You can take lessons, but that only helps you master the craft. Art is what you do with it."

"These are all excellent," Marti said. "Have you ever been exhibited?"

"Oh, certainly. Not at the major galleries or in the city, but locally, and at the Lake County Museum and all of the colleges and junior colleges in the area."

"Do you teach?"

"No, I'm afraid teaching is for those who cannot paint."

"Have you ever done a still life?"

"No, I prefer to use subjects that are . . . alive—in some way."

"Do you sell your work?" Marti asked.

"Oh, heavens no. It's mine."

Marti wanted to ask what her source of income was, but that was a personal question and this woman wasn't a suspect. Instead, she thanked Ms. Carlisle for taking the time to talk with them.

"We might be back," she said. "There's so much we don't know. I hope that's all right."

Lucy Carlisle assured them that another visit would be welcome.

"I don't think she remembered me," Vik said, as they retraced their steps down the walkway. "She comes from a wealthy family. Her father worked in Chicago, but I don't have a clue as to what he did. And she's still a Carlisle, so she must not have married. From the looks of this place, though, they didn't leave her much money."

"It's a nice place," Marti said.

"Small," Vik said, "and not in a part of town where you would expect her to live, somewhere closer to the lake. According to the *News-Times,* a deal is in the works to take the corner realty place down and put up a chain store with a pharmacy. Lucy Carlisle might not be living here much longer if the state wants her land. That corner lot isn't big enough if they're going to put in a drive-through window for the pharmacy like they want to."

"Maybe she won't sell."

"Oh, right. This street has dual zoning, commercial and residential. They'll get it all right if they want it. Eminent domain."

"Too bad," Marti said. "That house seems like the perfect place for her."

There wasn't a significant increase in the noise level as they moved from the quiet and shade of Carlisle's property to the street. It was more like time travel, leaving one era for another. Marti thought of the possibility that Lucy's house would be razed. Poor woman. Everything in that house belonged there, including the owner. There was no way it could ever be the same anyplace else.

While Vik pulled out his files on all of the cases as soon as they returned to the precinct—a sure sign that he hadn't checked them out earlier—Marti put in a request for the paint chip found under Lily Day's fingernail. The female property clerk who took the call responded with a loud groan. "Nineteen-seventy-nine. My God, it'll take at least seven days."

"No," Marti said, "you will send it to the crime lab for further analysis tomorrow."

"Do you know—"

"No, and I don't care. Tomorrow." She hung up muttering, "Seven days," just loud enough for Vik to hear.

"If it's that college grad they just hired to replace old Sally, it probably will take her that long," Vik said. "Word is out that if she gets more than six requests a day, she thinks she's overworked; and finding any evidence that's been here for more than a year becomes *Mission Impossible*."

"We'll see how impossible it is." Marti pulled out her notebook. "At least we have some place to start. We've got three more artists to talk with: Jimmy Binslow, Carrie Pinkham, and Arlene Johns, who was president of the art guild when our first two arms with hands were found."

She got on the phone and spoke with all three of them

within the hour. Nobody was available to talk with her today. She had to set up an appointment to talk with Carrie Pinkham. Whoever answered the phone said that Mrs. Pinkham was deaf and would require someone present who could sign. When Marti offered to locate someone, she was told that Mrs. Pinkham would take care of it.

"Not such a bad day's work after all, Jessenovik."

"I don't think three more interviews will get us anywhere."

"Not unless it flushes out one of the killers."

"And then what?" Vik asked. "Don't tell me you think we'll get a confession."

Marti shrugged. Who could tell.

4

It wasn't yet dark when Vik got home. The day had gone from cool and overcast this morning to warm with clear skies now. He pulled into the garage then took his time getting out and walking to the front door. Mildred had been using a walker ever since her last MS flare-up, and he wanted to give her enough time to be there to greet him. Although she was fine now, little weakness in her arms or legs, it was taking her a long time to recover. The doctor thought the walker might be permanent. They took a short walk around the block most evenings, but he didn't think they would ever hike through the woods again. At least she wasn't in a wheelchair, not yet anyway. He tried to be grateful.

When Mildred met him at the door, she was using her cane. He hugged her, glad that she had had a good day. There was a catch in his voice as he greeted her. Once, forever had seemed like a long time; but since this last bout with MS, he had come to realize that it might not be so very long after all. *"Moja serce,"* my heart, he whispered in Polish.

Her movements were stiff as she walked down the hall, her footsteps accompanied by the dull thump of the cane. He could remember her nimble as a ballet dancer and was glad. He could see that she was thinner. Her appetite wasn't good. Her hair, once long and thick and blonde, was now short and wispy and gray. *Moja serce,* he thought, grateful that, in his heart, she would always be the young girl he'd married.

"Krista came today and brought the baby. You should see how he's grown."

He wanted to ask if Krista had stayed long and tired her but did not.

"She helped me with dinner, so I made dumplings and a strudel."

He could smell the rich chicken broth as they reached the kitchen. Mildred liked it here almost as much as she liked the view from the den, which was now their bedroom, so he had put a rocking chair and footstool by the window. Her knitting was there and a book, pages open, face down. He felt reassured as he sat down and eased his feet out of his shoes. This *had* been a good day.

Mildred busied herself at the stove. "Stephen called. He said he'll have time tomorrow to cut the grass if you can't get to it."

"Good." He resisted the urge to tell her to sit down so that he could wait on her. There was a vase filled with yellow flowers and sprays of greenery on the table that hadn't been there this morning. "Krista brought flowers." He would have to call, let her know that he'd noticed. Krista didn't think he paid attention to things like that. Neither did Mildred, but she loved fresh flowers. If he brought them, she would worry that more was wrong with her than she was being told.

"I would order them when I order the groceries; but over the phone, Matthew, I'm not sure what to ask for. And besides, they do not deliver right away. I wouldn't want them to wilt."

While she served bowls of soup and potato rolls, Vik turned on a lamp and switched off the ceiling light. Then he cut slices of the still warm strudel, releasing apple and raisin and cinnamon aromas that mingled with that of the dumpling-rich chicken soup. He kissed her again on the nape of her neck. She turned and kissed his mouth. When he sat beside her at the table and bowed his head and said the blessing, he realized it might not get much better than this, and that this was pretty good, and moved his chair closer to hers.

Trouble, their guard dog, was patrolling the perimeters of the chain-link fence that enclosed the yard when Marti got home. She got a dog treat from a sack in the garage and gave it to him. "Good dog." Trouble was a working dog, not a pet, but they all made sure he got treats and attention.

Momma, Joanna, and Lisa were on the deck. Marti waved but didn't join them. This was the biggest house she had ever lived in. There was so much room to spread out that when she went inside she listened to where the voices were coming from, and the noise, and went there. Today it was what the kids called the "middle place," two large rooms between the main level and the third.

Ben, Theo, and Mike were planning another weekend camping trip while the weather was still good. Although they would stay at Ben's place in Wisconsin, they were going to rough it instead of staying in the cabin. The boys' best friends, Peter and Patrick, were going, too, along with their father. Camping gear was everywhere. Two tents had been unfolded and sleeping bags unzipped. Marti noticed six new orange life vests. Ben and the four boys were sitting in a large circle.

"Why the vests?" Marti asked, as she sank down beside Ben and sat with her legs crossed, Indian style.

"We're going to go canoeing on the lake," Theo said.

"Oh?"

"The lake about a mile from the cabin," Ben said. "The one that's not real deep."

"Mostly because of my arm," Mike said. When he held up the cast, she saw that it was decorated with drawings and autographs.

"As long as its not white-water rafting," she said. The boys were all excellent swimmers, but they weren't ready for that yet. And if they were, she wasn't. "And, Mike, keep your cast dry."

"The menu looks okay," Ben said. "Mike, you, and Patrick can break it down to a shopping list. And Theo and Peter will be in charge of entertainment Friday night. . . ."

"Great!" Peter said. "A campfire, smores, and scary stories!"

"That's what we were going to do," Mike said.

"We can see who has the scariest stories," Patrick said.

"And," Mike added, "we can make popcorn like the settlers did. Remember when we went to that encampment at Glacier Park."

Theo rounded out the entertainment by suggesting they get in some fishing.

When Marti left them, they were counting tent pegs.

Momma was standing at the grill turning the chicken when Marti went outside. They had talked about screening in the deck but decided not to when they realized how much more than mosquitoes they would be keeping out. Two mourning doves kept to the edge of the deck as they pecked at some seed that had scattered from a bird feeder, and sparrows chirped evening songs in a melodic stacatto. The deck was shaded by tall, leafy oak trees. A young cardinal gave three charoops then glided from one low branch to the railing on the deck where Theo had scattered sunflower seeds. He cocked his head and looked at them with bright, dark eyes, and kept watching them as he ate.

"Ma, you're home early." Joanna smiled.

Lisa looked at her but didn't speak. According to Momma, Lisa seemed depressed. She had stayed close to home for the past week and had not seen her current boyfriend. Marti was concerned about the depression and relieved about the boyfriend, since her main worries concerning Lisa involved the possibility of sex and pregnancy.

"So," Marti said, "what have you two been up to?"

Neither girl answered. A green sweatband encircled Joanna's forehead and damp, auburn hair. She was wearing an overlarge T-shirt and smelled like she had been either biking or jogging. Lisa, who was shorter than Joanna and disdained anything that could be remotely associated with athleticism, had a visor perched on her head to keep the sun off her face. Instead of the usual spandex, she was wearing a loose-fitting blouse.

"You're home early," Momma said. "Supper's almost ready. Joanna, why don't you warm up the dressing for the spinach salad, and Lisa, pop the rolls in the microwave. We don't seem to be attracting any bugs so I think it's safe to bring out the dishes and tableware."

"What's up with those two?" Marti asked, as soon as the girls disappeared through the patio door.

"I'm not sure. Lisa talked with her mother today, ended up yelling, 'I hate you,' and slamming down the phone. Then of course the two of them disappeared upstairs for a couple of hours. When they came down, they did a lot of whispering. Then Joanna got her afternoon exercise, and Lisa stayed in their room until she got back."

"That tells us a lot."

"At this age, they don't tell you anything."

"Well, I'm just going to have to ask, Momma. I don't have the patience for these little mystery games."

"I don't think they're being secretive on purpose, Marti. I think it just comes with the hormone changes."

After dinner, Marti followed the girls when they went upstairs. They were lying across their beds facedown, with their heads over the edges of the beds, reading magazines. Marti sat on the carpet and leaned her back against Joanna's bed.

"Okay, ladies. I can remember the need for privacy and secrets and girl talk; but if there is something I need to know, you had better tell me."

"Oh, Ma."

"I'm tactless, I know. Talk to me anyway."

Neither girl said anything.

"Look, I don't mean to be so abrupt, but I never know when I'm going to get caught up in a case; then all I have time for is worrying."

"It's nothing important," Lisa said. "Sharon's got another boyfriend."

Sharon. Not Mom.

"She took Lisa's keys," Joanna volunteered.

Marti didn't have to wonder why, but it surprised her to know that Sharon was bringing a man where she lived.

"I don't care," Lisa said. She flipped the page of the magazine.

Joanna disagreed. "She does."

"*Joanna!* Like I'd want to be around him."

"What do you mean?" Marti asked.

Lisa gave a deep sigh but didn't speak.

"You've met him?" Marti asked. Sharon had always kept each Mr. Wonderful as far away from home and child as possible.

"No," Lisa said. "But he comes there, to the apartment; and if I call while he's there, she acts like I'm just a friend or it's a wrong number. If I want to go home, I have to call first."

Marti went over to the bed and sat beside Lisa. "I've known your mom for a long time. I know she loves you. But she also knows you are safe and well taken care of here with us." She touched Lisa's hair. It was short, but thick and coarse, even with a perm. Lisa looked more like Frank than Sharon. She was taller than Sharon and had Frank's darker complexion, round face, and deep-set brown eyes.

"I think Sharon thinks I've kind of abandoned her," Marti said. It wasn't what she'd intended to say; but it was, she feared, the truth. "I told her she could move into the apartment over the garage, but she doesn't want to."

"She likes things the way they are," Lisa said. Marti could hear the bitterness in her voice.

"Right now," Marti said. "Maybe."

"She's avoiding responsibility, and you're helping her," Joanna said, with adolescent arrogance. "She hasn't gotten over the divorce, and she's got some weird idea that by dating all of these guys she can get even with Frank."

Marti chose her words. "She's an adult; Lisa is not. If providing a home for Lisa means I'm enabling her mother, then I just have to do that."

"Oh, Ma, I like having Lisa here, too, even if she is . . ." She ducked as Lisa threw a balled-up sock in her direction. Both girls laughed. "It's just that . . ."

"It's just that we are two families now, not one the way we were when we first came here. And I'm married. That has to be hard for Sharon to deal with, too. So let's give her some time. She's had a lot of changes, no—a lot of losses to deal with lately. And I know you have, too, Lisa, but you have us. I'm not sure your mother feels that she has anyone. Can you be patient with things the way they are, just for a while?"

Lisa nodded. She still seemed dejected, but when Marti left, the girls were giggling over an article in one of the magazines.

It was dark when Marti pulled up at the apartment house where Sharon lived. There was a pause when she identified herself through the intercom, then Sharon said, "Oh, okay, come on up."

"Shhh," Sharon said, as she let Marti in. Sharon was just over five feet. Marti was accustomed to seeing her in high-heeled mules with her hair in some elaborate weave to give the illusion of height and wearing a multicolored caftan that added volume to her slenderness. Tonight she looked like a different person. The braids were gone, and her hair was short and straight, almost boyish. Her slippers were flat, and her robe was a plain gray satin. For a moment that bothered Marti. Then she thought, *Same old Sharon. This is how Mr. Wonderful wants her to look.*

"He's sleeping," Sharon whispered. "We have to be quiet." She led Marti through a darkened apartment down a hall to the kitchen, where the only light came from the microwave just above the stove. Everything in the kitchen was in order. There was nothing in the sink. The stove gleamed. Marti sat at the table.

"Shhh," Sharon cautioned again as she took a jar of instant coffee out of a cabinet and a can of ground coffee as well. She set them down, careful not to make any noise. She ran the water until it was hot and filled the cups, then measured coffee into a filter and put that into the coffeemaker. Marti knew that was for Mr. Wonderful in the morning. This was a side of Sharon she had not seen in a long time. Some might refer to it as domestic. Some, who were used to Sharon's almost militant feminism, might see a softer, gentler Sharon. Marti saw Sharon the doormat, Sharon as she had been with Frank, always compliant, always subservient. Marti saw a Sharon that she didn't like. Maybe that was why Sharon didn't want her to be here. Maybe Mr. Wonderful was a nice, ordinary man who still thought he had died and gone to heaven and didn't feel as if he was suffocating yet.

"Here we go." Sharon put the cups down with the instant coffee already stirred in. "Yours is black."

Before she sat down, Sharon wiped the microwave turntable and the countertop, folded the dishcloth diagonally, and hung it inside the cabinet door beneath the sink.

Marti was ready to leave. Instead, she said, "Sharon, Lisa says you took her keys."

Sharon looked away. "Marti . . . please . . . I just need a little time . . . a little space. You know I can't have a man around Lisa. It's not right."

Marti stirred her coffee, then tasted it. It was tepid and weak. She thought of Rayveena and all of the times Sharon had stayed with her and Momma when her mother was entertaining a man.

"So how's Rayveena?" she asked.

Sharon jumped up so fast she tipped over her coffee cup. "Oh," she whispered. By the time she got back to the table with the dishcloth, some of the coffee had dripped on the floor. She cleaned it up with paper towels, then rinsed the dishcloth and put it away. She looked about the room before she sat down.

"I just saw her," Sharon said, "and she is fine. As long as she can get her hands on some dope, she's always fine."

"You told me she had cancer."

"She's fine," Sharon insisted, voice quiet. "You know Rayveena; she'll beat it."

"I'll try to drive into the city soon. Momma's been asking me about going to see her."

"No. No. She's fine. Really. How's Momma? Nice having her with you, isn't it?"

Marti wondered if the reason Lisa was calling Sharon by her first name was because now she had chosen to call Marti "Ma" like the other kids. "Sharon, I know things have changed a lot, I know that this is a difficult time for you, and I love having Lisa with me. But you are still her mother. She does still need you. You are not like Rayveena. You've always been a good mother. Lisa has always come first."

Sharon sat with her hands in her lap and looked down at the table. "I love her," she said. "She knows that I love her." Her eyes brimmed with tears. "This is hard, with Rayveena sick and everything. I need just a little time. Can you make Lisa understand that? Please?"

"Sure," Marti said.

"I don't worry about her when she's with you. Please help me."

Marti pushed the chair back and stood up. When Sharon didn't move, she went over and put her arm about her shoulders. "It's okay," she said. "Be all right." Leaning down she kissed Sharon's forehead.

She left Sharon sitting at the table. As she made her way down the hallway, she saw that a door that had been closed when she came in was now ajar. She slowed down, then stopped to look in as she passed. A man was standing there. He was tall, light skinned, and nice looking, just the way Sharon seemed to like them. He was also naked and made no attempt to cover himself as he smiled at her.

5

Sharon woke before dawn. She hadn't slept well at all. She never should have gone to see Rayveena. Now the woman was coming to her in her dreams. Every time she dozed off, there she was—bald and old, witch-like in a ragged black dress, skeletal thin, one bony finger pointing. At least her nightmare hadn't disturbed DeVonte. She'd wanted to wake him, ask him to hold her; but he was sleeping so soundly, so peacefully. She looked at him instead, watched a smile tug at the corners of his mouth, heard him sigh. Mr. Wonderful and it had happened just like everyone said it would when it was the furthest thought from her mind.

When Frank had filed for a divorce, Sharon had promised herself that she would never go alone to a bar. Then she amended that to not going out with a man she met at a bar. At first she had kept that promise. Then it became easier not to. Good thing or DeVonte would not be here now. She would not be entertaining a proposal of marriage. Mr. Wonderful. How had she gotten this lucky? How had he come into her life? Everything was so different with him. She had pursued Frank. Hell, she had proposed to Frank. But DeVonte—he wanted her. And she . . . liked him . . . enjoyed being so wanted . . . but she didn't love him the way she had loved Frank. Thank God she didn't. DeVonte would never be able to hurt her the way Frank had. And because she was the one who loved less, DeVonte would want her all the more, try harder to please her, put her happiness above his own. That was how she had been with Frank. Now it was her turn.

Marti wasn't there when the two new computers were delivered to their office, which was just as well. The man who set them up was just that, a set-up man, but Vik said he had been full of advice and he had to stop listening to him to avoid getting confused. They were having April-in-September weather again. The day had begun with warm temperatures and cloudy skies and now thunder rumbled and lightning flashed and rain tapped against the window in a rapid, wind-driven barrage that was much faster than Marti could type. She stopped trying to keep up and reached for *WordPerfect for Dummies* again. Beside her, Vik smiled. The desks for the computers had been set up side by side, and she hated the lack of privacy. Too bad she couldn't throw the computer out the window.

At first it had been fun, playing solitaire; then the lieutenant had told them he expected them to replicate all of their forms and use them. She flipped through the book, then turned to the index. Changing margins on a word-processing program was a lot harder than setting them on a typewriter, even if Vik had already figured it out. Not that he was any happier about this than she was.

"Damned shame about that chat room," he said.

"Tell me about it." In May they had almost let one get away because they missed a reference to "chatting," which she now knew meant going on-line to a "chat room."

"Chat, chat, chat," she said. "Damned if I intend to." She still wasn't sure of exactly what it was, and she had no idea of how one did it. Until now, accessing the computer meant requesting that someone else get the information, and computer literacy meant identifying the right person. At home, when her kids went on-line, it seemed easier than using the telephone. As she read the instructions and set the left margin, she realized she had somehow managed to unset the right margin. Now she would have to repeat the whole process. So far today, she had learned nothing. She should have found the time to join her kids.

Beside her, Vik's chair squeaked as he leaned back and folded his arms. "This is what happens when business is slow. There's nothing new on the arm with hand, and I don't see much point in talking to a bunch of artists. What can they tell us? We don't know for sure that any of the arms with hands had anything to do with art. One paint chip does not an artist make. Maybe it's a flake from a car. Maybe we're the flakes for pursuing it."

Marti could see that despite the fact that he seemed to be learning faster than she was, he wasn't happy about it at all. "You know, Jessenovik, maybe we should just go ahead and take the class like the lieutenant said."

Vik gave her a look that implied she was suggesting the surrender of the Left Bank. "I'm not having any problems, MacAlister, but if you want to . . ."

Oh no. There was no way he would ever be able to say that *she* couldn't handle this. She had been the butt of enough precinct jokes to last the rest of her career.

By ten minutes to nine the rain had gone from torrential to a steady downpour and there was at least a ten-second interval between thunder and lightning. Marti had set all of her margins and was ready to figure out how to format a document.

"Someone else should be doing this, and if I find out who . . . ," she said. "There's nothing in my job description that says 'secretary.' "

"The lieutenant said this would be a good way for us to get used to the damned things," Vik reminded her.

Gordon McIntosh called a few minutes later.

"Says he has something," Marti said.

"Something he can't tell us over the phone?"

"Probably not."

Vik looked at her and then at the computer. "Let's walk over without our umbrellas. Drowning will be a lot better than this. Too bad we can't leave a window open while we're gone."

When he pushed his coffee cup close to the keyboard, Marti could see that it was almost filled.

"Vik, if that spills . . ."

"I know." His grin was almost demonic.

When Marti walked into Gordon's office, the first thing she noticed was that he had about half a dozen catalogs spread out on his desk that featured knives and other weapons with blades and sharp edges. Her umbrella and rain scarf were dripping. As she debated what to do with them, she turned to Vik and whispered, "Think he's found the needle in the haystack?"

"Get serious." His eyebrows almost met in a ferocious scowl. "Short of some flaw on the blade that was used and our ability to track it down, it's impossible."

Gordon was standing by the window. He turned to them with a smile that made Marti think of the Cheshire cat.

"Arsenic," he announced.

"And?" Vik said.

"I found significant traces of arsenic in the remains."

"What remains?" Vik asked.

"The arm and hand we just found in the woods."

"I walked all the way over here in the rain so you could tell me that?"

"Think about it, Jessenovik. We've got premeditation."

"What we've got here, McIntosh, is a doctor who wants to become a detective."

Gordon nodded. He was still smiling. "That's what forensic medicine is all about."

"Have you tested the other three arms with hands for arsenic yet?"

Gordon gave him a blank look, then realization dawned. "You mean . . . ?"

Vik gestured toward the catalogs. "I mean that instead of trying to figure out if the same weapon was used to dismember them, it would be a lot smarter to see if you could rule out arsenic poisoning. Even if you can determine with absolute certainty that the same weapon was used, the odds on determining that a specific person purchased one twenty years ago are damned slim. With arsenic, we would at least have something to base a process of elimination on."

"Damn," Gordon said, "you're right. Why didn't I think of that?"

"Because you were too damned busy trying to do one of those knife routines like they did at a certain trial in LA a number of years back?"

Gordon got red in the face, but Marti could tell by the way he was shaking his head that he was embarrassed, not angry.

"So," Vik said, "let's get to work on what we do have before we start looking for what we don't have and might never have, okay? In fact, it might be better if you just did whatever it is that pathologists do and didn't put any additional strain on your brain by trying to do my job, too."

"Have you got anything else?" Marti asked. This case was veering close to unsolvable.

"Well, since we have the ulnus and radius for all of the arms, I did a little math using the Trotter formula."

"And?" Marti said. She didn't have a clue as to what the formula was, but she did know that correctly applied it could give an accurate estimate of height.

"No tall people," Gordon said. "Even the young man wasn't more than five feet seven. The young woman was about five feet two. Ms. Nineteen-ninety-four was about five-four, and our most recent find was about five-five."

"How about weight?" she asked.

"Ah yes, the Rohrer body-build index. According to those calculations, the young man was of medium build; the women were all slender. Oh, and although I only have one arm and not the other for each victim for comparison, the arm strength in all of the bones, except for Ms. Nineteen-ninety-four, is well developed."

"As in above average?" Vik asked.

"I would say that they did something specific with that arm, sports related, occupational, I don't know, but something; and they probably wrote with the severed hand."

"Except for Ms. Nineteen-ninety-four," Marti clarified.

"Yes."

Marti left Gordon's office with a better sense of the body parts once belonging to whole people, people who played, worked, exercised.

"They're more real to me now," she said, as they walked back to the precinct. She wasn't sure she liked that. It would make it that much more difficult to let go of the cases if the victims couldn't be identified. "Damn." The rain had slowed to an annoying drizzle that dripped off her rain scarf and onto her jacket. She turned up her collar.

"Try to maintain a little professional detachment with this one, MacAlister. What McIntosh has told us so far isn't going to do us any good unless we can come up with a possible victim. Then maybe it'll be of some help"—he took a few more steps—"if we ever come up with any possibilities."

"It looks like we've got three different cases," she said. "Similarities with the first two that don't exist with the third victim. Now this one."

"Looks that way," Vik agreed. "Although it's hard to believe that three different people within such a limited area would all come up with the same idea. Mildred and her sister can't even agree on what to serve for family Sunday dinners."

Marti wished for an umbrella. The wind had picked up, blowing the rain in her face. "I was beginning to worry about Gordon," she said, "he's really fixated on identifying the weapon. At least he's not stopping there."

"I'm not so sure," Vik said. "Arsenic stays in the body forever, and instead of looking for it, he's trying to figure out if all of the limbs were severed with the same weapon. The man is paying no attention to the obvious. Good thing he's not a cop; he'd have problems working traffic." He stepped in a puddle and cussed. "Damn. Now my feet are wet. This is

54

enough to make you wish we'd find a ripe one. What do you want to bet that my wet socks and trace of arsenic are as close as we come to solving this one?"

Marti didn't say so, but she agreed with him. "Arsenic poisoning also increases the odds that we're looking for a female."

"Unless we've got a guy out there smart enough to want to make us think so. Or three guys. Or four." They walked the rest of the way in silence.

Sharon stood outside of the hospital room until the odors in the hallway made her feel sick to her stomach: food, urine, medicine, disinfectant. She wanted to throw up. She wanted to run. Instead, she pushed open the door to Rayveena's room and stepped inside. Worse smells greeted her. She dropped the bag she was carrying, rushed to the bathroom, and retched until her stomach hurt. Then she rinsed out her mouth, took a few deep breaths to ease the lingering queasiness, and tried not to think of a young, sassy woman with flowing black hair as she went to see Rayveena.

This Rayveena looked years older than her time on this earth. Her eyes flickered open, then closed.

"Why are you here?" Her raspy voice was little more than a whisper.

"They called."

"I'm not that sick. Better stay away. They might expect you to pay what the insurance doesn't cover."

"I've taken care of that."

Rayveena licked her lips and sighed, as if what little she had said had exhausted her. Sharon looked at the chair but didn't sit. She waited, listening to Raveena's shallow breaths, poised to leave as soon as she was asleep. Instead, Rayveena's eyes flickered open again.

"Why did you come?' " she asked.

"I don't know."

Rayveena sucked in her breath, then said, "When you come out of me, I was a month short of being twelve. They told me

I had swallowed too many watermelon seeds. One day there was pain and blood and water and then you, lying between my legs, looking like someone had smeared you with blood and buttermilk. You come from one of my mama's men. Can't say which one."

Sharon felt as if her stomach was clenched like a fist. Bile rose in her throat, sour and bitter.

"Nobody asked me did I want a baby. Just like nobody asked me did I want to get poked by some old man. I didn't want you, so they took you away. I didn't see you no more until you were four. I didn't want you then neither. You understand that, girl? You understand what I'm telling you?"

The pain was sudden and sharp. Sharon doubled over, clutching her stomach and gasping. When the spasms eased, she straightened, looked at Rayveena, and said, "Yes, ma'am. I understand. I brought you some lotion and nightgowns and a few other things, but I won't be bothering you anymore. You take care of yourself, okay?"

Rayveena closed her eyes then opened them again and nodded. As she turned her face toward the window, Sharon left.

When Marti located Jimmy Binslow, he lived in an unincorporated area of northern Lake County not far from the Wisconsin border. It would have been a pleasant drive if it wasn't for the rain, which had tapered off to a steady drizzle. While she drove, Vik used a map to navigate. They turned off of Route 173 and made their way along a paved but narrow road. Tall trees, some bent and twisted, and a few with severed branches where lightning had struck, formed a dense barrier preventing them from seeing anything on either side of the road. They missed the turnoff twice, and had to go back when they reached the place where the road forked. On the third try, Vik spotted a dirt road just wide enough for one vehicle.

"There'd better be a turnaround," he said. "We could get stuck trying to back up if anyone comes toward us."

Their unmarked car bumped along over the ruts in the

road. There were no turnarounds. The road ended in a clearing, and they were facing a cabin with an RV parked on one side and beside it a pickup truck. An antenna attached to the roof was high enough to clear the tall treetops. Before they could get out of the car, the cabin door opened and a tall man stood waiting.

Marti rolled down the window and stuck out her head. "Mr. Binslow?"

"Who wants to know?"

"Great," Vik muttered, "a Native-American Davy Crockett."

Marti took another look at the man. His high forehead and rounded, less prominent features confirmed that he was Potawatomi.

After Binslow checked their IDs, he admitted them to the cabin. It was one room with a sitting, sleeping, and kitchen area. Sparsely furnished, it looked comfortable without being crowded. As soon as she saw the photographs, unframed and tacked to the walls, Marti knew why Nan Conser had directed them here. Binslow waved them to the sofa.

"This is a long way to come to see an old man."

He *was* old. Straight silver gray hair was tied at the nape of his neck and hung down his back. His hands were gnarled with age and shook with tremors.

"You did these?" Marti asked, indicating the photographs.

"Yes, they are mine. But that was a very long time ago. Now I cannot hold the camera." Although his voice was strong, his speech was slow and deliberate, and he stopped to swallow as he spoke.

"May I look at them?"

"Of course." Binslow smiled, as if he was pleased by her interest.

All of the photos were in black-and-white. All of the subjects were people. A young Indian woman laughed into the camera as she looked up from the child she was holding. Another woman, tall, with classic American Indian features but dark, African-American skin, stood rigid and unsmiling beside an unfurled American flag. An old man with a gap-toothed smile danced in ceremonial garb. Marti took a step back. She had taken so many photos of so many crime scenes that the life and vitality in Binslow's were strong enough to almost bring her to tears. She had never thought of photography as anything more than a way to capture a moment. These captured much more. She could tell stories about these people based, not just on what she saw, but what she felt.

"These are wonderful, Mr. Binslow."

"Some of them are in books," he said.

He pointed to a small bookcase. Half a dozen oversized books lay flat on the shelves. Three of the titles and cover photos indicated that they were about Native Americans. She chose one and found Binslow's name in the index. Half a dozen of his photographs were included, all black-and-white. One captured a family in native dress as they sat around a campfire. The effect of light and shadow was startling.

"You have not come here to see an old man's pictures," he said.

"No," Marti admitted, although she would like to stay long enough to look at them all. "Years ago, maybe nineteen-seventy-nine or nineteen-eighty, a man died here. All we know about him is that he had a substance on his hands that is used in developing film."

Binslow regarded her for a moment, his expression serious. "That is not such a long time ago. What did this man look like?"

"I don't know."

He considered that. "Did this man die young?"

"Yes. He wasn't twenty-one."

"And since you are police, it was by someone else's hand."

"We assume so, yes."

"How can I help you?"

Marti glanced at Vik. That was a good question; one that she didn't have an answer for. "Traces of metallic silver were found on his fingers."

Binslow nodded. "I'm not sure of the easiest way to explain

this." He thought for a moment. "The first thing we must do when we are developing the film is use a chemical called the developer to change the silver salts on the film's emulsion to metallic silver."

That change from salts to metallic must be what pointed McIntosh toward photography. "If you had some residue on your hand, would it come off or go away during some later stage of the process, or would it come off when you washed your hands?"

Binslow shook his head. "These are chemicals. I have no idea. How often do you hear of some process or another making people sick years after they stopped doing it?" He looked away for a moment, then looked at her and asked, "What brings you here to me? Who sent you?"

There was no recognition in his eyes when she told him it was Nan Conser.

"Did you exhibit your work locally?" she asked.

"Exhibit?" he asked with a wry smile. "Ah, yes. On occasion I was that Indian who took pictures. There is a word for it when there is only one—"

"Token," Marti said.

"Yes. That is what I was, but only because of a picture I took at a powwow that was published in *LIFE* magazine with my name and where I lived printed underneath. After that, each year there was an exhibit, and I was invited. Of course I went, otherwise they would have thought that there was nothing of value my people could do. A camera is a little thing, but a picture in a magazine is mighty." He leaned back in his chair and seemed deep in thought. "I cannot think of anyone that young taking pictures when I was. Sometimes there were one or two others who would have photographs at these exhibits. Perhaps one of them would know."

"Did you attend any of the art league meetings?"

"No. But I was invited occasionally to tell them about the camera. What I saw when I looked through the viewfinder? Why I took a picture? Things like that."

"Were there young artists there?"

"Sometimes there were. Most everyone believed they knew everything they needed to know or knew nothing and wanted someone to give them what they did not have. So I seldom went. When I did, if there was someone who would listen, I would take the time to speak to them. Most often it was the young. If you had a picture or a description of this young man you are seeking, perhaps I could help you. The year does not mean anything to me. I cannot place people in time; I am too often alone." He swallowed hard, then wiped a bit of spittle from the corner of his mouth. "There were not many around here who worked with the camera. I will call the number on your card if I remember anyone who was young."

Before they left, he said, "If you can stay a few minutes longer, I will make you a sacred bundle to take with you." He went into the kitchen area and returned about ten minutes later with two small bags made out of animal skin and closed at the top with hide laces. "I have put a bit of tobacco inside, as an offering to the gods, and sage for good health. Also, I have tied a small piece of hemp so that you may bind those who harm and trouble others. There is a bit of flint for strength and seed for knowledge."

"Thank you," Marti said. "I can't wait to show this to my sons." Theo and Mike would really be impressed.

To her surprise, Vik gave the old man just the slightest smile as he accepted his bundle. He weighed it in his hand, and looked as if he was about to speak, but said nothing, nodding instead.

"Well," Vik said, as she turned the car around in the clearing in front of the cabin, "health, strength, and knowledge." He held up the bag. "Not that I believe you can package it like this and give it away. But I do think they have one hell of a lot of knowledge that we think we are too damned smart to listen to."

* * *

Sharon met DeVonte at the door. As soon as he stepped inside, she opened her robe so that he could see that she was wearing nothing underneath. Her tongue probed his mouth as she kissed him. She undressed him there in the hallway, kissing, licking, as she took off his clothes. Then she pulled him down on the carpet beside her. He didn't have to do anything at all.

Later, she brought lunch to him in the bed they'd retired to and fed him shrimp and crab and strawberries. Then, slowly, she began kissing him again. Much later, when he was stretched out on the bed with a satisfied, sated expression on his face, she made him turn over, straddled the small of his back, and gave him a massage.

"Damn, baby, I don't know what I did to deserve all of this; but whatever it was, tell me, so I can do it again."

"Were you serious about getting married?"

"Serious? That's not something I'd joke about."

"When?" she asked.

"Let's get the license tomorrow. I'll talk to a lawyer about getting the waiting period waived."

He couldn't wait. He loved her. Tired and aching, she stretched out beside him. "Sharon Lutrell," she said. "Sounds good."

DeVonte agreed. "Sounds damned good."

When he was snoring softly beside her, Sharon got up and took a sleeping pill so that she wouldn't dream, or if she did, she wouldn't remember.

Marti didn't know anything about sacred Indian bundles, but she knew the boys would be excited. She made a special trip home. Vik came with her. Theo and Mike were upstairs with Patrick and Peter. The four boys crowded around her and Vik as they put the small pouches on the card table.

"Deerskin," Peter said.

"No, I bet it's otter," Theo disagreed. "The Potawatomi used that a lot."

"I don't think there are any otter around here anymore," Patrick said.

"There aren't too many Potawatomi either," Mike said. "They put their chief in a cage made of tree branches and made them go to Kansas."

"Maybe this is old otter skin," Theo said.

Two blonde heads almost touched two thatches of thick, kinky hair as the boys examined the bundles. They sniffed them, guessed what the smells were, weighed them, held them up, and finally looked inside. Marti explained what each item was.

"Awesome," they agreed, almost in unison.

Momma fixed sandwiches and they ate a late lunch or, as Vik suggested, an early dinner. When they returned to the precinct, there was a message from Carrie Pinkham. She could see them at seven that evening. Marti wondered what kind of an artist she was.

"The joke is on us this time," Vik said. "After years of tracking down nutcases, we're the nutcases this time, off on some wild-goose chase. Acting on the premise that one victim could be an artist and the other a photographer based on a paint chip the size of a pinhead and traces of metallic silver makes about as much sense as pronouncing an undertaker dead because he smells of embalming fluid."

"Not one of your better analogies, Jessenovik, and morbid."

"Four different arms without heads are morbid, too. Everything about this job is morbid. At least with an entire body we can make some kind of sense out of it."

Marti checked the coffeepot. There was nothing but hot dregs at the bottom. Vik hurried over. "Don't bother, Marti. I'll make it myself."

"You make swill, not coffee."

"I know, but when I make it I, can stir it, and the spoon doesn't stand at attention in the middle of the cup."

She relented.

6

The rain had stopped by the time Marti and Vik walked to their unmarked car. The wind was blowing cold off the lake and they both put on their jackets to ward off the chill. Maybe, for a few days between now and the middle of October, they might get a few days of Indian summer. Right now, it didn't seem likely.

Carrie Pinkham lived in a small, wood-framed house on the southeast side of town. It was a quiet, tree-lined street with small, one-family houses in various stages of decline and—here and there—restoration. The houses squatted behind chain-link or picket fences and most had neatly trimmed yards with late-blooming flowers. Pinkham's house looked recently painted, white with blue trim. There was a swing set in the yard, along with tricycles, bicycles, and other wheeled toys. The noise coming from inside the house suggested that most of the riders were at home. Twins greeted them when they knocked, two girls almost identical, with honey brown faces and barrette-bound braids.

"You want Granny?" one asked. She looked to be six or seven.

"That's right," Marti said. "Is she at home?"

"Course, she's always at home. I'll go ask her if she wants to see you."

"No, I'll go."

"You went last time, Angelique, and Granny will remember."

That settled, the other twin flounced away.

"Why you want my granny?" Angelique asked.

"We heard she painted pictures," Marti said. "We want to talk to her about it."

The little girl grinned. "She don't paint no more, lessin' it's when she colors with us, which ain't often."

"Maybe you just don't color often," Marti said.

"No, it ain't that, it's Tameka. She breaks the crayons every chance she gets. Or Jameel. He eats them."

The other twin returned. "Miss Lindsey's not here yet, but Granny says to come in."

"What's your name?" Marti asked.

"Ebonique," the girl said.

As Marti followed Vik inside, she wondered why Nan had suggested she come here. The front door opened into a living room crowded with furniture and toys. A baby slept in a play-pen, and two preschoolers sat in front of a large-screen television with the sound turned up so loud it hurt Marti's ears. She wondered how the baby could sleep through it.

"Tameka!" one of the twins yelled. "We got company! Turn that down!" She turned to Marti. "Granny can't hear nothin'. They make noise all the time."

Vik nudged her and nodded toward four oil paintings lined up along one wall.

"Real people," he said. "Doing things real people do. I like these a lot better than Lucy's."

The paintings looked almost like something a child would draw. Primary colors, no pastels, no shading, one-dimensional. Each depicted an event Marti could remember from her childhood: women gathered around a newborn; a family picnic; a beauty parlor with beauticians wielding flame-heated straightening combs and curling irons; old women—church mothers—sitting on a church pew, wearing white dresses and fancy hats and fanning themselves. As she looked at them, Marti thought of Momma and for some reason felt close to tears.

A tall, slender woman came into the room. She wore slacks and a short-sleeved blouse. Gray hair and a slight stoop of her shoulders indicated that she might be older than she looked.

"Angie, Ebbie," the woman said. "Turn off that television set and take your sister and brother into the other room." Her speech was without inflection and sounded as if she were holding her nose. She turned to Marti and Vik. "I am Carrie Pinkham." She moved a bag of Pampers and a stack of folded clothes from the sofa. "Please sit down."

Before she could say anything else, there was a knock on the door and a young, brown-haired girl came in. They began speaking in sign at once. Miss Pinkham seemed relieved to see her. The young woman's lips moved as she signed, but Pinkham's did not. Sign was not silent, as it appeared to be. Both women made noises with their fingers and hands. After a minute or two, Pinkham sat in a chair opposite Marti and Vik, and the young woman left the room and returned with a kitchen chair. She placed the chair where she could see everyone.

"Hi, I'm Lindsey Kirch. I teach speech pathology at Northwestern. My father is a doctor, and Mrs. Pinkham is one of his patients. We're also friends. I went to school with one of her sons who is hearing impaired, and I've taught sign to two of Mrs. Pinkham's grandchildren who are also deaf. She's not used to speaking with the police and wanted to be sure that you understood each other."

Mrs. Pinkham tapped Lindsey's arm and began signing. They conversed for a minute, then Lindsey asked, "Would you like coffee or pop?"

"No, thank you. This shouldn't take long." As Marti spoke, Lindsey signed, so she continued. "We are here because we heard Mrs. Pinkham is an artist, and now we see that she is."

The two women signed. "Why is that important to the police?"

"We're not sure."

When Lindsey translated that, Mrs. Pinkham's hands moved in rapid gestures.

"That's a bit strange, but if I can help you, I will."

Marti liked the way Lindsey spoke without saying "she says." She spoke directly to Mrs. Pinkham. "What was it like being an artist here in the later seventies, early eighties?"

"I wasn't considered an artist. Not like the others. I could bring a painting once a year to their exhibit, and I did that for many years, from the time I was in high school. One of my teachers arranged it. But that was a time when you wanted to have one colored friend or one colored artist. I, too, am a twin. My sister is not deaf. She played the viola and piano, but for fun."

The excluded, Marti thought, *only good enough to visit once a year.*

"What was it about your paintings that made them want to exhibit them?"

" 'Oh,' they would say, 'how primitive.' As a young girl, I thought that was good, like saying, Oh, how impressionist, or, Oh, how cubist. As I got older, I came to realize that 'oh, how primitive,' meant Oh, how simple, Oh, how inferior. I came to see that they were using my work so that others could see how much better theirs was. My sister had told me that all along, but I loved the attention so I chose not to listen."

"How did you feel about that?"

Tears came to Mrs. Pinkham's eyes. "I was deaf, you see. I could sign, read lips; they did not always know that. So, though I knew they pitied me, for a long while I did think they liked my work. They would buy it, you see, smaller paintings that I did. I thought that meant that they liked it until I heard one woman ask another where she would hang it. 'Hang it?' she said. 'Why, I throw them away.' "

"Tell them about these four," Lindsey interjected.

Mrs. Pinkham wiped her eyes. "They are not just paintings," she said. "I did not sit and see this picture in my head one day. My mother died and I wanted to remember her. I could have drawn her face, but I wanted to remember who she was, not just what she looked liked."

Her hands paused; then she continued. "My mother did not

have many children of her own, but like me they were always around her. She did not just feed and tend them, she loved them. Even when she was old, the new mothers would bring their babies to her, as if by holding them in her arms she was giving them a blessing. And family, she was forever gathering us, in prayer, in thought, in the dozens of pictures of us on her walls and sideboard and dresser, always she was gathering us, urging us together, to be family." She laughed. "And believe it or not she was vain. Even when she was dying, she insisted that her false teeth be in her mouth. 'Carrie,' she said, 'I don't care if people don't have shoes on when they're laid out. You put stockings on my legs and shoes on my feet and make sure that my shoes match my dress.' And there she is, with all of the church mothers, all of them gone now but one—all of them together now with the Lord—just as they were together most all of their lives. Good Christian women, all of them. Real Christians, not just churchgoing, church living." Tears streamed down her face almost as fast as she wiped them away. Lindsey stopped signing and patted her hands.

"All of her paintings are like this," Lindsey said. "They all represent someone in her family in a way that symbolizes who they were. They're quite moving, aren't they? Even before you know the stories behind them."

Marti hesitated. How did she want to proceed? "We have the remains of some people who died about twenty years ago. We cannot identify them but we think they might have been artists or maybe worked or lived with or around art or artists. Can you think of anyone in the late seventies or early eighties who was involved in art who moved away or left unexpectedly? I know this is an unusual question, but can you think of anyone, by name or even description?"

Mrs. Pinkham gave her question so much thought that for a moment Marti thought she might be remembering something. Then she shook her head. "No, but I didn't go to the meetings or anything. Once I graduated high school, I was never even around anyone who did any painting."

The baby in the playpen stirred, then began crying. The twin sisters ran in. One tugged at Mrs. Pinkham's blouse to get her attention while the other lifted up the baby.

"Bring him here," Mrs. Pinkham said, holding out her arms.

"He pooped," the twin said.

Vik's nose twitched and he stood up to leave. "Anything else, MacAlister?" he asked.

"Not that I can think of." She thanked Lindsey for interpreting, although once they'd got started talking, she had hardly noticed the young woman at all.

"This is getting us nowhere," Vik said, as they drove back to the precinct.

"Unless we've got someone like Binslow or Pinkham out there who thinks they're another van Gogh and feels angry and excluded."

"Maybe," Vik conceded, "provided they are also a psychopath. Binslow didn't strike me that way. Neither did Mrs. Pinkham. She is a hell of a good artist though. That picture of the beauty parlor made me think of Mildred."

He was silent. Marti couldn't imagine how black women getting their hair done could make Vik think of his wife, but she didn't question the painting's power to do that.

"She's gone from a walker to a cane," he said. "At least most of the time. Her birthday is coming up in a couple of weeks. I don't think we'll be doing the polka at her party."

"Maybe not," Marti said, "but at least you'll still be together."

"I know, Marti. I know. And that's enough, for me anyway. But Mildred, she remembers when things were different. I tell her that's not what's important, but she remembers. We both do." With that he turned on the radio and tuned into a news station, something he never did.

Sharon checked her watch again. It was almost nine o'clock. Lisa was twenty minutes late. Maybe she wasn't coming. The restaurant was family oriented, which meant frequented primarily by middle-aged couples and senior citizens. It was the eating place nearest the high school that didn't attract students. She was seated at a booth by the window not far from the door. The window was foggy where she had peered into the parking lot. When the waitress came over and poured more coffee, she ordered a club sandwich. She couldn't wait much longer. DeVonte didn't know about Lisa, and she wasn't sure how she was going to tell him. She had told DeVonte she was going to a PTO meeting, which was true, and that she would be home by ten. She checked her watch again. DeVonte was so insistent upon punctuality. The one time she had been late meeting him, he had sulked for the rest of the evening and pretended to go right to sleep when they went to bed.

The sandwich came with fries. She was trying to get the ketchup out of the bottle when Lisa showed up. "You're late." She was sorry as soon as she said it. "That's okay. Sit down. Here." She handed Lisa a menu and motioned to the waitress. Maybe, just once, Lisa would choose something without changing her mind two or three times. If they didn't take too long getting Lisa's order to the table, there was still a good chance that she could get home to DeVonte by ten.

"I'll have a burger with fries. No lettuce, no pickle, and mayonnaise and mustard on the bun."

Sharon almost held her breath. She bit back a complaint as Lisa looked at the menu again.

"No, make that the fried chicken sandwich. No mustard, just mayo. Fries, and do you have bread and butter pickles?"

The waitress smiled and nodded.

"Good. I'll have some of those on the side. And did I say fries?"

The waitress nodded again, then hesitated. Sharon wanted to shoo her away but sat with her hands clenched in her lap and her jaw clamped shut.

"Oh, and a Coke," Lisa said. "Easy on the ice. No. Iced tea. With lemon. Thanks."

This time the waitress didn't waste any time getting away.

"So," Lisa said, "what's up? I just came from a basketball game. Latrese dropped me off, and I've still got homework. You'll have to take me home . . . to Joanna's."

Sharon tried not to focus on the hostility she heard in Lisa's voice. "Lisa, I only wanted the keys because I'm having the locks changed."

"Right, Sharon, like I'm retarded."

She wanted to wince when Lisa said her name. Lisa had stopped calling her Ma on Mother's Day, as if that was some kind of gift. Is that what Lisa thought? That she didn't want her to call her Ma anymore? If she did, it was Rayveena's fault. They had made their annual trek to Chicago the day before Mother's Day to bring Miss Rayveena candy and flowers. Lisa had slipped and called Rayveena Grandma and been reprimanded, no—cussed at. Lisa hadn't called her Ma since.

The waitress brought iced tea. "What's this?" Lisa asked. "Didn't I order Coke?"

"No, but I'd be glad to bring you some." She said it as if she meant it.

"No, this will be okay. Do you have any honey?"

"Sure. I'll get it."

Lisa looked down at the silverware. "Oh, and could you replace this," she asked, holding out a fork.

Water stains probably, Sharon thought.

Lisa rubbed her eyes. It was a childlike gesture and for a moment, Sharon wished Lisa was a child again or even just a few years younger. Just a couple of years ago she was wishing that Lisa was older so that she could have her life back. She almost laughed but caught herself. She wished she could tell Lisa how pretty she looked tonight, not because she was wearing anything special, just because she was growing up. She wished she could tell her how much she loved her. But saying things like that had never been easy for either of them.

The waitress brought a bowl filled with packets of honey. "So?" Lisa asked, as she opened one and squeezed the gooey golden contents into the glass of iced tea. "You must want something."

"I just wanted to talk to you."

"About what? My grades are up, and I'm not seeing Rory, at least not right now."

Sharon was sure that had more to do with Marti than anything else. "That's good. Now I won't worry about you while I'm gone."

"Gone? Gone where?"

"I, um, I'm a little stressed out. I'm going to go to the Bahamas for about a week. I won't be gone long. I just need to get away."

"From whom? Me or Rayveena."

"Not you, Lisa, not you."

"Right. I know."

Sharon reached across the table to take her hand, but Lisa moved her hand away. "Please, Lisa, I really do need to get away."

"That's fine, Sharon. Get away anytime you want to. It is Rayveena, isn't it? She's worse. You know, if you time it right, not only can your mother die while you're gone, but some stranger, a social worker or minister maybe, can take care of the funeral before you get back."

"Do you want to go and see her, Lisa?"

"No, but she's not *my* mother."

"She's your grandmother."

"No, she's not even that."

Sharon met her gaze for a moment, saw the challenge there, the question—How much of a mother are you?—and looked away. "A week, Lisa, a week. That's not very long." Not long enough for Rayveena to die, unfortunately. "Besides, you've got Joanna and Marti and her momma."

The waitress brought Lisa's order and another fork. Sharon glanced at her watch, 9:35. She resisted the impulse to ask Lisa to hurry up. DeVonte would not be pleased when she came in late.

"I can see you're in a hurry," Lisa said. She motioned to the waitress. "Could you wrap this up for me please?"

"Lisa, it's okay."

"No, Sharon, it's not okay. You've got a man waiting for you. You'd better be getting home to him. Maybe I'll see you when you get back from the Bahamas."

The waitress brought a plastic foam box and Lisa slid everything off of her plate and closed the lid. "We can talk when you have more time. I won't bother to get in touch if Rayveena dies while you're gone."

"Give me a minute." Sharon caught the waitress's attention and pointed to Lisa's Styrofoam box. While she was waiting, she picked up a french fry and swirled it in the ketchup. When she bit into it, it was cold.

7

Sharon looked at DeVonte. He hadn't been upset with her last night, even though she was ten minutes late. He was changing. He loved her and she was going to marry him and he was becoming a different person already. Soon all of his bad habits would be gone—because he loved her. He had worked some magic, or more likely paid someone, and they would be married this morning. This was her wedding day; the first day of the rest of her life with Mr. Wonderful. They would spend the night in Fort Lauderdale and board a boat to the islands tomorrow.

The boat. The Atlantic Ocean. Her stomach began churning at the thought of sailing across so much water. It would only be for five or six hours, but they wouldn't even be able to see land. And the flight to Fort Lauderdale. She didn't want to think about that either. She hated flying. But she would be with DeVonte. She would be his wife. For one of the few times in her life, she was happy, happier than she had ever been with Frank. They would only have a week together on Grand Bahama Island before she would have to face Lisa and everyone else, but she wouldn't have to face them alone. It would be fun telling Rayveena that she was married again. Not once but twice she would have the one thing Rayveena could never get, a husband.

She looked at the sweet, brown sugarman sleeping beside her. Mr. Wonderful, and he was. How quickly he had fallen in love with her. He would make her happy. He would. She was happy already.

After roll call Marti barely had time to turn on the new computer before she got a call from Gordon McIntosh.

"Don't tell me," she said, "you've narrowed the list of possible weapons to three hundred and seventy-five."

"No, I've found more arsenic. There are traces in all four of our arms with hands."

A connection! A valid connection. But why?

"That's great," she said.

"You don't sound as excited as I thought you would."

"That's because this is the beginning of the investigation, Gordon. We've still got a long way to go."

"Oh. Well, I haven't gotten anywhere with the weapon yet."

"How about looking at the area of amputation on each of the arms," she said. "See how many points of similarity you can find, if any." She didn't tell him that she thought identifying or locating a specific weapon was impossible. She might want to send him off on that tangent again just to keep him busy and out of the way.

She told Vik as soon as he came in with four large cups of coffee from McDonald's. She didn't like the way he brewed coffee any more than he liked the way she did, so they had compromised. They would each have to bring in their own coffeemaker if Slim and Cowboy spent much more time before the grand jury.

"Arsenic," Vik said. He took the lid off his paper cup and frowned as he poured the contents into his mug. "Maybe tomorrow I'll bring in a couple of thermoses of Mildred's coffee."

"That would be nice," Marti said, encouraging. She took the lid off her cup, too, but just so the contents would cool faster.

Vik leaned back in his chair and held his mug with both hands. "Arsenic," he said again. "Poison is usually a woman's method of choice. And a sharp instrument, usually a man's.

It's nice to know, but it doesn't tell us a hell of a lot. Arsenic is almost as easy to get your hands on as a pack of cigarettes. And, so far, we don't have any likely suspects."

"But we do have something that links all of the victims, arsenic and the dismemberment at the elbow." She told Vik what she had just asked Gordon to do. "If he gets in the way, let's refocus his attention on identifying the weapon. That should be just about impossible and it will keep him busy for a few days."

"Now you're catching on, MacAlister. The best thing to do is keep him out of our way until Cyprian gets back from vacation."

"Now," Vik said, "arsenic." She could see he wasn't pleased by that. She doubted that anything about these cases would make either of them happy, except resolution. "Another needle in a haystack, Marti. This is going to be one big pain in the butt no matter how many clues we turn up or how closely we relate one victim to another."

"That's it," Marti said. "Did these four people have something in common? Maybe the paint chip and the traces of metallic silver *do* mean something."

"And maybe we should interview the entire art community of Lincoln Prairie, no, all of Lake County, and see if we can find out. So far we've got a middle-aged spinster, an elderly American Indian, and an African-American grandmother. Which do you think is the most likely suspect?"

"None of them," she admitted. "But we have four victims with arsenic poisoning and two clues."

"Did Gordon have anything else on the processes that yield metallic silver?"

"He didn't mention anything." She would have to check back with him to make sure he was still looking into it.

"There might be a lot of things those clues could point to other than art."

It sounded like a long search to her, but the odds were about the same as those two victims being somehow involved with any local artists. The odds against an art connection seemed to increase significantly when she considered all four victims.

Sharon tried not to seem nervous as she waited with DeVonte outside the courtroom. It was a court where they set bail for misdemeanors, and she was sure Marti didn't attend those kinds of hearings. Just a few more minutes, the sheriff's deputy who would act as their witness had said. His Honor will marry you between this case and the next. She smoothed down her skirt. She was wearing a navy blue suit with a powder blue blouse. Not that she would have wanted to wear white again, but something pastel maybe. DeVonte had suggested that they both dress conservatively. She would have liked to have had flowers, just a corsage, but he was right. This would be their secret, for the time being at least, and they might run into somebody she knew.

She looked into the courtroom and then up at DeVonte. He was staring off into the distance, trying to look serious, with a smile tugging at the corners of his mouth. She shouldn't be here, she thought with sudden panic. It was too soon. She didn't know him well enough. This wasn't the right thing to do now or the right way to do it. Lisa should be here. Marti should be standing up for her like when she'd married Frank. DeVonte's hand gripped her elbow. He smiled down at her. He had such a mischievous smile.

"DeVonte . . ."

"Shh . . . it's almost time."

Why on earth was she doing this? She wanted to shake his hand free and turn and run. It had not been right the last time, and she had known Frank much longer, made much more formal preparations, been married in a church. She had been so sure of everything then. Now she was just as certain that this was wrong. She had only known DeVonte for a few weeks. None of her friends knew him at all. She could walk away right now without having to explain anything to anyone.

She took a step, stopped only by the pressure on her arm and the questioning look in his eyes.

"I love you," he said. "I need you."

I need you. That was what Frank had said. She'd always had to beg Frank to say he loved her, words that came easy to DeVonte. Did he mean it?

DeVonte pulled her closer. She could smell the breath mint he had popped into his mouth a few minutes ago. She inhaled his cologne, which she thought was too sweet, too feminine. She would change that, just as she had changed his attitude last night when she wasn't on time. He was Mr. Wonderful. He would always be Mr. Wonderful. He was not like Frank. He was not like any man she had ever known.

After an uneventful morning, a lot happened while Marti and Vik were out to lunch. When they got back to the office, Arlene Johns had left a message indicating that she could see them at seven that evening at her pottery workshop, and Jimmy Binslow had called. His sons and daughter did have a few albums. Some of the pictures had been taken during the time period they were interested in. He would call back as soon as they dropped off the albums at his place, maybe later today. In addition, Nan Conser had been there and left two pairs of white gloves, a box filled with photographs taken in 1979 and 1980, with a promise of more to come and a note instructing them to use the gloves when handling the photos. The box of photographs seemed to beckon her, so Marti put on a pair of gloves and went through them, sorting them by year. That done, she dialed Lucy Carlisle's number, intending to find out if she had any photos, but hung up after the phone rang ten times.

"Going through these could be time-consuming, Vik. Especially since we've got more coming. What do you say we talk to Lupe and Denise?"

"Why?"

"Well, Lupe can sort them and make a list of the names on

the backs. Once she has that, she can check them against what's in the *News-Times* archives. Denise can run checks on anyone whose name we have who looks like a minor. And they'll probably think of something else that could be helpful. You never know, something might turn up."

"Right, MacAlister. I say we just look for the guy with the rose tattoo, and Jane Doe Lily Day's lily."

He sounded grumpier than usual, but she didn't say anything. She knew he was not going to be happy about working this case. And she was already checking each photo for anything that could possibly be a tattoo.

Lupe Torres arrived a little after five. She was still in uniform and wore twenty-odd pounds of equipment with the grace of a dancer. She was tough and self-assured. Marti remembered when Lupe was a rookie, with as much bluff as confidence, and felt as if she had watched her grow into the job.

Lupe checked the coffeepot. "Yuck. You guys on your own this week? I heard Slim and Cowboy are nailing them at the grand jury hearings. It's about time those two made a meaningful contribution."

Without waiting to be asked, she got out the can of coffee, measured some into a filter, and went to fill the pot with water.

"Thank God," Vik said, as the door closed behind her.

Marti agreed. "Too bad it's not a bigger pot."

By the time Denise Stevens arrived at five-thirty, the room was scented with the pleasant aroma of full-bodied Colombian, and Marti, Vik, and Lupe were sitting back and trading war stories.

Denise was just a little shorter and about 10 pounds heavier than Marti's 165. They were both healthy, as Momma would say; but unlike Marti, Denise was not pleased with her size. She wore dark-colored clothing and colorful hats, which called attention away from her hips and directed it to her face. Denise had the full, generous features that some black women are blessed with and sloe, almond-shaped eyes. Today's hat was a wide-brimmed gold felt with a pheasant feather that curled around the crown almost like a ribbon.

She, too, headed for the coffeepot. "Not bad," she said, after she cooled hers with what was left of a half-pint container of milk. "What's up?"

Marti filled them in on what they had so far on the four dismemberments.

"That's not a hell of a lot," Lupe said.

Denise said, "Three victims were under twenty-one. It seems like at that age someone would notice if you weren't around anymore, but there was a lot of hippie stuff in the sixties and seventies; I suppose some kids disappeared into cults and communes. Even so, you would think there would be a report filed somewhere to say they existed."

"We weren't as organized then as we are now," Lupe said. "A lot of information about juveniles wasn't just classified, it was inaccessible—to everyone."

Marti explained the potential link with the arts.

"That's stretching it," Lupe said. "You really don't have much to go on, do you?"

"At the rate we're going," Marti said, "we might be inundated with photographs pretty soon. That's why we wanted to meet with you." She reached for the box of photos Nan had brought in and explained why she was putting on the gloves. "These have names on the back, not everyone's but most of them. Tomorrow we're going to pick up some albums with photos, and we need to look at whatever the *News-Times* has on file, see if any of these names made the news. Maybe, by an organized process of elimination, we can come up with something."

"Do all of the pictures pertain to something artistic?" Lupe asked.

"Most of those we'll be looking at were taken at local exhibits and art fairs between nineteen-seventy-seven and nineteen-eighty-two."

"And if there is no art connection," Lupe said, "we'll probably come up empty."

"So far the possibility of an art connection is all we have. Our man at the Coroner's Office is looking into other processes that produce metallic silver. He hasn't called us with anything yet. And as soon as they find the paint chip, we'll take another look at that." Just thinking about how long it was taking annoyed her.

"Nice computers you've got," Lupe said.

"Right," Vik said, scowling as he looked at his.

Marti remembered that Lupe seemed to like them. "Want to use mine?" she asked.

"Can I?"

"Depends on how good you are at getting our forms into a standardized format for the files."

"That could be arranged," Lupe said. "You planning on sharing them with Vik?"

"Only if he says please and thank you."

Lupe grinned. "I'll think about it. What I really want to do is come in when my shift is over and get these pictures organized by name and date and place. See what correlations we can come up with, check out what happened to everyone, and also identify who we don't have a name for."

"Sounds like a plan to me," Denise said. "I can run the names for you and work on identifying those without names and tracking them down."

"That's a great plan," Vik said.

"You're just saying that because you're not doing the work," Lupe said. "What you'd better do while I'm working on this is figure out how to make a decent cup of coffee."

"You're not going to throw that in?" Vik asked.

"Depends. Are you going to bring in some of Mildred's strudel? A little of that dumpling soup would be good, too. How is she doing?"

"Much better," Vik said.

Marti could tell by the tone of his voice that he wanted to believe she was. She could also hear the small voice saying "maybe not." She promised to give Lupe all the photographs as soon as she got them, and they all agreed to meet again for breakfast in two days.

It was a little before seven when Marti and Vik pulled into the strip mall where Arlene Johns's pottery shop was located. Joanna had gone through an artistic phase when she was in the Girl Scouts, and Marti could remember that she "threw the clay on the wheel," "poured the slip into the mold," and molded clay with her hands. She thought that all related to pottery.

A tall, hefty woman met them at the door. She was wearing bib overalls and had short, curly hair that was somewhere between auburn and gray. Her eyes, behind wire-rimmed glasses, were brown. Marti looked at her hands and guessed she was at least sixty.

The woman extended her hand. "Arlene Johns."

"Detective MacAlister." Ms. Johns's handshake was firm. "And my partner, Detective Jessenovik."

They showed her their badges, but she didn't pay much attention.

"I can't remember the last time I've spoken to a police officer. What on earth brings you here?"

"You've been doing this for a while?" Marti asked, waving in the direction of shelves filled with vases and covered and uncovered bowls.

"For a good many years now, yes."

"Were you doing this in the late seventies, early eighties?"

"Yes, in fact, I was president of the Lake County Art Guild back then."

Marti took a closer look at what was on the shelves. Everything in this room was finished, complete with price tags about half the circumference of a dime.

"Can I take a look at where you work?" Marti asked.

Johns let them into a large, open room with shelves against

every wall, large worktables to the center, and small, square tables arranged in two groups, each with a potter's wheel, a foot pedal, and a stool.

"This is what they call a studio?" she asked.

Arlene Johns gave her a big smile. "Yes," she said, "it is."

She led them to one set of shelves. "These were done by my students." And then another. "Those on the top shelf are mine."

The finishes on everything that wasn't still just clay were dull and flat. None of the colors were bright. Marti hadn't seen the chip of sky blue paint yet, but she didn't think she would be able to match it with anything here.

"Do you ever use metals?" she asked.

"Occasionally."

"Silver?"

"No, not very often."

"If you did, would you get any traces of metallic silver on your fingers or hands?"

"I hope not. Everything we do here is fired at about two thousand degrees. If you got that close to any of the metals at that point . . ."

Marti walked over to a table where trivets made of wet, red-brown clay were drying.

"My students' work."

"Children?"

"Junior high."

"My daughter made me something in ceramics once, a cup. The colors were bright though. She told me I had to use it for pencils."

Arlene laughed. "Clay sculptures. Nonfunctional pieces. That's a different process. We don't do that here. You can drink out of our cups."

Marti wondered if that's why the finishes weren't shiny, but she thought she might offend Johns if she asked.

"This can't be why you came to see me, Officers."

"No," Marti admitted. "We have the unidentified remains of two people who died in the late seventies, early eighties. We're trying to find out who they were."

"And something buried in the questions you've been asking makes you think I might have known them?"

"Or something about them. There's a possibility at least that they were somehow involved with the arts. You wouldn't remember any twenty-year-old males or females back then who disappeared?"

Johns ran her fingers through her hair, thought for a moment, then held her hands palm up. "I coordinated art shows." Her hands kind of fluttered. "There were all kinds of people there. We did one by the lake, another up in Zion in the park, um, what can I tell you? All kinds of people came. If you mean someone who might have exhibited, I don't think so. Everyone in the shows lived in the county, but that doesn't mean I knew all of them. Frankly, I seriously doubt that anyone that age would have been an exhibitor. *That* I would remember." She clasped her hands together and shook her head. "I'm sorry, but your question is so far-fetched. . . . I really would like to help you, but I have no idea."

Marti seldom purchased anything from those she questioned, but on her way out she chose lotion bottles for Joanna and Lisa that were painted in muted brown tones and a vase with what looked like a cameo attached near the fluted top that she thought Momma would like.

As they exited the parking area, Vik said, "I'm glad you distracted her with that purchase. The woman obviously thought we were nuts. And she's right. Who's going to remember some twenty-year-old kid unless they make a public nuisance of themselves."

"Maybe we should mention the tattoos," she said.

"Not yet," Vik said. "If this doesn't pan out and we've got to look elsewhere, that could be an important clue."

Even though she agreed that they had made the right decision about the tattoos, her conversation with Arlene Johns, or rather the lack of substance, had pointed out just how flimsy the possibility of any art connection really was.

Marti was dozing in the recliner when the telephone awakened her. It was almost ten o'clock. Ben had been dozing beside her, but now he was awake, too. Momma took the call, but handed the receiver to her. Marti yawned as she reached for it. Someone from Cook County Hospital was calling for Sharon. She listened to the male voice at the other end, then said, "I'm sorry, but her daughter is out of the country right now. I'll be down as soon as I can get there."

"It's Rayveena," Momma said.

Marti nodded.

"Then I'm coming, too."

Neither of them was dressed to go anywhere.

"That phone call did not surprise me," Momma said, as Marti headed south on I-94. "As soon as Lisa told us about this vacation Sharon was taking, I thought Rayveena might be a lot sicker than Sharon was telling us. Someone called from school today asking about Sharon. They think she's on family leave."

"Too bad they're not closer," Marti said. "Miss Rayveena shouldn't be dying alone." Sharon's mother wasn't like the other mothers on the block. She didn't hold a regular job, and they got some kind of public assistance. Miss Rayveena wasn't married either, something that Sharon worked hard to forget, or at least ignore.

"Rayveena was much too young when she had that child. She said she was fifteen when Sharon was born, but one of my church sisters knew the family back then and said she was closer to twelve."

"Twelve? My God!" Sharon had never told her that.

"Rayveena wasn't nothing but a baby herself," Momma said.

84

Marti checked the speedometer as they passed under the Lake Forest Oasis. Eighty-five. When she glanced sideways, Momma didn't seem to notice. "Miss Rayveena was turning tricks, wasn't she?"

"She seemed to have a regular clientele. I always wondered why you never asked about it."

Marti wasn't sure either. She and Momma had always been able to talk about anything. "It was Sharon, I think. She was always so . . . everything had to be perfect in her life. She had to be just like everyone else, and she wasn't, and she just could not admit to anyone that life where she lived was different. Not too many of the other girls in the neighborhood hung out with her. Mostly it was her and me. At school she had more friends, but she made sure nobody ever came home with her."

"No telling what she would find when she got there," Momma said.

Marti reached for the travel cup filled with coffee even though she was now wide-awake. Good thing she had slept for over an hour. She had brought a thermos, too, just in case. There was no telling how long they would be at the hospital.

"I thought that maybe when her uncle started coming around things would be different. But he didn't last too long."

"Long enough," Momma said.

"He was her uncle, wasn't he? She never wanted me around when he was there."

"He could have been," Momma said, "but I don't think those Sunday afternoon rides out of the city were anything but trouble."

"Why?"

"I don't know. It just didn't feel right, that's all. Sharon sort of got an attitude after that."

Marti knew what Momma meant. Sharon wasn't fast or careless, and she didn't get a reputation; but boys became much more important, in an odd kind of way, like now. It wasn't about sex or even affection. It was more like Sharon became less herself and more what someone else wanted her to be. Like she didn't know who she was anymore and needed some boy to tell her.

Marti took the Route 41 exit to Chicago, and they reached Cook County Hospital about eleven. As often as she had come to County when she was a Chicago cop, she could no longer remember her way around and had to ask for directions twice. When they finally found the room number they had been given, Marti thought someone must have made a mistake. That skeletal, nearly bald woman in the bed couldn't be Miss Rayveena.

Momma walked right over to her. "Rayveena, honey, it's me, Sister Lydia. Can you hear me?"

There was no response. Machines beeped and half a dozen small plastic bags joined with larger bags of IV solutions to drip medication and nutrients into her veins. She was on oxygen. Marti walked closer. Miss Rayveena's eyes were half-open, but she wasn't looking at anything. Her stomach was bloated and her skin scaly and dry. Her chest hardly moved the sheet as it rose and fell, but she was still alive. The smell was awful, like several things left out much too long and beginning to spoil.

"Miss Rayveena," Marti said. "Miss Rayveena." Tears came to her eyes, and she wiped them away as they slipped down her cheeks. Marti knew the signs; this wasn't cancer, this was AIDS; and nobody deserved either. Some would say Miss Rayveena did, but she would not agree with them. Sharon's mother was just human. She had never known her to say one word against anyone. If anything, she would defend the worst of them.

And she was much too young when Sharon was born. She wasn't old enough to be anybody's momma. That must have been why the other women overlooked the things she did, or failed to do, and why they tried to take up the slack where Sharon was concerned, making sure that she had clothes just like everyone else's and that they weren't hand-me-downs, and school supplies, and Sunday shoes as well as Sunday school. Marti didn't think Sharon liked being the object of everyone's charity, but Sharon had known it was done out of love. That was how it was back then; people looked out for each other.

Momma fetched a basin of water while she was standing there thinking. As Marti watched, Momma bathed Rayveena as well as she could—given the tubes and the IV drips—from face to feet. The almost bald head she left alone. "Need some baby oil," she said. "She does have some cocoa butter and lotion with aloe vera." Momma straightened the sheets and held her hand just above Rayveena's forehead, with her eyes closed in prayer.

A nurse came in, checked everything, then said, "She seems quieter now." She was a small, dark-skinned woman with a short, gray Afro and a wrinkled face. "She is much better now than she was when we admitted her this morning. I thought she'd be gone before the night was over. She should have been in here a long time ago." She shook her head. "Not much we can do for her now. She's got meningitis. Maybe it will take her. Be a blessing if it did."

"Did she ask for her daughter, Sharon?" Momma asked.

"She told us she didn't want to see anyone. Her daughter's name was on her records, but when the social worker called, it was your phone number."

Momma was right, Marti decided. Sharon must have been expecting this. That was why she'd run away. Marti looked at Rayveena, thin, jaundiced, and wondered how long she would last. Sharon hadn't left any information about where she was going or how to get in touch with her. Maybe Lisa knew, although she'd denied it this morning.

Momma pulled a chair close to the bed and sat with her face near Rayveena's. She talked with her quietly until the nurse came in again and then the doctor.

"She is a very sick woman," the doctor said. "I didn't think she would make it through the night. But her vital signs are improving. She seems to be resting quite comfortably right now."

"Is she in pain?" Momma asked.

"Not now."

"Good. You keep it that way. There's no need for her to suffer now. No need at all."

"Yes, ma'am," the doctor said. "We'll do everything we can to make her comfortable."

After he left, Momma said, "And I'll be right here to see that he does. Ben will drop me off in the morning. If I'm not back in time to fix supper tomorrow night, just look in the freezer. There's a pan of lasagna and a container of chili. All you have to do is heat something up."

Momma returned to Rayveena's side, but she didn't sit down. "I've got to be going now, child, but I'll be here in the morning to sit with you. I will not leave you alone, Rayveena. I promise I will not leave you alone." She patted the hand without the IV and stroked Rayveena's brow. When she turned, her eyes were bright with tears. Neither of them said much on the drive home.

DeVonte had the seat by the window. A cloud cover spread as far as he could see. It was almost like looking at snow. He didn't like snow, or cold weather, or the rain they had left behind in Chicago. One day he would go to the islands and never return. He loved flying almost as much as he loved sailing. Sharon didn't. She was afraid. Too bad he'd had to marry her, but there was no other way to get at her insurance and pension and 401K investments. He wanted to let go of her hand and wipe the sweat from her palm. Instead, he signaled the stewardess and ordered more drinks.

"You're sure you don't want to sit by the window?" he asked.

He wanted to laugh when Sharon gulped down the whiskey sour and shook her head. She put down the plastic glass and clutched his hand again. This was going to be a wonderful trip. Sharon was afraid of flying, afraid of heights, afraid of water. He chuckled.

"What are you laughing at?" she asked.

"I was just thinking about what a fantastic time we're going to have. Wait until you see my condo. It'll be just the two of us this time of year. We'll swim, sit in the sun. I haven't had time to buy a boat yet, but we'll rent one and go sailing." There was a low pressure area that was threatening to become a hurricane. If it did, Grand Bahama Island would be right in its path. The plane rocked as they hit some turbulence, and the seat belt light came on. Her hand tightened in his.

He smiled. "We are going to have a wonderful time, Mrs. Lutrell." The "Mrs. Lutrell" brought a smile to her face that would have disappeared if she'd known there had been five others. "You'll love it. I promise." He chuckled again.

8

SEPTEMBER 17

Sharon shivered as seagulls whirled and screeched overhead. Even though they would only be in Florida until tomorrow morning, and it was the first time she had ever been here, she had hoped to sleep in and then do some shopping. Instead, DeVonte had ordered room service for 8:00 A.M. Then they were up, dressed, and out—to the swimming pool, she thought—but DeVonte headed right for the shore. Instead of taking long, slow strokes in warm water contained by four sides and a bottom, cold, foamy water swirled about her legs. Her mouth was filled with the briny taste of salt. She could hear the clatter of pebbles and shells as they were dragged into the ocean. Waves crashed just inches away. Sand was sucked from beneath her feet. Sea-weed, green and slimy, touched her skin. Children ran and splashed and squealed nearby, ignorant of the danger of the undertow. She was afraid.

"Sharon, come on!" DeVonte called. He waved, then dived into the foam-capped swell of wave. "Come on!"

She walked against the incoming force of the waves as she went toward him. Water swirled about her waist and then her shoulders. She stopped. He was out too far. The water was getting too deep.

"Come on!" DeVonte urged. "Come swim with me! Look! I'm out here all alone!"

He grinned at her and beckoned. There was one cold shock of water as she began swimming toward him. She concentrated on the rhythm of her strokes and told herself that she could touch bottom if she had to, even though she knew she could not.

"See! This is great! What did I tell you!"

She tried to tread water as he reached out and held her.

"Come on," he said, and swam away.

"DeVonte!" She was not a strong swimmer. She was afraid to go farther out.

"Sharon, I'm right over here. Come on."

He was at least fifteen feet away. Her arms felt heavy as she swam toward him. She couldn't see his head for the height of the waves. Something seemed to tug at her legs, the undertow, and she was below the water, gulping it in, sputtering as she came to the surface, then down in the water again.

A hand grabbed her arm and pulled her up. She could see the sky. She gasped and choked and coughed up water and held on to DeVonte for dear life.

Marti had gotten up in time to let Lisa know her grandmother was sick without alarming her. Rayveena was not any closer to Lisa than she was to Sharon, and Lisa did not seem concerned at all. Momma was so worried that she had Ben take her to the hospital before the children left for school. Marti left a message for Sharon on the machine, just in case she called.

Marti joined Vik for breakfast at the Barrister. Wood was laid in the fireplace, awaiting a day cool enough to light it. The dark wood paneling and Tiffany-style lampshades made the place seem cozy without the fire.

Nan Conser called about an hour after they arrived at the precinct. When Marti thanked her for dropping off the photos, Nan said, "Oh, I've got another box I'm working on. And this is probably far-fetched, but I thought of someone else you might like to get acquainted with, Dexter Penwell. He died a few years ago, but his sons still run the business."

Marti didn't mention that so far they had struck out.

"I have thought and thought about this, and I can't come up with anyone involved with photography other than Jimmy Binslow. But then I thought of Dexter. He was an excellent artist but made his living as a photographer and a sign painter. Like I said, this is far-fetched, but his sons have always worked in the business and they're old enough to remember how the guild ignored their dad. Maybe this photographer you're trying to identify is someone who was ignored, too."

The excluded, Marti thought again. Something about that intrigued her.

After a morning of accomplishing very little, they were at Jimmy Binslow's around early afternoon. Inside, something smelled good.

"Rabbit stew," Binslow said. "Fresh rabbit. We've got a lot of them around here."

Marti smiled as Vik made a face. It was obvious he didn't know that you could get frozen domestic rabbits at the grocery store. It was probably a delicacy now. Momma used to cook them. Fried and then smothered in gravy, they didn't taste much different than chicken. The smell of wild rabbit was different, but still delicious. Binslow had seasoned his stew with onions and celery and bay leaf. Her stomach grumbled.

Binslow went to the bookcase. "I've got the albums here for you. I looked through 'em, but I didn't see anyone I remembered. No one in particular anyway. Nan's there, and that Johns woman who ran the shows. No other photographers though. I think I was there mostly because I'm Potawatomi or American Indian or Native American or whatever they're calling us now." He spoke without rancor. "Arlene Johns called last night. I haven't spoken to her in years. She wanted to know if I would be interested in exhibiting again. I'm thinking about it. Be nice for my children, especially now that I've got grandkids."

Marti thought so, too.

Binslow moved slowly as he went to the stove and checked

the pot. "It sounds like Arlene has finally found something she's good at. She's says she's a potter now with a studio. And she's teaching classes. She used to teach art for the public schools, but I don't think she was happy doing that. It sounds like she likes what she's doing now much better. You're sure you won't have some lunch? There's always plenty when I make rabbit stew."

Marti took one look at the expression on Vik's face and declined. She accepted the albums. Vik was already moving toward the door as she thanked Binslow and promised to take good care of the photos and return them as soon as possible.

"Well, so much for Lucy Carlisle, Jimmy Binslow, and Carrie Pinkham," Vik said, as they turned onto Route 41 and headed for Lincoln Prairie. "A painter, a photographer, and our very own Grandma Moses. We've struck out with everyone your friend Nan suggested."

"Not exactly," Marti disagreed. "I think we can be reasonably certain that if there was a young photographer in these parts back then, he definitely didn't have any contact with anyone in the art guild."

"And," Vik said, "does that blow our artist theory? What about Lily Day? We have nothing to go on with the latest arm with hand. Do we throw in the towel on these cases? It seems like a waste of time to me."

Marti didn't have any answers.

It was early evening and pleasantly cool when Sharon left the hotel with DeVonte. The concierge had suggested an Italian restaurant about four blocks away. Several stores were still open.

"Let's go in, just for a minute," she said.

"With all those suitcases you brought, I can't imagine what you could need."

"Stronger suntan lotion," she said. "And I only brought two suitcases and a carry-on."

DeVonte grinned. "As heavy as they are, and as full, what else could you possibly need?"

Pulling him by the arm, she went into a store. It was filled with souvenirs and racks of T-shirts and bathing suits.

"See," she said, rushing to a rack of bikinis.

Laughing, he helped her pick one out. It was hot pink and skimpy. "But you are not going to wear it until we get to the condo," he cautioned.

"You like the one-piece better?" she asked.

"Only if the beach is crowded. On the island, it will just be you and me."

She looked at the shelves of souvenirs, thought of Lisa and Marti and all of the kids, but decided to wait. They would be staying here overnight on their way back to Lincoln Prairie. She could get something then if she didn't find anything she liked on the island.

"Ready for pasta?" she asked, as they went outside.

"Ready for you," DeVonte said.

"Again?" She laughed. "Already?" It felt good to be loved.

Marti stopped at the building with the DEXTER PENWELL AND SON sign above the door. Beside her, Vik grunted but he didn't complain. They had stopped for something to eat so he wasn't hungry, just tired, which didn't matter. They were both tired most of the time, at least when they were working a case.

The door was ajar. Marti rang the bell then went inside, with Vik right behind her.

"The door was open," she said, as a slender man wearing glasses, with smooth, chocolate latte skin and a goatee came toward her.

"What brings you here?" Penwell Jr. asked when they showed their ID.

"We've been talking to some of the members of the art guild," Marti said.

"Then like I said, what brings you here?"

They followed him into a room so large that it didn't seem

crowded despite the array of materials and supplies. Signs, complete and incomplete, lined the walls, along with wooden racks that held large jars of paint and shelves filled with brushes and other supplies. Paint-splattered wooden tables had been pushed to the center of the room.

"According to Nan Conser, your father was an artist and a photographer as well as a sign maker."

"True," Penwell Jr. agreed. "He was a damned good artist. Studied at the art institute in Chicago. He wasn't good enough for the art guild though. Here, take a look."

They followed him to an office. The large metal desk was crowded with papers—invoices, advertisements, bills, mail. Matted and framed caricatures were on the wall behind the desk—Muhammad Ali, Joe Louis, Barbara Jordan, Wilma Rudolph, Aretha Franklin, Shirley Chisholm. Two oil paintings hung on the opposite wall. Both were of three boys and a girl. They were children in one, teenagers in the other. Marti didn't know a lot about painting, but she could pick out which of the boys was Penwell Jr.; she could tell the middle boy was mischievous and that the girl was bossy and maternal. She didn't know how the paintings conveyed that, but they did.

The photographs were commercial; weddings, christenings, children. Marti asked their standard questions about the metallic silver and got the same answers.

"Do you remember anything at all your father might have said, back in the late seventies or early eighties, about a particular photographer or photography in general and its exclusion by the guild?"

"Except for Jimmy Binslow," Penwell Jr. said. He thought for a minute, then shook his head. "No, photography was part of how he earned his living. He didn't think of it as an art form. The artwork," he waved his hand toward it, "that was different; but they discovered Carrie Pinkham first and didn't need anything from him." The bitterness in his voice was reflected in his expression.

"How is it," Vik said, "that someone this good painted signs?"

"He had a family. We had to eat. He painted signs that were good, too. And people liked that better. Being a sign painter was much more appropriate for a black man than being an artist back then."

Vik's eyebrows almost met. He leaned against the edge of the desk and stared at the paintings of the children for a moment, then said, "Fools, all of them, damned fools. It started with the Indians, and they never got any smarter." With that, he strode out of the room.

Marti caught up with him just as he reached the car.

"Damnit, Marti, what in the hell is wrong with people? A hundred and fifty years ago we put the chief of the Potawatomis in a cart made out of tree branches and sent the tribe to Oklahoma. Twenty-five or thirty years ago we sent this man to this shop to paint signs. This winter we'll send dozens of indigents from one church to the next, night after night, for food and shelter. Don't we ever learn anything? Will we ever get any of this right?"

Marti didn't say anything. What Vik was talking about was the tip of an iceberg, and she didn't have any answers.

After the boys were in bed, Marti retreated to the middle room and the card table, where a jigsaw puzzle was in progress. This was one in a series described on the box as Americana country art. Each was a homey scene that looked like something out of the late-nineteenth or early-twentieth century. Johnny always said that when she put jigsaw puzzles together, they looked like anacrostics. That was what this puzzle looked like now, except for the sky. Someone else had been working on it since she last had the time, and the sky was almost completed.

Once she got the frame in place, she just let the puzzle come together. Eventually she reached the point she was at tonight. She sifted through the pieces in the box without focusing on anything in particular and found a piece with a touch of brown that was part of the horse, then another with a diagonal strip of red that was part of a sign, and two that were a dappled, drab, olive green that completed the curtain in one of the windows. She liked the randomness of not looking for the autumn-colored leaves or the gnarled tree trunk or the variegated blues of the sky. Sometimes a section came together. Other times, like tonight, she just added a piece here and there. By the time the puzzle was finished, she would understand the parts as well as the whole.

"Ma, you still up?" It was Joanna.

"Everything okay?"

"Umm. We won tonight."

Marti sighed. Volleyball season had just started. She had missed the first game.

"That's okay, Ma. At least you try." Joanna sat on the opposite side of the table and rummaged around in the box until she found a couple more pieces of blue. Then she traversed the length of the skyline until she figured out where they went. "I know I've never told you this, but you are always there when I need you. And I appreciate that."

Marti wondered what had brought that on and decided it must have something to do with Sharon and Lisa. She found the tip of the horse's tail and then a doorknob.

"Want some tea?" Joanna offered.

"In a couple of minutes. First, I want to hear a little more about how wonderful I am."

Joanna didn't smile. "Really, Ma, I know I can depend on you. Let's not worry about whether or not you make it to a game."

With that, Joanna came around to her side of the table and gave her a hug.

When she was alone again, Marti thought about the arms with hands, about the hand they had found in the woods, fingers protruding from the leaves, curved as if it was beckoning her, whispering from its shallow grave, asking her to find out who it belonged to and how it had gotten there. They knew so little. Would they ever know anything more? What was she missing? How would she ever connect a hand with a chip of paint under the fingernail and a finger with traces of metallic silver to any of them? And, if she did, would that bring her any closer to identifying the more recent two, even though all four had traces of arsenic?

She reached into the box of puzzle pieces and began turning over the ones with the colored side down. The orange of one tree's leaves caught her eye, then the maroon of another, then the white wisp of smoke from a chimney. Soon this puzzle would be completed. She might never find enough of the pieces to the others.

Sharon sat on the balcony and looked up at the stars. They were on the ninth floor and a cool wind blew in from the ocean. She tried not to think about how high up they were. The railing was only waist high. She was afraid to go close enough to it to see how secure it was.

"Here we are," DeVonte said. He put glasses, a bottle of Chevas Regal, and some soda water on the small table. Heavy-handed, he put more liquor in her drink than she wanted. She didn't say anything.

"To us." He raised his drink in a toast.

"To us." Us. At last. Us. Wait until she got back to Lincoln Prairie and Frank found out. To make it even sweeter, DeVonte was a financial advisor and loaded. Not that that was why she'd married him, but it beat the hell out of marrying another loser. They were going to look at houses in Lake Forest when they got back. Too bad she couldn't invite Frank to the house-warming.

"You're miles away," DeVonte said.

"No, not really."

"Let me refresh that." He took her glass before she could protest and topped it off with Chevas. "Drink up."

She gulped down half a glass. It burned all the way to her stomach. She hadn't eaten much for dinner. She hadn't eaten much all day. DeVonte had made a few remarks about women being fat who didn't look fat to her at all. With her lack of height, she was going to have to be careful. She didn't ever want him to say that about her.

"Tomorrow we sail to the Bahamas," he said. "Just wait. The condo is in the middle of nowhere. I got in on the ground floor on one of the few places on the island where they are just beginning to develop. We'll have enough privacy to make love on the beach in broad daylight, and we'll be within fifty feet of the water. You'll love it. More open space than some of the islands. Not too much of the tourist stuff, and we can avoid what there is. We'll rent a boat. Maybe we'll buy one. I've been meaning to. I love to sail."

Sharon listened with a mixture of pleasure and anxiety. Ocean, boat, she didn't like either. But she would learn to enjoy them, be less afraid. They were going to be so happy together. She would learn to enjoy all the things he liked to do. DeVonte topped her glass again. He raised his in another toast.

"Listen," he said.

She could hear the sound of the incoming tide as waves crashed against the shore.

"Here. Come look. It's incredible."

He went to the railing. She shook her head.

"Oh, come on, Sharon, look. It's beautiful."

She stood and he grabbed her hand. When she reached the railing and looked down, she felt dizzy.

"Whoa," DeVonte said, as she leaned against him. "Here." He put his arm around her. She was safe. With DeVonte she would always be safe. She lifted her lips to his and they kissed.

Marti's breakfast meeting with Lupe Torres and Denise Stevens turned out to be bagels, cream cheese, doughnut holes, and a pot of Lupe's coffee—strong, black, and heavy on the chicory. They met in a conference room at the precinct, and Marti brought the albums Jimmy Binslow had given them yesterday. Lupe was in uniform, with her visored cap pushed back on her head, strands of straight, black hair escaping in short tendrils. Denise was wearing a hunter green roller-brimmed hat. When Denise took the hat off and began laying out the photographs on the scarred oak table, taking up most of the space, Marti smiled. When Denise took off the hat, it usually meant that she was having a good day and feeling good enough about herself to risk having someone pay more attention to the size of her broad hips than the slant of her dark eyes.

The photographs were in plastic sleeves and Marti could see small white dots with numbers in the lower right and left corners with a narrow label between them. Marti checked her watch. Vik was late. She immediately thought of Mildred. He hadn't called in. They would wait.

Vik arrived a few minutes later with a foil-wrapped package. "Stollen," he said. "Mildred made it yesterday. Hot out of the oven. It had to rise overnight."

The smell of raisins, walnuts, and cinnamon was almost overwhelming.

"Mildred really is feeling better," Lupe said.

Vik's smile was tight and cautious. "Today," he said. "Today."

As soon as he put the bread on the small corner table where they had set up everything for breakfast, Marti cut a hunk off one end. The butter was sweet and had been left out to get soft. "Mildred thinks of everything," she said.

"She's overdoing it, as usual," Vik said. His voice was gruff.

"Let her," Marti said.

"You think so?"

"I think she needs to do the things she enjoys. She's always loved to cook."

He looked at Marti for a moment, then nodded.

Denise had arranged the photographs by year. The labels at the bottom listed the names of everyone Lupe and Denise had been able to identify. Those they could not had been circled in red on the plastic.

"Don't rub off the red marker," Denise cautioned, as Vik reached for a photo. "And just look. They're in order."

Marti put both hands on the table and leaned forward. She found Nan Conser right away. Not because she hadn't changed—there were laugh lines at the corners of her eyes and mouth that hadn't been there twenty years ago, the skin under her chin was not as firm, and gray was beginning to streak her hair—but her smile was the same and the way she threw her head back when she laughed.

"I didn't know Nan worked with jewelry," Marti said. "I didn't know Nan did anything artistic."

Vik stood closer. "Maybe it's someone else's and she's just standing there."

Marti found a snapshot taken in 1980 and another in 1981, and in both, Nan was sitting or standing at a table where jewelry was displayed. "I wonder why she doesn't do it any-more?"

"Maybe she does," Vik said.

Marti turned and saw that half the loaf of stollen was gone. She went to the table and cut another thick slice and slathered on the butter. She might not see butter again for days. According to Joanna, butter was a real killer and the only acceptable substitute, other than grape and olive oils, was liquid margarine. Worse, Joanna had managed to convince Momma to go along with it.

Denise was hovering over the photos when she returned to the table.

Marti held out her hands. "No butter. Besides, they're protected by the plastic bags."

"Nan has called me three times," Denise said, "to make sure we're not near heat, moisture, or the air-conditioning. I'm not taking any chances." She checked Marti's hands. "I don't think she was supposed to let us borrow them."

Marti found one photo of Carrie Pinkham. She had expected more. Carrie was standing in the center of a group of women that included Arlene Johns and Nan. Marti spotted a woman with a large Afro in the background, took a closer look, saw the woman's resemblance to Mrs. Pinkham, and wondered if it was her twin. From the expression on the woman's face, Marti guessed that at best she was not pleased. She scanned the other photos and did not see anyone else who was African-American. Arlene Johns was in a lot of the photographs, but she didn't see Lucy Carlisle at all.

"Arlene Johns sure looks different, doesn't she?" Marti said. Her hair was long and blonde and she was at least twenty pounds thinner. "What's this?" The photo was in color, and the pottery arranged on the table in front of her looked like something out of one of Theo's books on American Indians. The designs were jagged and pointed, the colors bright. It was nothing like what Arlene had at her pottery shop now. Marti checked the other pictures of Arlene. By 1981, her hair was shoulder length and brown and she had gained a few pounds. Her pottery was painted in subdued shades of brown and gray.

"Unrequited love?" Lupe said. "Look at these." She pointed to one of the earlier photographs. In both, there was a young man with dark hair that hung, shaggy and uneven, to his shoulders. A red circle had been drawn around his face. Marti checked the year. "John Doe number seventeen?" she asked.

"He doesn't show up in any of the others," Lupe said. "I'm trying to track him down. No luck so far, but I haven't shown this to anyone; figured you'd better handle that. I wouldn't want to spook a killer—if he is John Doe number seventeen."

"Maybe I'll just borrow those," Marti said. "Talk to Arlene about him sometime today." She took another look at the pictures. Whoever he was, he was right behind or beside Arlene. The expression on Arlene's face suggested that having him in such close proximity was just fine.

There were only two photos of Jimmy Binslow. One was a wide-angle shot that took in at least a dozen photographs arranged on some kind of screen. In both photos, Jimmy was wearing a felt hat with a feather in it, a short-sleeved plaid shirt, and jeans. A long-stemmed pipe dangled from his mouth, and he was wearing some type of necklace. She wondered if he was calling attention to the fact that he was an American Indian on purpose.

When Denise began rearranging the photographs, Marti realized that the numbers in the circles on the right aligned them by year. The numbers on the circles to the left aligned them in chronological order by primary subject. Only Carrie Pinkham was alone.

"Arlene Johns sure did gain weight," Vik said. "She started wearing glasses, too."

Marti looked. "Cat's eye glasses," she said. Johns wasn't wearing glasses when they went to see her—contacts maybe?

"Ugly," Vik said. "Real ugly. I never saw a woman who looked good in them. Mildred's got an aunt who still owns a pair and wears them. She can't see for crap with them, but she likes the style."

Marti checked everyone with a red circle around their head—the unidentified.

"Forty-three people," Denise said. "Thirty-one of them adults and eleven who could fit in the seventy-nine to eighties time frame. No tattoos that we can see." She snapped open her briefcase and took out some enlargements. "These seemed like the ones you'd be most interested in. Maybe you can show them around. It's the best we could do."

"How did you get the names for those you did identify?" Marti asked.

"Nan had already named quite a few. Most were guild members or local artists. We didn't worry too much about figuring out who the children were."

Marti looked at the photographs of the young man again. His face was one of those enlarged. She could see the scattering of freckles across the bridge of his nose. The corner of his left front tooth had a tiny chip. His smile was lopsided; his posture relaxed. Could this be John Doe #17—arm with hand #2? She passed his photos to Vik. "Anyone you know?"

"Sure, Marti, my second cousin's sister-in-law's third cousin's uncle. How's that?"

"Just thought I'd ask."

There were five women young enough to be Lily Day, all just part of the crowd. Because of where they were standing when their pictures were taken, it was impossible to see their hands, and very little of their arms was visible. There wasn't even a smudge that could have been the tattoo.

"We'll have Nan and Lucy and Arlene Johns take a look at this young man," Marti said. "Carrie Pinkham, too. Who knows."

Only the heel of the loaf of stollen was left. When Vik reached for it, Marti protested. "You've got more at home."

"So? I'm hungry now."

"Yeah, well, this might be my last chance until Thanksgiving to eat real butter."

He handed her the butter. "Go for it."

"Vik!"

With just a hint of a smile, he tore the piece of stollen in half. "My contribution to your cholesterol count. Don't tell Joanna it was me."

Over doughnut holes and coffee, they agreed that they had

probably gotten as much from the pictures as they were going to. Then Marti helped pack the ones Nan had contributed, while Lupe thumbed through Jimmy Binslow's albums.

DeVonte tried not to show how irritated he was by the delays in going through customs, boarding the ship, and securing a cabin. The ship was so crowded that getting to the cabin had been a hassle. Now he was in a space that wasn't as wide as a walk-in closet, while Sharon went to find out what time the casino opened and when they would be serving breakfast.

He threw their carry-on, his camera case, and Sharon's purse on the narrow bunk. Sharon's purse was one of the few things he had never had the opportunity to look through. He made sure the cabin door was locked, opened the purse, and pulled out her wallet. Driver's licenses, credit cards, wedding picture—first husband, that was interesting—and an infant in a pink dress who, in successive photos, became a pouting toddler, a smiling cheerleader, and a black-gowned prom date. What the hell? She didn't look anything like Sharon. He took out the most recent and looked on the back. "To Mom, with love, Lisa." It was dated May tenth. He looked again. Mom.

Lisa. He remembered several phone calls where Sharon's voice dropped, became deliberately casual. Had he heard her say that name? Had she lied to him about having a child? Child, hell. That was a woman in that black dress, young maybe, but with curves. Yes, this must be her child. Poor, insecure Sharon would have a hard time introducing him to another woman this lovely, daughter or not, at least not until she was certain that he was all hers. As if any man could ever belong to just one woman, or wanted to.

He returned the picture to the little plastic sleeve and went through the purse's zippered compartments. In case of accident notify . . . two names, Lisa, her daughter, and a Marti MacAlister, friend. DeVonte wrote down MacAlister's name, address, and phone number. It seemed logical that Lisa would be staying with Sharon's friend. Lisa. Sharon's daughter. Another beneficiary. Damn. He replaced the wallet and unlocked the door. Now what was he going to do about that?

Marti kept the list of names that Lupe had put together based on who was in the photographs, along with the records that Nan had provided; membership lists for the art guild, various programs of events with lists of participating artists, newspaper clippings. While Vik talked with missing persons specialists about the photos taken thirty years ago, she sat down at the new computer, pulled up the word processor, and referenced and cross-referenced everyone according to what they did artistically. Next she sorted them according to first year of membership. Then, pleased because she knew how to do that, she put them in alpha order, reversed that, and put everyone together by name and year. When everything was printed, there were so many correlations they seemed meaningless.

The box of photos sat on the floor between her desk and Vik's. Vik refused to look at it, choosing to read the newspaper instead. Marti couldn't look away. "Damn it, Vik. There has to be something there."

She began looking at them again in random order.

"Jimmy Binslow is just standing there all by himself," she said.

Vik shifted in his chair, turned to another page in the newspaper, but said nothing.

There were no photos where Nan and Arlene were standing near each other. If they were in the same photo, they were standing with other people. "From the looks of it, Nan and Arlene were not close friends."

Vik grunted. "Professional jealousy."

"That's something to think about."

"Only if you're running out of ideas." Newspaper rustled.

She took the stack of printouts and found the one where she had sorted everyone according to what they did. Then she went through the photos again.

"Vik, here's Arlene with some pottery that has the same

color blue painted on it as our chip. And Nan. Vik, the setting for the jewelry looks like silver. Why didn't she tell me she worked with silver?"

"The guy isn't with Nan. At least not in any of the pictures. And why aren't there any pictures of Lucy Carlisle? Or her mother."

"Her mother was dead by then. Damned shame her property is so close to Clark Avenue. With any luck, this reporter doesn't know what he's talking about and they're not going to take her property."

"Eminent domain?" Marti asked.

"This article doesn't mention that," Vik said. "It just says there are ways for a determined developer to get the land. That must mean money. I wonder what she'd be willing to sell for. Not at any price, she's quoted as saying, but I don't believe that. That's prime property for another strip mall, close as it is to those new houses they put up and the golf course. They want to anchor it with a major chain store and pharmacy on that corner. Makes you wonder about what the developer might try."

Marti was more curious about why Lucy wasn't in any of the pictures. She checked out all of the photos with the red circles. Nobody else who was unidentified was standing with or near any of the artists, except for that one young man and Arlene. She picked up the phone. There was no answer at Arlene's pottery shop or her home. Nan wasn't at home or at the museum. She slammed down the receiver.

"Another one of those days," Vik said. He wasn't being sarcastic.

Sharon waited in line ten minutes to use the restroom, then closed the door to the bathroom stall and leaned against it. She squeezed her eyes tight shut and tried not to cry, but tears slipped out anyway. She wanted to be with DeVonte, but she didn't want to be here. She was afraid of sailing on water this deep, even for the five or six hours it would take them to dock at the island. Even the first deck was too high above the water. The roll of the boat was making her feel sick to her stomach, and there were too many people. What if the ship capsized? She didn't even know where the life jackets or life-boats were kept.

Worse, she had a whole week of sand and surf ahead of her. There was no way DeVonte would agree to swim in a pool, if there was one. She took two deep breaths. She loved him. She did. And he loved her. He wasn't like the others. He would protect her. He would keep her safe. DeVonte wasn't like the others.

When she reached the cabin, it was empty. There was a note. "Meet me on the second deck, aft, DeVonte." What the hell did "aft" mean? And second deck, was that this deck? She didn't have to look out the window to know it was higher than the first deck and she was afraid at that height. She sat on the bunk. The mattress was thin and it was rock hard. Maybe she could get DeVonte to come here, stay here with her, make love. No. There was something about that that re-pulsed her. Not DeVonte, just this bed, this room. But it wasn't like . . . no, it wasn't.

"No," she said aloud. She shook her head from side to side. "No . . . not here." But it wasn't like . . .

"Damn, damn damn!" Damn Rayveena for being sick enough to die with a disease that wasn't even mentionable, thanks to the stigma attached. Damn Rayveena for everything. Sharon had dreamed about her last night. She dreamed about her every night. The dreams were getting so familiar that they didn't always awaken her. Damn her! "Damn!"

She heard the key in the lock and jumped up and went to the window.

"Here you are, baby. I was waiting."

Late, she was late again. Was he upset? She didn't turn around to see. He came up behind her. His hands were gentle on her shoulders as he turned her toward him, began kissing her neck. No, not here, not here.

His hands began caressing her. She tried to respond. This was not that room. It was not the room with the narrow bed where she had sat with the man who had pictures of her mother having sex, pictures of her without her clothes on. DeVonte was not going to pose her on that bunk and point a camera at her. DeVonte was her husband. He was not that man. This was now, not then.

"What's the matter, baby, don't you want me?"

Sharon put her arms around him. They were married now. She returned his kiss and began pretending.

As Marti watched, Vik sorted through her computer printouts. From the expression on his face, she guessed that he was impressed. She wasn't sure she wanted him to feel that way about anything even remotely connected with generating reports.

"Not bad," he said. "Nan's mother was an artist, too. Better check and see if she made the jewelry. Maybe that's why Nan was snapped sitting at the table."

"Her mother wasn't with her."

"Maybe she was dead, Marti. Lucy Carlisle's mother was dead by then. There's a picture she painted here somewhere."

"You recognized it?"

"Yeah."

"Funny then that Lucy's mother's pictures were there, but Lucy's were not."

"The mother gave a lot of her stuff away in her will. There're a couple in the library, the historic society, and the Lake County Museum."

"I wonder why."

He thought for a minute. "I can remember hearing that Lucy wasn't the artist her mother was, but her paintings aren't all that bad. I just like the mother's better because they're places I know."

"I liked that about them, too."

"Well, one thing is for sure, I know a hell of a lot more

about art than I ever wanted to." He looked down at his desk. "You didn't eat my bagel, did you?"

"Vik, we went out to lunch, remember."

"That was then." He checked his top drawer "Oh, I know where it is. At the library."

"Your bagel?"

"No, MacAlister, Mrs. Carlisle did do at least one still life."

"And?"

"Ugly," he said. "That is one ugly painting."

"Maybe you just don't understand it."

"A table, an apple, a thick black line down the middle, and on the other half of the canvas a table, an apple that's half peeled, the knife, and the peel. What's to understand?"

"Too bad she isn't here to explain it. Maybe it was a phase, like those her daughter has."

"Where the hell is that bagel? I know I brought one back." He went through his desk drawers and came up empty. "I think the painting is in the library because Lucy gave it to the city. That's about the only way anything that bad would be hung where people could see it."

"Why would Lucy do that?"

"How would you like it if somebody compared what you did to what your mother did and you came up short?"

Marti thought of her cooking. "How did the mother kill herself?" she asked, not because she was interested, but because maybe if she distracted Vik he would remember where he put the bagel and settle down.

Vik thought about that. "Can't remember. It might not have been mentioned."

"And Lucy was a teenager when it happened."

"Yeah, there was a lot of crap in the paper about local artist passes legacy to daughter, or something just as foolish. A bunch of crap, like that article today about Lucy being forced to give up her house."

"Have you ever seen any of Lucy's work exhibited?"

"Of course not. Why would I purposely go look at a bunch

of stuff like what she had on the walls? Especially the lines. And the stuff she did in high school, which they hung in the hallways, was a lot worse. Real crap."

"All of it?" He remembered a lot more than she'd thought he did.

"I know where it is!" He jumped up, went to the closet, and retrieved the bagel from his coat pocket. He looked happy as he sat down and began eating it. "So what are we missing here? Anything?" He waved the hand holding the bagel in the general direction of the box of photographs and the computer printouts that he had returned to her desk.

"A better question might be, what do we have?"

"Damned little," Vik said. "Maybe if we come up with a reasonable explanation for the most recent arm with hand . . ." Vik glared at the box. His eyebrows almost met in the middle of his forehead. "Nothing," he said. "Nothing."

"A face maybe," Marti said.

"Right, and if we knew where to circulate it . . ."

"We'll have to start here," she said. "I'll talk to one of our local friendly reporters." After she arranged to have the photo in tomorrow's edition of the *News-Times*, she tried reaching Nan and Arlene Johns again, without success. She hoped they would get more out of these cases than a course in art appreciation.

As DeVonte walked toward the railing where the black man in the ship steward's uniform stood smiling at him, three children ran past. He had to step to one side to avoid colliding with one of them. Behind him, a door opened and he heard a woman laughing. He almost turned, but didn't. He didn't want the woman to notice or remember seeing him here. The man in the uniform turned so that his back was to DeVonte. For most of the cruise he had been smiling and pleasant as he followed DeVonte about the ship.

When he was certain no one was nearby, DeVonte joined the man at the railing. They were midship, on the starboard side. Grand Bahama Island was still too far away to be seen on the horizon. The sun was hot, the wind warm. The water, a deep, clear blue, was capped with white. Two seagulls whirled and screamed as they followed in the ship's wake.

"I know you, man?" DeVonte asked.

"No, but I know you." The man spoke in the soft, rolling accent of the islands. He was short, dark, and thin.

DeVonte looked down at him. "How is that, man?"

"Was June, was it not, when you sailed with that woman who wore her hair in curls going to the island but returned to the ship with many braids."

This one was observant. "And?"

"Then there was one, when, in April? The one with the hair that was once nappy and black, but was then straight and blonde. The high yellow woman with these." He made a motion with cupped hands indicating large breasts.

He was very observant. Both women had been married and cautious. He had been careful not to be too close to either of them. He had eaten at the same table with one, a communal table on board ship, and danced once with the other.

"The reason I remember," the man said, "is because we have to answer questions about both of them that the police in Fort Lauderdale ask us. It seems they are missing. There are other women who are missing also who came on board one of our ships; but I only work on this ship, and I did not see you with them."

"What makes you think I might have been with these women? I go to the island a lot to gamble at the casino. That place is lucky for me. I board alone. A casual flirtation, a drink, a dance maybe, what does that mean? I'm not here with anyone."

"Oh, it is not you who look like you are with them. It is they who let me know that they are with you. A woman has a way about her when she is with her man. Even if it is just for a dance or a drink. She is not possessed, she possesses. You know what I mean?"

"Yes. I think I do." His hand tightened on the rail. "And what did you tell the police?"

"What the others tell them. That I know nothing. But I was certain that I would see you again. It's been awhile, but time now that we talk about it."

You see too much, DeVonte thought. Aloud, he said, "Not here."

"In this cabin," the man said. He smiled, gold caps flashing as he held out a key.

"How much does that cost?" DeVonte asked.

"Two thousand American dollars. I have also seen that you carry much money, Mr. DeVonte Lutrell."

DeVonte pocketed the key. "Twenty minutes."

"No man, fifteen." The man in the steward's uniform walked away.

DeVonte went to his and Sharon's cabin first and retrieved a piece of wire and a pair of the latex gloves he had packed. It was a good thing he was always prepared for anything. He found the steward's room without any difficulty. It was on a lower deck just above the waterline and in a forward section. The corridor was empty. He went into the room, which was just wide enough to walk to the window, where he could see the ocean and a thin line of sky. There were two seats attached to a small table, which was bolted to the deck, a double bunk, and a small bathroom with a shower. Familiar with the layout, DeVonte left.

There was a twist in the walkway, and he waited there until he heard the lock in the cabin door turn and the door open. He slipped on the latex gloves. In four steps he covered the distance to the cabin and entered the narrow space right behind the man in the uniform. Before the man could speak or turn, DeVonte pushed the door closed. He was careful to stay behind the man as he swung the wire around his neck. When the man stopped struggling, he let him slip to the floor. Ignoring the man's bulging eyes and protruding tongue, he checked the side of his neck and detected no pulse.

Satisfied that the man was dead, DeVonte took the key that had fallen to the floor and pocketed it along with the one the man had given him. He dragged the man into the small shower and pulled the curtain. He used a towel to clean up, tossed it into the shower, and pulled the plastic curtain across the opening. He turned the lock on the bathroom door before he closed it. There was nobody in the hallway. He used the key to lock the cabin door and walked to the ladder.

The adrenaline rush made him feel hyped. He went up to third deck and forced himself to take deep breaths as he stood at the rail and looked over the side at the Atlantic far below. The water was the deepest, darkest shade of blue he had ever seen. It was so pure, so perfect; he often stood here when he came aboard, almost mesmerized, looking at it. He felt an affinity with the ocean, something he had never felt before, not even when he was a young boy with his mother. He should have been a sailor. One day soon he would buy a boat. One day soon he would be one with the sea.

At this distance the air didn't feel damp, and the sound of the water as it was parted by the steel prow of the ship was little more than a splash and a hum. Soon they would arrive at the island. Freeport. Flat, hot, and poor. Away from the turquoise water that tempered the heat and eased the glare of the sun, away from the almost white sand, Freeport was little more than dusty roads, grass that flared into fires without the spark from a match, dying fish that were sold from the back of a rusty truck, and *The Sound of Music* played with a reggae beat in the marketplace. The only thing he liked about Freeport was its proximity to the States and the casino.

He leaned against the bulkhead that eliminated his view of the main deck. Another deck jutted above and slightly over the main deck. That bulkhead extended here to the third, uppermost deck, and between here and the opposite side of the ship was the room where the coxswain, or maybe the captain, kept the ship on course.

It was quiet here. The steel bulkheads buffered the voices of the tourists and the tinny rhythms of the steel band that played two decks below—aft, near the fantail where the pool was. He had found this spot a number of cruises ago. It was a perfect place for assignations. There was no view unless you went to the rail and looked down at the water. And because there was so little to see, he had never encountered anyone when he came here. And he had come here a number of times; twice he had been met by a woman. The women the steward remembered, in fact.

He closed his eyes. He could remember their names but chose not to. Instead, he recalled the darkness of the night, where dark water met dark sky, with only a crescent moon high above and a scattering of stars. His fingertips had seemed to vibrate as he'd stroked a neck, a face. His hands went to the throat as he kissed them; and still kissing them, he'd pushed them against the wall. Then he'd pressed his thumbs into the sides of their necks until they'd stopped struggling and their bodies went limp. They disappeared as soon as they hit the white foam frothing at the side of the ship.

And now, despite careful planning and his insistence on secrecy, since both women were married—he had not been quite as careful as he thought—he had been required to kill again. In the future he would have to remember what the steward had told him about a woman sending implicit proprietary messages about the man she was with. That was not a mistake he ever intended to make again.

10

Marti didn't have any trouble finding the house where Arlene Johns lived. Two black and whites were parked in front, the Animal Control officer's van, an evidence tech's station wagon, and a car from the Coroner's Office. The house was one of the smaller Victorians on a quiet street on the east side of town, just a few blocks north of the precinct. Marti liked the wraparound porch, but she wasn't sure how they came up with the color scheme—a medium shade of olive green with maroon-and-pink gables and trim.

Overcast skies and rain had given way to sunshine at last, but it was still cool for September. Neighbors and onlookers stood in small clusters. Marti caught Vik's eye and nodded toward several women who stood with bare arms folded.

"Afraid they'll miss something," he muttered.

As soon as the call came in, Marti had dispatched a uniformed officer to the pottery shop. He'd reported back that there were no signs of forced entry. He would stay there until she and Vik had time to check out the place.

A female uniform met them at the door, which had not been forcibly opened. "Body's right over here." She escorted them inside. The area was cordoned off and still being processed by two crime scene technicians.

Gordon McIntosh stopped pacing and said, "Not your ordinary fall, but they could have waited to call me."

Arlene Johns lay crumpled at the foot of a staircase that paused at a window two-thirds of the way up then swiveled to the second floor. Both arms were pinned beneath her body. Her head was twisted at an angle only an owl could achieve and survive. In profile, one eye was open. She was wearing one shoe. The globe-shaped top of a newel post was just inches from her stocking-clad toes.

Marti turned to the uniform who had let them in. "Who found her?"

The dog warden stepped forward. "I did," he said, and hitched up his pants.

"Oh? No neighbor?"

"Dispatch got a call about a dog. When I got here, the dog was hoarse from barking. He's tied up out back, no food and out of water. Probably just hungry and thirsty. I knocked and when I didn't get an answer, I looked through the window and there she was, so I called it in."

"Who is the neighbor who complained about the dog?"

The dog warden pulled out his notebook and read off the name and address.

Jean Cozier was a harried-looking young woman wearing faded, tight-fitting jeans and a food-stained sweatshirt. She lived two houses down in another Victorian. Hers was salmon pink. The white-and-brown trim made Marti think of cake icing. Six children, all preschoolers, played on the porch.

"They need their naps," Cozier said, hands on hips. "I need their naps. And that dog has been barking all day. Can't you do something to get it to stop? She's done this before, left it out and ignored it. I told her I was calling the pound the next time it happened. What did she do this time? Resist arrest?"

Vik said, "I take it she would bring the dog in or feed it or whatever when you complained."

"Of course not! That would have been neighborly, considerate. Arlene is an artist. Artists don't give a damn about anything but their 'work.' Not that I consider turning out one useless bowl after another work. I don't think Arlene Johns has done an honest day's work in her life."

Marti managed to listen to another five minutes on the subject of Arlene Johns from her neighbor. "Mrs. Cozier"

"Miss Cozier. None of these are mine. I'm a day-care provider during the day so that I can buy this house and go to school at night. I'm studying law with a minor in urbanology."

As they walked back to Johns's house, Vik said, "Mind telling me what an urbanologist is? Don't tell me it means she's going to save Chicago?"

"That's what it sounds like."

"Hah," Vik said. "She can't even manage six kids and a barking dog. How does she expect to take on a city?"

Gordon was squatting beside Arlene Johns. "Classic," he said.

Marti looked at Vik. He shrugged and mouthed, "*Quincy* again."

"Can you tell what it is?" Gordon asked.

"Oh, come on, McIntosh," Vik said. "This one's too easy."

"Aha! You don't know!"

"It's the arms, McIntosh, the arms. You don't do a pirouette off the stair landing and hug yourself to keep from falling."

Gordon gave them a good-natured grin. "No, Jessenovik, that one's too easy. It's the newel post. There are just a couple of chips in the wood, but I bet it's how someone loosened it."

Vik walked around the perimeter of the yellow crime scene tape. "It's too close to the body," he said. "Unless she grabbed it, carried it like a football as she fell, and released it when she landed."

"Nope," Gordon countered. "She might have been alive when she landed, but she wasn't conscious."

"There's a lump on the side of her head that you can't see that's about the size of a golf ball. Bruising, too. What do you want to bet this whole fall down the stairs was staged, and she was hit with the newel post while she lay here?"

Vik rubbed his hands together. The expression on his face was almost cheerful. "I'll bet you one hundred and twenty milligrams of arsenic," he said.

"Aha! A fatal dose of inheritance powder. It's too easy, Jessenovik, but you're on!"

Marti went into the living room and left the two of them talking. Gordon's expansive bantering was okay, but there was something reassuring about Dr. Cyprian's monosyllabic reticence. Arlene Johns collected things, too. Maybe it was some kind of artistic inclination. Marti had rarely seen anything she wanted more than one of. Arlene's taste ran to brass. Anything brass. The smallest was an angel that sat beneath a lamp shade, the largest an elephant about a foot and a half tall that sat by the fireplace and saluted with a raised trunk. The thin layer of dust that covered tabletops and mantel indicated that nothing in the room had been disturbed.

Marti went into the kitchen. The objective here seemed to be to hang as many little shelves as possible, fill them with tiny little teacups, and allow the dust to stick to the thin layer of grease that covered them. Aside from a reluctance to dust, Arlene had been a tidy housekeeper, and there wasn't even an unwashed glass in the sink. Tucked beside the stove was a door that opened onto steps going up and down. Marti went up.

There were two large rooms upstairs. Here, Marti found Arlene's pottery from her bright color period. Every piece had been thrown on the floor and had shattered. She picked up one jagged piece painted sky blue and shook her head. Even if it did match the cerulean blue chip found under Jane Doe Lily Day's fingernail, she still wouldn't know any more than she did now. She put the shard of baked clay into a baggy. If it weren't for the fact that Arlene Johns was dead, blue pottery wouldn't mean a thing.

Elsewhere in the room, everything on two bookcases had been thrown on the floor. Books and papers were scattered everywhere. An overturned bureau blocked her entrance to a second room, where Arlene must have slept. Drawers had been dumped, nightstands overturned, and shelves ripped from the walls. Pale green drapes and lace panels hung at odd angles from the windows. The matching bedspread and the sheets had been pulled off the mattress. Clothing had been snatched from the closet, some still on the hangers, and thrown everywhere.

At first glance Marti could see that someone had been quite angry. But only the upstairs rooms were in a shambles. Controlled anger, maybe. Everything downstairs was tidy. Perhaps someone wanted this to look like vandalism, as if they had not been looking for something in particular. If Arlene Johns had not lost her balance and fallen down the stairs—if she had been pushed—then why this? Why try to make it look like an accident and a home invasion as well?

Sharon tried not to feel disappointed as the taxi took them from the ship to DeVonte's condo. After they drove past the casino and the marketplace, a McDonald's, Pizza Hut, and five or six churches, there was nothing but open space interrupted by little clusters of one-story buildings with three or four small stores, eateries, and open markets. She had imagined something like Vegas. Where were the nightclubs and the hotels? There was one big supermarket—for the tourists, the taxi driver said and laughed. Then she saw a few more shops clustered together. Now there was nothing but bush and grass, a few stubby palm trees, and here and there a single-story, cinder-block house, or maybe one made of brick with a chain-link fence around it. She couldn't even see the Atlantic. Maybe that was good. DeVonte said they would be right by the water, but maybe "right by" meant farther away, like these houses were.

"Go here," DeVonte said. The driver detoured around a group of stalls filled with T-shirts and things made of shells. He drove to a stall a short distance from the others and pulled up alongside a pile of conch shells.

"I'll fry it for supper," DeVonte said. "I like mine fresh from the ocean."

Sharon tried to block out thoughts like refrigeration and salmonella. Cooking it should make it okay, if it didn't taste too bad.

The condo was close to the ocean, too close, not more than fifty feet away. Sharon counted six balconies on the second floor and six down. The two-story building, painted pink with wrought-iron trim, was surrounded by sand and banana trees and hibiscus. There were no cars. Maybe everyone called a taxi. No, DeVonte said there was no phone. No television either. They had passed a small motel, also painted pink, but not as recently, about three or four miles back. There was another two-story condo across from the motel, small like this one, and a restaurant. There must be a pay phone there. They went past some construction still at the foundation stage; then there were low bushes and beyond that a turquoise view of the ocean, off-white sand and nothing.

A week. She would be here for a week. There was nothing to do. It was a tropical island; there had to be something somewhere. But what? Snorkeling, deep-sea diving, glass-bottom boats, all things she was afraid of. Perhaps she should be glad to be in such a small, secluded place. Too bad they were so close to the water.

The interior of the condo didn't surprise her. It had probably been furnished by the builder. The other apartments probably looked much the same. It had been built during the mauve-and-gray decorating craze of a few years ago. Every room was mauve, gray, and stark white. DeVonte was right. There was plenty of food—canned or stored in Tupperware—none fresh, but if he bought everything off the street the way he'd bought that conch, a lack of fresh fruit and vegetables might be a good thing. She found tea bags and instant coffee and put water on to boil. She wasn't taking any chances on getting sick. She assumed there was a hospital on the island, but she didn't want to pay the local doctors any visits.

The view of the beach would have been beautiful if she didn't dread going back into the water. As she stood by the window, there was a loud pop. She jumped. Behind her, DeVonte laughed.

"Champagne," he said, and named a vintage and year that meant nothing to her. He poured it into tall stemmed, crystal glasses.

"Umm," she said. It was good. When the champagne was gone, they made love.

When Marti and Vik left Arlene Johns's house, it was getting dark. Two uniforms were tossing the place. Marti and Vic would return to do the same and go to the pottery shop after they had talked with a few of Arlene's friends. Her nearest relative was an older brother who lived in Champaign. They had spoken with him by phone. He explained that Arlene had been married briefly, but that her husband had died in a car accident. He said he would drive up as early as possible tomorrow.

"I think this was personal, Jessenovik, very personal," Marti said, as they got into the car.

"Could be."

"Those upstairs rooms were attacked, just as Arlene Johns was." Gordon had found additional trauma to the body. It looked as if Johns had been kicked in the ribs and abdomen at least half a dozen times as she lay at the foot of the stairs. "There were no defense marks."

"Maybe she was taken by surprise; she didn't have time to react," Vik said. "There was no forced entry, which indicates she let in whoever it was. That could mean that she knew her attacker."

"Makes sense," Marti agreed. "It would have been nice to have some scrapings under her fingernails though." Maybe when the forensics team went through what they had vacuumed up at the scene, there would be some trace evidence to work with. "So," she said, "what do you think? Have we said or done something to stir up a killer? Or could this be a coincidence?"

"Stirring something up implies that Arlene knew something. All we've got are those old photographs. If John Doe number seventeen is standing there with her, he can't be the killer."

"Someone who knew him *and* her then."

"But why, Marti?"

That was where she began drawing a blank. "Unless someone killed him and didn't know there was any reason to kill Arlene Johns until we started asking questions."

"Well then, we'd better move our butts on this one and find out who he or she is, although the odds on anyone we talked with having the strength to do something like this are slim. Maybe we should check the emergency rooms, see if anyone has come in with a heart attack."

"Oh, Vik, Lucy Carlisle and Carrie Pinkham might be getting up there in age, but Nan Conser isn't that old."

"Nan Conser was around the same time as the rest of them. She has to be about the same age."

Vik was right. Nan did have to be at least in her early fifties. That came as a small shock to Marti. Nan didn't look as old as the others. Marti had grouped Nan with women friends her own age, closer to forty.

Neither Nan nor Lucy Carlisle answered the phone. Carrie Pinkham was at home. Carrie's house was quiet when they arrived, the grandchildren either with their parents or sleeping. Lindsey Kirch arrived ten minutes after they did. Marti thanked her for coming on such short notice. By the time Lindsey arrived, Carrie had led them into the kitchen and fixed them all coffee. Now she brought Lindsey a can of diet pop.

A wall had been knocked out so the kitchen took up the entire back half of the house. They sat at a big, round table. Three high chairs were lined up along the wall. The room smelled of gingerbread, and Carrie cut thick squares from a large pan and served them on paper napkins.

With Lindsey, conversation became easy. No, Carrie had not had any contact with Arlene Johns. Marti showed her the picture of Arlene with the scraggly-haired young man.

Carrie's only comment was, "I never noticed him, but he certainly would have been out of place. These exhibits were much more formal, by invitation only. Only Jimmy Binslow could have gotten away with hair like that, but his was much neater, tied in a ponytail at the nape of his neck."

So this young man would have been noticeable and would have called attention to himself and Arlene. Why did she seem so friendly toward him in the photos if he didn't belong there?

Lucy Carlisle answered the phone the next time Marti called. There was one light on at the rear of the house when they arrived. Marti had to ring the bell seven times before Lucy came to the door. Instead of opening it, she slid open a small panel, then said, "Oh, it's you," a greeting less than welcoming. Her voice quavered. She sounded old and tired.

"Are you all right, ma'am?" Vik asked. "Is there anything we can do?"

"No. Just a minute."

She unlocked the door, removed a safety chain, and admitted them. Again they went to the kitchen. The room made Marti think of Snow White or Cinderella, but she couldn't say why. It was small and cozy. One wall was brick. Both cats were curled up in wicker baskets. They noted Marti and Vik's presence and went back to sleep.

"Can I get you something?"

"No, ma'am," Vik said.

Lucy looked as if she wasn't feeling well. She smelled of camphor and moved as if her joints were stiff.

"Are you all right, ma'am?" Marti asked again.

"Oh, it's just these developers. They're hounding me so. Sometimes I feel like selling them the house just so they'll leave me alone. But I don't want to. Where would I go? Where would I find another house like this?" Tears welled up in her eyes and she brushed them away with the back of her hand. "I don't want another house; I just want to keep this one. I just want them to leave me alone."

When asked if she had talked with Arlene Johns recently, she seemed surprised.

"Arlene? Good heavens no. We're not friends or anything. We're not even associates anymore. I haven't seen or talked with Arlene in years."

Marti debated whether or not to tell her Arlene was dead. Before she could make up her mind, Vik said, "She died today, ma'am."

"Good heavens!" Lucy exclaimed. "Was it her heart? She didn't have cancer or anything like that, did she? That is such a painful way to go, and with her brother downstate and her sister, Grace, in Hawaii . . . Grace must be nearing seventy-five now, and I hear her emphysema is real bad, which doesn't surprise me. She must smoke two or three packs a day. I don't think she and Arlene were close. Arlene was a change-of-life baby, you know; her mother was over forty when she was born. I'm sure another child was the furthest thought from her mind. Well now, I'll have to find something to wear to the funeral."

When Marti showed her the picture of the unidentified young man, she seemed taken aback.

"A hippy? Why do you have this?"

"Oh, he's just a young man who was at one of the art guild exhibits."

"At a guild exhibit? When? Good heavens, this looks old, that hair; though I guess they are wearing it long again now, aren't they? When was this taken?"

"Nineteen-eighty."

"Well, I didn't go to any of the art guild's activities back then. I wasn't even here. I was abroad. I wasn't a member; my mother was. I'm not sure I would remember him if I had seen him somewhere. A lot of people looked like this in those days, even here in Lincoln Prairie. He probably just wandered into the exhibit. I bet he was using drugs. What's his name?"

"That's what we don't know."

She offered them coffee again and again they declined. When they went to Nan Conser's house, nobody was home.

It was late when Marti and Vik returned to the precinct. It had turned cold and the wind had picked up. There was a flagpole outside their window with a chain that clanged like a bell. Most of the time Marti could ignore it. Tonight it was annoying. They had spent two hours going through Arlene Johns's house after the team of scene-of-crime technicians and a couple of uniforms had finished tossing it. Everyone came away empty. Either the person who first tossed the place had found what he or she was looking for or hadn't, and neither Marti nor Vik nor any of the other officers had been able to figure out what it was or what it meant.

When they finally had time to go by the pottery shop, it was just as Marti remembered it and, as far as she could determine, undisturbed. All of the papers and files relevant to the business were kept in unlocked file cabinets. Vik hummed as he packed them into boxes for transport to the precinct, eager to start reading through them. Maybe she could come up with some way to get whatever information there was— assuming there was any—on the computer. Not that she wanted to, but Vik had been impressed with her last effort.

The coffeepot at the station house was empty. They hadn't had a decent cup in two days, except for what Vik had brought from home, unless they drove over to Dunkin' Donuts. The grand jury hearings were almost over, which meant that Slim and Cowboy would be back soon. For once she was looking forward to seeing them.

"We don't need coffee," she said. "We need sleep." Ben was off tonight, not that she had the energy to take advantage of that, but it would be nice to snuggle up to a warm body. "Let's pack it in, Jessenovik. I'm too tired to think straight. The autopsy is in the morning. Then we'll start getting reports. We need to check Johns's phone records ASAP and get the lab reports." What would they do if Arlene Johns had ingested arsenic recently? It would make the probability much greater that their arms-with-hands killer had struck again, but they were still no closer to figuring out who that was.

Sharon stood on the balcony and looked out at the ocean, surprised by how let down she felt. Not disappointed, just . . . she wished she were back in the States. What little she had seen of Freeport wasn't anything like the television commercials. It was flat and hot and poor. It hurt to see children selling home-baked goods, and it was depressing to see the tiny vans with tired women and dust-covered men going home from work. And this condo, she didn't even know where she was in relationship to the rest of the island. They had been in the taxi so long that she knew it was quite a distance from the boat, but she didn't know enough about Freeport to have any sense of direction or distance.

She would have to find a phone in the morning. She had promised to let Marti know where she was. There was no place to shop out here, not even the little native-run stalls, and apparently no large department stores. The only other inhabitants in their condo were a gray-haired man who wore a thong for a bathing suit, his three children, all under five, and his wife, also beginning to gray; and they all spoke French, no English.

The crowded beaches, friendly natives, and frosty glasses of piña colata that she had expected had not materialized. The breeze was nice, the air warm this late at night, the sky clear and dark with a scattering of stars and a half-moon hanging low. The ocean moved in soft hisses followed by deep rumbles. She shivered when she thought of the water but not because she was cold. DeVonte said he would rent a boat tomorrow so they could go sailing. A boat, something not much bigger than they were, on an ocean that was thousands of miles deep!

He laughed when she asked if it was a small boat. Like most men, he thought her fears were amusing. She wished he was different and understood. He said he would teach her to sail while they were here; and when they came back the next time, they would buy a boat of their own. But she didn't want to come back, and Lord knew she didn't want a boat. She just wanted to go home.

11

DeVonte left the condo at 6:30 A.M. the next morning. Sharon was still sleeping. He walked the three miles to the lake, where a water taxi would take him nearer the center of the island. He needed to find out the status of the tropical depression that had been developing when they left the States yesterday. There were no telephone, television, or even radio at the condo. After he found out about the weather, he was going to have to go to a pay phone and try to get through to the States. He needed to talk with Lisa, Sharon's daughter.

The day was already getting hot, but it was not unpleasant. This close to the ocean, the breeze off the water tempered the heat. His feet, shod in sandals, would be covered with the dry, tan dust that packed the road long before he reached the small dock, where there would be a boat to ferry him across the small lake, a shortcut that would take less time than calling a cab or waiting for a van bus and driving the distance to the center of town. Hibiscus were in bloom and small, curly-tailed lizards darted in and out of the spiky, dry grass along the side of the road. The sky was a bright, clear blue. He saw something off in the distance that could be clouds; but if so, they were far away.

He spotted a narrow path through the grass and bushes and among a stumpy bunch of palm trees and veered off the road toward the sound of the ocean. The water here was most often calm and lazy; the waves, even at high tide, lapped

129

against the shore and receded with little undertow. Today the waves were higher and crashed against the sand with more energy than usual. A harbinger of an approaching storm? Perhaps, or perhaps just a little of the turbulence that danced at the edge of the storm. This was the place of his birth, the place where he felt most himself, but also most like a stranger. He had been through storms here before. A hurricane would be nothing more to him than the means to lose a wife . . . and her daughter.

He could hear the boat's engine idling before he walked to the rear of the small motel where the boat was docked. He boarded, then gave the smiling, dark-skinned driver two dollars. The man could see that he was not a tourist and did not attempt to make conversation, which was good. It was too early to talk with anyone, and he did have things to think about. The boat would seat about twelve, six on either side, sitting on a long, narrow bench. The tourists who came here were not kind to the island. Paper cups, beer bottles, and pop cans floated in the water. Other debris was trapped in the tall grasses along the concrete wall that abutted the water and created a walkway between the lake and the motel. DeVonte stood and cupped his hand over his eyes, scanning the five piers that were built on old pilings and jutted about fifteen feet into the water. He was looking for Captain Bob. He had rented the old man's boat a few times, always going out alone. He might need to rent it tomorrow, but neither captain nor boat were docked here.

"I want to rent a boat," he told the driver. "But I don't see Captain Bob."

"For here or to go on the ocean?"

That was a thought. This lake would be fine when it was time for Sharon to drown in the storm while they were trying to move farther inland to escape the flooding. But for tomorrow's outing, the ocean would be great.

"You know someone who would rent one?"

"Sure," the man said with a smile.

DeVonte liked that about the island. The economy, or lack of it, was such that anything could be rented or bought.

"Give me his name."

"He is William. Tell him I sent you. I am his cousin, Maurice."

"Where can I find him?"

"You know that marketplace another two miles down the road? That way?" He pointed in a direction farther down the road from the motel.

"Where they have stalls and there's a restaurant not too far away?"

"Yes, that is the one. Just ask for William. Someone will know where he is."

"Thank you." It was a tiny place, half a dozen small, dark stalls packed with T-shirts and shell jewelry, a desperation stop just off the road where tourists could stop at the last minute and find a souvenir to bring home. Everything was priced higher than at the big market near the casino, a water taxi's ride and a short walk away.

It was a ten-minute ride to the dock at the opposite side of the lake. DeVonte stopped at a small restaurant nearby. As early as it was, the tables were already set with smooth, white cotton tablecloths and decorated with small vases of hibiscus. Inside, he knew that the bathroom was clean. The menu was limited. He ordered two muffins, warmed with butter, and a cup of coffee.

"Have you heard any news of the storm?" he asked. "Is it still likely to come?"

The waitress with a round face the color of roasted chestnuts gave him a wide, gap-toothed smile. "Storm?" she said. "There will be no storm here. You watch and see. Always they say the storm is coming. See how the sun smiles today? Enjoy your stay with us. Do not be frightened into leaving."

She thought he was just a tourist. "Is there still a phone around back?" he asked.

"You have been here before!"

He should not have said that. He didn't like doing things that might cause someone to remember him. He knew the food would be slow in coming. He decided to call. Lisa looked young enough to be in high school. He would have to catch her while she was still at home. And if she was not staying with this Marti MacAlister, it might take longer to get in touch with her.

It was never easy to call from the island. After several attempts to dial direct with a credit card, he had to get an international operator and use coins.

"Hello?" Good, a young girl, not an adult.

"Could I please speak with Lisa?" If pressed, he would have to assume that Sharon and Lisa had the same last name.

"Who's this?"

"Is this Lisa?"

"Who wants to know?"

"Her mother's new husband." No point in not saying that. It was part of the bait to lure her to the island. Everyone would know in a few days. Although, he thought, once Sharon and her daughter were dead, he would stay here, at least for a while. Here everything would be accidental. And in the aftermath of a storm, even one that only gave the island a glancing blow, there would not be time for the authorities to ask questions.

"Hello?"

There was silence on the other end of the line, then, "She *married* you?"

"Yes. You *are* Lisa!" He let just a touch of the island slip into his voice. Sometimes Americans trusted him more once they knew he was not an American, not that he ever let them know he was from such a poor island. If he just said the West Indies, they most often assumed he had come to the States and made his fortune, which in an unconventional sense was true.

132

"Why do you want to know? Why isn't *she* calling me?"

He could hear the anger in her voice and rushed to soothe her. "I am so glad to finally talk with you. Your mother, well, she didn't think you would approve."

"Why not? How old are you? You're not like, twenty, are you?"

He laughed. "No, it's nothing like that." He thought of the wedding photo in Sharon's wallet and wondered if that man was Lisa's father. "You know how she is when it comes to your father," he said, guessing. Whoever the man was, Sharon still had some problem with or connection to him or the photograph would not be there. Not that it mattered to him.

"She likes to surprise him," the girl said.

"And I have surprised you."

"Yes."

"Good. Now let's both surprise your mother." It took less than he thought it would to convince her to fly to Nassau. Perhaps once he got her here, there would be no need to travel any farther than a few miles across the Atlantic. If he killed her there, Sharon would never know anything. Maybe, if the storm came. Then he could tell them whatever he wanted to about mother and daughter, accurate or not.

It only took another three-quarters of an hour to make flight reservations for that afternoon. When he called back, she became reluctant.

"Sharon told me she was going alone."

Sharon. They were either best friends or not close. It seemed more likely the latter. And Sharon had not kept this trip a secret. Who else had she told?

"She is very concerned that you will be angry with her. That is why I am calling. It is so beautiful here. It is a hard place for anyone to stay angry for long. I want this to be a happy time for her, and for you, too. I do not want to return to a household of angry women."

"She misses me?"

"Yes, very much. And she is not happy."

There was silence on the other end of the line. He decided to wait.

"When does the flight leave?"

Good! "Twelve-fifteen. Make sure you're there an hour early. Do you have money for cab fare? I can arrange . . ."

"No. I've got enough. That's fine. And thanks."

The waitress waited until he returned to bring the coffee and muffins. He folded two dollar bills and slipped them under the saucer. After he had eaten, he shunned the small vans that served as taxis and would be filled with workers who smelled of perspiration even though their workday had not yet begun and walked the rest of the way to town instead. Along the way he tipped his cap to a local police officer, who was dressed in the quaint but colorful uniform of the Queen's Gendarme. Often he came here and stayed a week without seeing a member of the local constabulary. He wondered if it was because the crime rates here were low or because the island was so small. He was certain that crime was well controlled here, not out of hand the way it was becoming in Jamaica. As he walked, he glanced up at the sky. A few clouds, not dark, certainly not ominous. Maybe the tropical depression had dissipated or wandered off in another direction.

He went into several small stores. As usual, gospel music played on local radio stations and nobody was tuned into the news. He stopped at an open bar where two elderly gentlemen were having a morning shot of rum, sat on a stool beneath the grasslike roof, and ordered a Bloody Mary. It was too early for anything else.

He caught one of the men's attention and tipped his glass toward the sky.

The man gave him a brown-toothed smile that was more gaps than teeth. "Yes, man, she is out there," he said, "and headed right toward us. Tomorrow maybe, or the next day, unless she picks up speed. They say she is moving slowly."

"Gaining strength," the bartender said. DeVonte intercepted his glance and indicated that he wanted a refill.

"I like storms," he said when the bartender came over. "I'm staying, riding this one out."

"This one, she might ride you. Perhaps you should be leaving. These storms, they are nothing to play with. They come, man, and strip the leaves from the trees. Uproot them. Topple the houses, cave in the roofs. And water, there is water everywhere for days after the rain stops. It is the flooding that is so awful, not the wind or the rain."

DeVonte downed what was left of the first drink and reached for the second.

The bartender took the empty glass and turned away. "Hey, old man!" DeVonte said. "They are leaving yet? The tourists?"

"Not the ones who stay at the casino. But I hear that the ships going to the States today are full, and those coming from the States have just the gamblers."

Water splashed as the bartender gave the glass a quick wash.

"There are storm warnings yet?"

"No, nothing," the old man said. "They say this one has not made up her mind yet which way she will go; but Sister Matiwilda, she says it is coming here. And that one knows what she is talking about."

Satisfied that the storm, however slow, was still heading this way, DeVonte finished off his drink, caught a cab to the small airport, and arranged a round-trip flight to Nassau in a prop job that he had flown in before. He allowed for enough time in Nassau to rent a boat. If the water wasn't too choppy, he could tell Lisa it was his boat and let her think it was just a short sail to Freeport. It would be easy enough to help her drown. Once the storm hit, even if it sideswiped the islands, nobody would remember something as trivial as him walking with a young girl. Everything depended on that hurricane. It would come, though. It would.

* * *

The pilot was nervous about taking off with a storm on the horizon, but more money than he would see again anytime soon convinced him to go ahead. DeVonte returned to the waiting taxi and directed the driver to take him to the big market. He did not care much for what was offered at the local eateries, especially not the place nearest the condo, about three miles away. Except for the conch, too much of it was American, but not cooked quite the way Americans cooked it, or the way that he liked it.

He arrived at the stall where the conch was pulled from the shell and sold, just as a truck was pulling up with a fresh catch. By the time he returned to the dock where the water taxi was waiting, he had bought bread, the last tub of margarine in a small grocery store, and fresh vegetables. If he got back in time tonight, he would prepare a conch stew.

Now he just needed a reason to leave his new bride once again. He thought about that for a minute and smiled. They would go for a swim, and he would suggest the boat ride—just the two of them—and go off, supposedly to make the arrangements. He would let her know that sometimes Captain Bob was hard to find and remind her that there was no way he could call if he was delayed. And then, even if he was late getting back, and if Sharon was angry with him, so what? She wouldn't live long enough for it to matter.

Marti and Vik had time for roll call and a quick breakfast before Arlene Johns's autopsy began a little after 9:00 A.M. Unlike Dr. Cyprian, Gordon McIntosh was not an early riser, if given the choice. The autopsy told them little that they didn't already know. Arlene Johns had had surgery twice, had never been pregnant, and was a healthy, postmenopausal, fifty-nine-year-old female. After the autopsy, with what Marti was beginning to think was either showmanship or a strong need for drama, Gordon gave them the toxicology results they had been waiting for. There was no indication of arsenic present in the remains.

"No arsenic," Vik said.

"So this could have been an impulsive killing and not premeditated."

"Too bad we don't have a clue as to who it is."

"We have clues," Marti said. "We just haven't got enough of them yet or figured out how to put them together."

Marti had been sitting at her computer for about ten minutes when Arlene Johns's brother came in. He seemed surprised to be shown upstairs to the office, but unless the bereaved were also considered suspects, she couldn't come up with a good reason to interview him at the Coroner's Office or in one of the small cubbyholes downstairs. The brother, Davis Holt, was at least six feet two. He was a gaunt man, with suspenders holding his pants over a potbelly. Thick-lensed glasses indicated something more than a routine vision problem. Marti wondered if he was able to drive. She guessed his age at the late sixties.

"What happened to Arlene?" he asked. "Did someone rob her?" His voice shook, but Marti couldn't tell if it was emotion or a health- or age-related tremor.

"We haven't found any indication of that yet, sir."

"I don't understand. Arlene was always such a gentle person. She tried to paint, tried hard, took lessons, then she began dabbling in ceramics, which led to making pottery. Her sister and I thought it was a bit frivolous; but it was what she wanted to do—something she could do. It wasn't anything useful, but she wasn't hurting anyone. Why would anyone hurt her?"

Marti seldom had an answer for that. She didn't try to find one now.

Vik offered Mr. Holt some coffee, which he accepted. That done, Vik retreated to his desk, content to let Marti handle the interview. She rubbed her jaw and Vik nodded. He would jump in if he thought of anything she'd missed.

"A good girl, Arlene was," Mr. Holt said. "Much younger

than me and Grace, but she was never any trouble. Oh, she went off to that commune for a couple of months one summer, but a lot of young people did things like that in the seventies. And she did get disillusioned quickly and come home. A lot of those dropouts just dropped out forever. And it wasn't like the commune was one of those cults."

The word "commune" caught Marti's attention. "But there were no communes in this area." She had already asked about that.

"Oh no, certainly not," Holt agreed.

She decided to show Mr. Holt the photographs. He recognized most of the older people but couldn't place the young man they thought might be John Doe #17. His comments sounded like one long reminiscence. As he rambled, Marti thought back to her conversation with Nan Conser, not what was said so much as her impressions. The art guild sounded like a close-knit group, one that protected its image of itself and didn't allow anyone in who did not conform to that. They also sounded competitive, perhaps even petty. Dexter Penwell was just a sign painter, a cartoonist; Carrie Pinkham was just an imitation Grandma Moses; and Jimmy Binslow? An amateur shutterbug maybe. Insiders and the excluded. An interesting mix. Volatile? How did the members get along among themselves?

"Was your mother or father a member of the guild?" she asked Mr. Holt.

"Oh yes," he said. "My mother was a gifted watercolorist. My sister Grace paints marvelous landscapes."

"Then you come from an artistic family?"

"No, just Mother and Grace. Arlene is a potter. None of us consider that art. If Mother hadn't been a founding member of the guild, Arlene never would have been allowed to join, let alone be elected president, which was done for my mother's sake."

Marti pointed to a photo of Arlene. "Her work is quite colorful."

"Yes," her brother agreed, "and very mundane. Not much

has changed over the years, but at least she figured out a way to make money at it."

Marti wasn't sure she agreed with Holt's assessment of his sister. She liked Arlene's work. Everyone loved the pieces she had brought home. She thought art should be something that pleased you, that made you think, or perhaps remember. The more she looked at Arlene's pottery, the more she realized that she hadn't just bought it as gifts. There was something about it, the texture, the muted browns and grays, that she found soothing. It made her think of Momma's kitchen, warm in the winter and smelling of supper and maybe peach cobbler or apple pie. It made her think ahead to their first winter in their new home and a fire crackling in the fireplace. That was the gift she had really wanted to give them when she brought home Arlene's pottery.

"Oh," Mr. Holt said, "there's Nan Riley; she's a Conser now." He turned the picture over and checked the date. "So that's why she's there. I wonder if that's her work or her father's. Of course the guild would never recognize being a silversmith or jewelry designing as an art, but her mother had just died. I think they were trying to be nice. Her mother had tried to join for years. I'm still not convinced they should have let Nan in."

Mr. Holt went on. "Her father thought she would stay in the business with him, keep it going after he passed; instead, she joined the guild and stopped working with him. I guess it was important to her to fulfill her mother's ambitions. Her mother was one of those people who always wanted to belong. Married beneath her, I think."

Marti tried to concentrate on what Holt was saying and not how snobbish he sounded. Nan had told her that her mother was an artist and not accepted by the guild, but she'd never mentioned that her father was a silversmith or that she knew the craft as well, not even when Marti had mentioned the metallic silver. The phone interrupted her concentration. Vik answered it.

"Did Nan go to the commune, too?" Marti asked.

"Oh no, although that does surprise me. I would have thought that once Arlene went, and then Lucy Carlisle, Nan's mother would have insisted that Nan be like the others."

"What did Nan's joining the guild have to do with her mother dying if her father was the one who considered himself the artist?"

"Oh, but he didn't. He knew he was just a craftsman. It was the mother, you see, always making more of what he did than what it was. Always pushing him to be something he wasn't and Nan as well. I think Nan did everything she could to please her; but as you can see, she was never anything more than an art historian."

"Who were Nan's friends?" Marti asked. "Anyone in the guild?"

"I don't think so."

"Were there many members Arlene's age?"

He glanced at the photos. "Some. The guild was always good about attracting new members."

Vik cleared his throat. "What about Lucy Carlisle?" he asked.

"Lucy? I don't think Arlene and Lucy were ever friends. They certainly wouldn't have been after Lucy came back from that commune. Arlene had nothing good to say about the place, and the guild didn't hold with that group. Besides which, Lucy must have stayed for at least a year, and there was certainly no excuse to be made for that, even though her family lied and said she was studying abroad."

"But it was okay for Arlene to go to the commune," Vik said.

"Well, it was only a couple of months and everyone chalked it up to youthful indiscretion, and of course Mother was a founding member of the guild."

"And Lucy?" Vik persisted.

"Lucy's mother had been an active guild member, a great fund-raiser. She couldn't admit to Lucy doing something as common as joining a commune, so everyone let it pass. Lucy was not exactly a teenager when she joined, closer to thirty at least. So there wasn't that excuse."

"Were Lucy and Arlene at the commune at the same time?" Vik asked.

There was a rasping sound as Mr. Holt scratched his cheek. "No," he said. "Now that I think of it, Arlene went the summer of seventy-three or maybe seventy-four. Lucy must have joined in seventy-nine, or maybe eighty, not long before her mother died. Lucy didn't join the guild, you see, even though her mother was a member. I think it might have been one of those mother-daughter rivalry things. And, Lucy Senior was always considered the better painter, at least until Lucy began exhibiting. That was when she was asked to join the guild. That made quite a difference, a formal invitation. Studying at the commune did help her quite a bit with technique."

"Are we talking about the same commune?" Marti asked.

"Oh yes, this was some kind of artists' colony in Indiana."

"Do you know where in Indiana?"

"Not exactly, somewhere near Michigan City."

"And Nan Conser never went to this or any commune?"

"No. I don't think Nan had any illusions about being an artist," Mr. Holt said. "She found her niche in art history and commuted to Northwestern University. As an art historian, she was eligible for guild membership, and her expertise would certainly be appreciated; but she resigned after a year. I think she joined as a gesture because of her mother."

Nan's mother, who had been excluded. And then there was the young man, whom Mr. Holt didn't recognize. Could that happy hippy with Arlene Johns have been part of the commune? He looked at least ten years younger than Arlene. It was unlikely given the age difference that they could have been at the commune at the same time. Arlene seemed quite pleased that he was there, not a typical reaction from the president of the guild.

*   *   *

Sharon found the storage area that was located between two first-floor apartments. Six areas were separated by waist-high plywood. Nothing was secure. DeVonte hadn't stored anything but beach chairs, a hibachi, and a Weber grill. She took one of the folding lounge chairs and walked through the sand toward the beach. She didn't believe in sunbathing and opened the chair among a stand of palm trees. The air was warm and there was just the rustle of palm fronds as she opened her magazine. She tried to ignore the hiss of the waves and the curly-tailed lizards that darted in and out of the grass. Lizards. The commercials never mentioned them.

Her view of ocean and sky was as perfect as an advertisement. Even though she would never choose to live here, she could enjoy this for a week if only she could stay away from the water. She read for a few minutes then tired of that and closed her eyes.

For a moment she thought of Rayveena. She didn't hate her mother, even if Rayveena did hate her. Mother. The last time she'd called Rayveena Mama, she wasn't more than seven. Rayveena had been drunk and slapped her. "Don't you call me that, girl. You call me by my name." For a long time she hadn't called Rayveena anything. She had hardly spoken to her at all. Rayveena didn't want her then, and she didn't want her now. And that was okay. She didn't want Rayveena either. Neither of them had ever needed the other. Sharon stretched her legs until her toes reached the sunshine that filtered through the palm leaves, glad that she was too far away for Rayveena to call. Maybe they would both get lucky and Rayveena would die while she was gone.

Instead of going to lunch, Marti ordered pizza. She was getting tired of pizza in particular and fast food in general, but right now she did not need the distraction of going out to eat. She assembled some of the photographs on her desk: Arlene with brightly colored pottery and an unidentified young man; Nan—who had not admitted being a guild member—with the silver jewelry she had never mentioned making; and Carrie, smiling and proud because she was included. There was no picture of Lucy, so Marti wrote her name on an index card.

She reviewed what she now knew about each of them. There was anger in the way the rooms at Arlene's house had been ransacked, in the way she had not just been shoved, but hit on the side of the head and kicked in her midsection as well. That anger could have had its beginnings back when the photos were taken or even before then. There were few connections among these four women other than the exhibits themselves. They certainly were acquaintances, but they did not become friends while they were guild members. If she could find one connection that led to Arlene's death, could she then find connections leading to the deaths of the arms with hands or, at least, the young man, John Doe #17? She came back to Nan. What was the real story about her parents and the art guild? Why had she lied?

Marti chose three pictures and the index card with Lucy Carlisle's name on it, went over to the computer, and turned it on. She lined up the photos and card on the worktable. Then she pulled up the word processor and typed the women's names in vertically. She created columns and began thinking of words to enter at the top. A computer had almost kept her from solving her last major case. Maybe this time a computer would help her.

She tried to think of some key words. Arsenic—she added the arms-and-hands victims to the list. Commune. Art. She cut that and listed each type of art. Next she keyed in guild. Then she was stuck. She added the years 1979 through 1981, then the current year. She keyed in the year of death above them. She had run out of topics. Maybe she should think in terms of relationships instead. But there were none, unless the unknown arms and hands were the connections. If Arlene's brother were to be believed, these people didn't even think they had art in common. Marti stared at her graph for at least fifteen minutes before she decided that what she needed was a chronology. She began with Arlene going to the commune in 1973 or '74. Then she got the notes she had taken while Arlene's brother was talking. When she finished, she gave a copy to Vik. Then she tried to reach Nan again. Still no answer.

Vik scanned the printout, then said, "So Lucy Carlisle is at the commune for maybe a year in seventy-nine or eighty, Arlene is there the summer of seventy-three or seventy-four, and Nan never went at all. Arlene became president of the guild in nineteen-seventy-nine, after her mother died." He tossed Marti's notes on his desk. "All of this is interesting, but what the hell does it have to do with our arms with hands? Does it have anything to do with why Arlene is dead, or does it mean nothing at all?"

He was right. Creating a chronology was interesting, but this one didn't tell them a hell of a lot. There were too many gaps.

"I like this though. You're getting pretty good with the damned machine. I think you should go through your notes and keep working on this," Vik said. "We could come up with something that will help."

We. If she wasn't careful, he would let her do all of the computer work, just as he let her do most of the driving. Good thing the lieutenant wanted their reports keyed into the computer. Vik would have to do that himself. As much as he liked detail and paperwork, you would think he would love having a computer.

"I wish we knew more about this commune, Vik. I wonder if there are records anywhere. Maybe Lily Day or John Doe number seventeen lived there too, if they were, in fact, artists. We need to find out." She tried calling Nan again, at home and at the museum. When there was no answer, she tried the Lincoln Prairie Cultural Center, the umbrella organization for the museum.

"No," the woman who answered said, "we haven't seen her. Nan is a volunteer so we can't complain. But her work is so vital right now, and she hasn't been in for two days."

Worried, Marti hung up. Two days. Arlene was dead. What if something had happened to Nan, too? Worse, what if Nan was their perp and had run away after she killed Arlene? But why? She didn't think there was enough motive in what she had heard so far. But how much more had Nan lied about or withheld? She had to find Nan and talk with her. It was hard to believe that Nan could be a killer, but it wouldn't be the first time the perp had turned out to be someone she knew.

12

Sharon felt the warm Atlantic water swirling about her ankles and was ready to cry. Farther out, much farther out, DeVonte beckoned to her. She did not want to go to him. She did not want to swim or even get near the ocean ever again. He was so happy here. He loved the water so much. How could he still not know how she felt?

She waded out to where the water was colder, walked until it was almost to her shoulders, and plunged in. She kept her strokes smooth and slow as she swam toward him. After a few minutes it seemed like the farther she swam, the farther away he became. By the time she reached him, her arms ached and she was panting.

"You're out of shape," he teased, holding her in his arms. "When we get back to Lincoln Prairie, it's the health club for you."

If she wasn't careful, he would think she was fat. "Okay," she said. She hadn't known him long enough to know how athletic he was. Did he like tennis, too? Wally ball?

"Come, on, Mrs. Lutrell, I'll race you back."

"DeVonte!"

But he released her and dove into the waves.

She flailed about for a minute, then floated on her back until she felt the tide carrying her away from land. Then once again, she began swimming. This time her arms ached. She *was* tired. Land was a long way away. She swam a bit farther, then floated again. Again she felt the movement of the water pulling her out to sea.

"DeVonte!" she called. "DeVonte! I can't make it! Help me!" She took in a mouthful of water, spit it out, and called again. "DeVonte! I can't make it in!"

Where in the hell were the lifeguards? Where were the other swimmers? Why was it just her and him?

"DeVonte!" she called again. "Come help me!"

She could see his head bobbing in the water, but he did not turn around or answer.

"DeVonte!" It was no use. He couldn't hear her. She felt her panic rising and tried to stay calm. There were no sharks, she hoped. And she could float, swim a little, float, and—get nowhere, drift out to sea.

"DeVonte!" she screamed. "Help! Help!"

A man came running from the condo. He dropped a bucket as he ran toward the water. He pointed and waved his arms. DeVonte turned.

"Help!" she called again.

The man stripped off his shirt and pants. He dove into the water in his underwear. DeVonte began swimming toward her. She floated, then swam, then floated again. DeVonte reached her first. The man was close behind. Together they helped her reach shallow water.

"Was close, ma'am," the man said, out of breath.

Sharon sank down on the sand. She was too exhausted to go any farther. Her arms and legs ached. She was cold. The condo seemed so far away.

"The water is too rough to be out in today, man," the man told DeVonte. "That is why nobody is out there. You must be careful. Even if the storm misses the island, the tides will be high for the next few days and the water no good for swimming or boating. You can see that nobody else is out there."

DeVonte said nothing except, "Thanks for helping."

"Is good thing I was here. You could not even hear her. I

brought in a load of plywood, just in case. It is in the storage area. Use it if you need to board up your windows. There is not enough for everyone, but none of the others are here now that the French-speaking man and his family have left."

"Let me know if you need help with anything," DeVonte told him.

Sharon didn't know what storm they were talking about. She didn't have the energy to ask.

"Come on," DeVonte said.

She shook her head. "I need to rest for a few minutes."

"You really are out of shape. I didn't know. It's definitely the health club as soon as we're back home."

Home. The best thing she had heard all day. And a storm. Maybe they could leave soon. She wanted to ask to leave now. Instead, she tried to get to her feet, felt dizzy, and sat on the sand, again with her head between her knees. She began shivering in violent spasms.

"I'll carry you," DeVonte said. He scooped her into his arms.

When they reached the condo, he held on to her as she walked up the stairs.

"Let me help you to the shower. It will warm you."

When she was on the couch, wrapped in a terry cloth robe, he covered her with blankets, then brought her a cup of coffee.

"Feeling better?"

"Yes. I'm fine now." She sounded a little hoarse.

"Good. I've got to go out for a while."

She listened as he talked about trying to find a man with a boat, nodded, and wished for a television. Maybe they could bring a small one if they came here again and a VCR and some movies.

"You get some sleep."

"What about the storm?" she asked.

"There is no storm coming here. There is one out there, but it's miles away and not even heading in this direction. Would I have brought you here if there was going to be bad weather?"

He leaned down and kissed her.

For once she didn't mind being alone. She hadn't expected him to leave her to go see about some damned boat, but she was learning things about him that she didn't like. Some little thing like her being afraid or not being a good swimmer wouldn't stop him from demanding that she do whatever *he* wanted to do. This marriage was a mistake. They should have dated longer. She shouldn't have married him so soon. Exhausted, she gulped down the coffee as soon as it had cooled enough and curled up under the blanket.

Based on the information she received from the woman at the cultural center, Marti sent two uniforms to gain access to Nan's apartment. Then she aligned the three photos and the index card with Lucy's name on it on her desk again, glancing at them as she read through her notes. Again the hand that protruded from the bed of leaves with its fingers curled in a beckoning gesture seemed to call to her. What was it Vik had said? Something about the arms being left as a message. Too bad neither of them could interpret that message. She turned her thoughts to the facts. Lucy could tell her about the commune. When she called, Lucy answered.

"What can you tell me about the commune in Indiana?"

"Oh," Lucy said, "that place is long gone. Closed in the late seventies or early eighties."

"Are you in contact with anyone who was there, maybe when you were or with someone who ran the place?"

"There wasn't any organization to speak of. The commune tended to run itself, assisted by whoever happened to be there at the time." Lucy did not express any surprise that Marti knew about her stay there. "We were artists, not a cult. I didn't stay that long. And in those days, there was no keeping in touch, no tomorrow. We lived in the moment. People drifted in and drifted out. We seldom even used last names. That was one of the reasons for going there, to get away from commitments and responsibilities, as well as other people's expectations, and just let your art happen."

Marti rubbed the back of her neck. She was tired, and this was slow going.

"Would you look at some photos if I brought them over?"

"Why certainly, but I won't be home until later this evening."

Marti shook her head. Slow, slower, slowest.

"Attention," Vik said, when she hung up.

"What are you talking about?"

"The arms with hands. It's as if whoever did it wanted to call attention to themselves," he said. "Not that they wanted us to know who they were. But attention. They wanted us to notice. You don't just leave an arm out like that. And the one we found this month was frozen, which means the person was probably killed this summer maybe, when the arm might decompose before it was found. Whoever did it tried to make sure that wouldn't happen."

Marti looked at the pictures. She stopped when she came to Nan. Nan was the only one she knew of who had lied or withheld information. Aloud, she said, "We need a motive. We need . . . it's as if we are looking at all of the pieces and just need to put them together. There's still too much we don't know."

Vik didn't answer.

"Arlene Johns is dead. What if it was someone from the commune? What if the first two arms with hands were at the commune? What if the others were killed because they knew something? What if Arlene was killed because of what she might know? What if Nan Conser is dead, too? Maybe Lucy is next."

She called Lucy again. "Where was the commune?" she asked.

"Near the lake."

"Someone told me it was near Michigan City."

"Yes, and near the lake."

150

"What street, Lucy? What was the address."

"I'm sorry. It was so long ago. I have no idea."

Marti got on the phone and called the Michigan City police. They didn't know what she was talking about. There was no art league there, at least not one listed by that title. She called the library. The librarian agreed to go through their archives and see what she could find. Marti made sure the woman had her name and left a fax number.

The uniforms called in from Nan's apartment. The landlord was cooperative. Everything was in order. Nobody was home. There was an address book by the telephone, which they had permission to remove. They would bring it in so someone could start checking around.

"No Nan," she said. What did that mean?

Some reports came in from Gordon. Marti glanced at her copies. No arsenic. What had Gordon called it? Inheritance powder. Inheritance.

"Vik, of these four women, who has gained the most since the early eighties?" They both thought about it.

"From a material standpoint," Vik said, "Nan seems to have gained the least."

"And Arlene seems to have gained the most."

"How do you figure that?"

"Well, I can't vouch for how happy she was, and I'm not talking about her business, but she seems to be the one who had the best perspective about herself, her talents, abilities, whatever; and she seems to have made the most of them. I don't get the impression that she was still living in her mother's shadow either. So I'm guessing that she had the most self-esteem!"

"And there's Lucy," Vik said. "She's gained the most recognition."

"I know, but nobody seems to consider her artistic ability above average."

Marti would have to remember that when she talked with Lucy again. Two thoughts kept nagging at her, inheritance powder and attention. What if . . . no, nobody killed people to steal their art and then cut off their arms to call attention to it. They couldn't have cut off the arms so that they couldn't paint anymore either. The arms were dismembered after the victims were dead. That was so illogical that she didn't even mention it to Vik.

Even though flying was the most awesome thing she had ever done, Lisa couldn't wait for the plane to touch down. A week in the Bahamas! Not that she was sure she would like being with Sharon and her new husband, not unless there were some cute boys around. Anything would beat having to go to the hospital and see Rayveena. Sharon had told her that Rayveena had cancer and looked really bad. She had never been around a really sick person and didn't even like Rayveena that much. Crabby old witch, never hugged her, never acted anything like a grandmother, wouldn't even let her call her that. All Rayveena wanted was Sharon's money so she could buy drugs.

She checked her watch. Even with the hour's time difference, Marti might know by now that she was gone. Good thing the call came when nobody was home but Joanna and her. She ducked out of school as soon as she got there, but she did send a note to Joanna via a friend; not just so nobody would worry about her, but so they would know where she was and with whom. It would be just like Sharon to pick some deadbeat loser. As soon as they landed, she would have to call home so everyone would know she was okay. Marti and Momma would be mad, but she couldn't have passed up a chance like this. Sharon didn't even like to fly, let alone swim. No way would she be coming to the islands again, unless her new husband insisted.

Besides, she wanted to tell Sharon herself that Rayveena was dying, wanted to make sure Sharon really knew how serious it was and wasn't pretending everything was going to be okay or just go on like this indefinitely. Sharon had a way of not seeing things as they really were when she didn't want to. It wasn't any of her business why Sharon and Rayveena didn't like each other. Sometimes things weren't much better between her and Sharon. But if Sharon were dying, she would own up to being her daughter and be there for her. She wouldn't run away. Sharon had to run away from everything. She hated it the way Sharon always ran away.

DeVonte made arrangements to rent a boat before he went to the airport. The water was choppy because of the proximity of the storm, but they wouldn't have to go very far out. The timing would be tight. He checked the pilot's license to be sure he was authorized to fly back to Freeport at night, but the pilot had warned him that based on current weather reports, they would have to leave Nassau by midnight. After that, he would make no guarantees.

Inside the airport, DeVonte found a place away from the gate where he could remain inconspicuous. He was wearing shorts, sandals, and a plain white golf shirt with a straw Panama hat. The few things he'd brought with him were in a sports bag. The natives were so used to tourists that, other than being friendly, they wouldn't pay any attention to him at all unless he gave them a reason.

He didn't have any problem spotting Lisa when she deplaned. She was the only teenager to come through the gate alone. She was taller than he expected, and her school pictures had been flattering. She was darker than he preferred and more ordinary than pretty. Hopefully, nobody on the plane had paid much attention to her during the flight—unless, like her mother, she was afraid to fly. He watched as she walked through the terminal, backpack in hand, looking like she had some place to go, and walked toward her.

"Lisa, you look just like your mother said you would. I'm DeVonte." He smiled and held out his hand. She hesitated, and he could see the apprehension on her face. "It's all right. Your mother will really be surprised."

"Where is she? Why isn't she with you?"

153

"She couldn't wait to go to the casino. I didn't want to spoil the surprise by insisting that she come."

"Oh."

She didn't take his hand. That displeased him.

"Where is she?"

"Freeport. I thought you knew that."

"And how do we get there?"

"We're going to take a boat ride."

"Oh, well, I have to go to the bathroom first."

"Hurry then."

"Freeport," she said again.

"Yes, we'll be staying at my condo on Grand Bahama Island. This was just the fastest way to get you here."

"Okay. Where is this boat?"

"It's just a few blocks away."

"What time does it leave?"

"Whenever we want it to. I'm the captain." He sensed her uneasiness, but it was too late for that now. She was here. And soon she would be dead. He smiled. "Go, but don't take long. You'll like this restroom better than the facilities on the boat. We'll get something to eat on the way. Have you ever had conch? It's the specialty of the island."

"Then maybe I'll try some."

This one was not like her mother. She was a lot different from the few teenagers that he had dealt with in the past. He didn't like young girls and did his best to avoid them. These days they were too spoiled, too emotional, and too smart.

"You did let Marti know you were coming?"

"Yes, I did."

"Do you need to call her? Will she be worried? Making a phone call from the islands isn't like dialing at home. It could take awhile to get through."

"Marti knows I can take care of myself."

He could see she believed that. Soon she would know better. "Good. We'll wait until we get to Freeport."

He would have to come up behind her when they were out

154

far enough. Her height wouldn't be a problem, but he wished she was as short as her mother. He had better knock her unconscious before throwing her overboard, although even if she was an Olympic swimmer, the roughness of the water and the distance to shore would be too much for her. If he needed any explanations as to why she was here, there would be plenty of time to come up with them after the storm passed and her mother was dead, too.

Lisa did not like the bathroom. Although it was superficially clean, it was worse than the shower room at an away game. DeVonte was not to her liking either. Sharon was worse than a fool for marrying someone like him. If Sharon's other boyfriends were anything like him, it was no wonder she didn't want anyone to meet them. As a stepfather, he was going to be an embarrassment. It wasn't just that though. He was . . . there was something about him . . . and now that she was here . . . there were a lot of things she didn't like—or trust.

Why hadn't he made flight arrangements to Freeport? Or if their airport was too small, why hadn't he arranged for a smaller, connecting flight from here? And for someone who wanted to surprise Sharon, he wasn't in any hurry. It was almost four o'clock. Freeport wasn't that close. They couldn't possibly get there by boat before dark. Even if he had a yacht, it wouldn't get there that fast. And Sharon? At a casino? Sharon didn't even buy lottery tickets. There was no way she would go to a casino unless it was to please him.

Besides that, he didn't like her. She could tell. She wasn't cute and cuddly like Sharon, and before long, he would find out that she wasn't as dumb and adoring. Being with Sharon wouldn't make for a happy vacation in the best of circumstances; their mutual dislike wouldn't help. No. This was not going to work. It wasn't just that she didn't like him . . . there was something about him . . . he was slick. She was sure all of Sharon's boyfriends were slick. But . . . she didn't trust him. He had to know that she wasn't getting along with Sharon.

And there was no way Sharon would want to share her honeymoon with anyone else. No. Whatever this surprise was that he was planning, it was going to be at her expense; and she didn't want any part of it. She would just have to tell him so and take the next flight home.

Lisa walked to the door then stopped, overcome with reluctance. She did not want to go near that man ever again. She could not leave this building with him and go to a place where she had never been before, a place where she would have to depend on him. Trust your instincts, Marti had always said that when she talked to them about boys. Trust your instincts. Her instincts told her to get as far away from DeVonte Lutrell as she could and as fast as she could. She backed up, looked for a window. There wasn't one. There was no way out of here except through that door. She walked over, opened it wide enough to see him sitting maybe twenty feet away from her. He wasn't facing in her direction, but it would be easy enough for him to turn his head and see her. There was an exit out of the airport in the other direction, about fifteen feet from the bathroom. What if he did look when the door opened? What if he did see someone come out. Marti always said people tended to see what they expected to. What if someone who didn't look like her came out?

She went into a stall, opened her duffel bag, and changed her clothes. She stuffed her hair under a Cubs baseball cap and put on lipstick and sunglasses. She put her money and ID in one pocket and a small can of hair spray and a whistle in the other. She tossed the duffel bag in the garbage can on her way out. As soon as she opened the door, she headed straight for the exit without looking left or right or looking back to see if he was watching her.

Outside, the sun hit her. It wasn't cool in the terminal, but it was much hotter out here. Just up the street she saw a bazaar. Stalls were filled with people. Brightly colored clothing hung on ropes that were strung across the entrances to the stalls. That would be the first place he would look. To her left there was a small restaurant. No, she did not need to be inside. She began walking, away from the vendors' stalls, away from the smell of food, toward a group of tourists. She joined them, keeping just ahead of them for about a block. She had better stay where there were people and yell like hell if he came anywhere near her. Fire, like Marti said. Not help. She didn't see a single police officer, but yelling "fire" would get a lot of attention.

Behind her, the tourists talked. ". . . storm . . ." one of them said. She hadn't been paying attention to what they were talking about, but she did now.

"Thank God we were able to book a flight out of here tonight, even if it is a small plane. Imagine, with all the frequent flyer miles we've got, they're not booking any flights after three P.M. tomorrow, and they couldn't find seats for us either."

A storm? What kind of storms did they have here? She didn't turn to ask. Typhoons? No, hurricanes. Well, they couldn't be that bad, not as bad as a tornado. She didn't have enough money to get a flight back if she could. Marti was a cop. That might help. But who was home now? She checked her watch and wondered if anyone was there. Momma Lydia had been going into Chicago every day and staying with Rayveena. She wouldn't be home before five or six. She hadn't checked the board before she left, so she didn't know what anyone else would be doing.

She should have made sure DeVonte had booked a return flight, but she had figured she'd be going back with them. She hadn't asked him, or herself, enough questions about anything before coming here. It was that damned French test. She was flunking the course and hadn't even opened the book in two weeks. This was the last time she was going to jump at a chance like this to get out of something like that. The last time.

And Sharon? Where was Sharon? Was she really in Freeport? Or was she here somewhere? Was she waiting on his boat? She sure as hell wasn't at a casino. Was that part of the surprise—*his* idea of a surprise? She couldn't leave without knowing Sharon was all right, even if Sharon didn't have any problems taking off when Rayveena was dying. She was not like Sharon. She would never marry a jerk like DeVonte. Were they really married? Was Sharon really that dumb?

DeVonte knew teenage girls spent a lot of time standing in front of a mirror, but he thought fifteen minutes were excessive. Besides, they had to get on that boat and soon. He walked to the door and pushed it ajar. "Lisa?"

There was no answer. He called her name again then went inside. Empty. Nobody was there. He spun around. There were no windows. How? Only one person had come out since Lisa came in here. Only that girl. Blue denim caught his eye and he looked in the wastebasket. Her backpack. Damn. She had tricked him. But why?

He walked outside. He wanted to run, but he didn't want to attract any attention. The marketplace! That's where she would go. He headed in that direction. What was the girl who came out of the bathroom wearing? He couldn't remember anything but a baseball cap and sunglasses. Smart, this one, not stupid like her mother. But not smart enough. He looked at his watch. There wasn't much time. In the distance he could see the clouds gathering; the storm front was coming closer. The natives had not begun putting up plywood yet because they did not want to scare off the tourists, but people were leaving the island. The hurricane was on track to hit here. The question was, would it be a direct hit or just a glancing blow?

Sellers beckoned to him from the stalls, women—all of them at least middle-aged. Most had broad hips and ready smiles. They all talked. "You would like some jewelry for your lady friend today?" "T-shirts, I have T-shirts." Some reached out as if they would pull him in to look at their wares. He pushed their hands away, looking past them. Today's crowds were smaller than usual, stragglers looking for a few markdowns, stragglers who did not know that the threat of stormy weather would not affect prices.

He walked past the stalls and looked in without knowing just what he was looking for. Sunglasses, but a lot of women were wearing them. And the cap. What color was the cap? He hadn't noticed then and couldn't recall anything about it now. Ahead of him a girl quickened her steps. He jostled a woman to get to her.

"Lisa!"

The girl turned and smiled. It was someone else.

He circled the stalls twice. There were only ten of them. Then he entered each, and asked the proprietor if she had seen a girl wearing sunglasses and a cap. What color cap? one woman asked. He shook his head. The others became disappointed when they saw he was not going to buy and gave him a mute shake of their heads, lips pursed with displeasure. When he was certain Lisa wasn't there, he walked back up the street. Nassau was bigger than Freeport. There were more casinos, more hotels, even a university, more places to hide. He would not find her now. What would he do? Or, perhaps the question was, what would *she* do?

Lisa walked for a while. She stayed near people who looked like tourists and avoided the natives, and got as far away from the airport as she could. When she stopped and looked about, she wasn't in a place that looked anything like what she had seen on TV. Overhead, the sky was blue, but off in the distance it was a muddy kind of gray. The sidewalk she had been walking on had become a dirt path. The houses were small, some wood, some cinder block. There was a lot of grass and short, thick bushes. She couldn't see the ocean at all. Men sold fish from the backs of pickup trucks, weighing them in their hands. Children with bare, dust-covered legs offered her slices of cake wrapped in plastic. She didn't know where she was. She couldn't find Sharon on her own. But she had to, and

159

soon. She thought about going to the police; but aside from not seeing one police officer, she wasn't sure that was the smart thing to do. This wasn't the United States. She didn't know anything about their laws. Teenagers were getting locked up in other countries all the time, and their parents couldn't get them out of jail. What if they put her in jail and didn't even notify anyone at home? What if she was there when the storm came? No. She was on her own, at least until she could get to a telephone, call home, and let Marti tell her what she should do.

13

The elderly owner of the hobby and craft store was behind a counter, visiting with and waiting on customers, when Marti and Vik arrived at his store. He was short, with murky gray hair neatly trimmed, and wore a flowered, short-sleeved shirt. They had agreed that this was a loose end that needed to be tied up, and Marti wanted a tube of artists' paint that could be matched with the chip that had finally been found by the evidence clerk. Marti walked around while she was waiting. There were aisles and shelves filled with different types of artists' paints and brushes, and all kinds of art supplies. She didn't have any trouble locating the tubes of cerulean blue acrylic paint. What if the composition of this paint and that of the paint chip found under Lily Day's fingernail were different?

The crafts sections had everything from Popsicle sticks and miniature dollhouse furniture to doll-making supplies and model airplanes. This spring, more than four years after Johnny's death, Theo had finally finished the model airplane he and his father had been working on when Johnny died. Ben had helped, and Mike had built a plane, too. Should she pick out airplanes for the boys now? Had completing the airplane brought some kind of closure for Theo? Did he like building them? Was he too old to build them? Did he want another one? She didn't know. She could always find out then come back later.

The old man was still doing as much talking as he was

ringing up sales. Marti spotted Vik at the other end of the store and headed that way.

"Model railroads," she said. "Your hobby?"

Vik got a little red in the face. He looked as if he had been caught doing something he shouldn't.

"My dad," he said. "Model railroads were his hobby. He built a platform in the basement so he could stand up and work on them. When I was a kid, every year about this time he'd rearrange everything so that by Christmas we'd have a new town, Santa's village and all."

"Do you still have any of it?"

"Every piece. I was thinking about setting it up again now that I've got a grandson."

"Good idea," Marti said. She told him about Theo, Ben, Mike, and the model airplanes.

The old man came over to them. "Well, Officer Jessenovik. Matthew, isn't it? Gus's son. I knew your dad. This stuff is plastic," he said. "Don't buy any of it. Your dad's trains are metal and real wood, hand carved. Hang on to them. You can't buy anything like that anymore. They must be worth a lot." He asked Vik about his older brothers and inquired after Mildred. "Prettiest little thing," he said. "I wasn't too sure about her marrying into the Jessenovik family. Nothing but men, and none of you used to having a woman around. Your brothers' wives had brothers of their own, but not Mildred." He considered Vik for a minute, then said, "You were really taken with her back then. I heard she was ailing. Is she doing better now?"

Vik nodded.

The old man's eyes narrowed. "You're still taken with her, aren't you?"

Another nod.

"Good. You need that, both of you. Everyone does. Now, what can I do for you? I'm sure you're not here to talk about old times, although we can do that too if you'd like. I came down to help out. At least that's what I told my son, but it's sure nice seeing the same familiar faces, older maybe, but friends and the children and grandchildren of friends."

Marti took a dozen of the pictures out of her purse and explained why they were protected by plastic bags.

"Jimmy Binslow," the old man said. "Is he still around?"

"He's got a place north of here," Vik said.

"Good. He could do things with a camera that would have made him a fortune if he hadn't been an Indian. And there's Nan Riley. Married a Conser. That's probably her father's silver." He got a magnifying glass from the stock on one of the shelves. "No, she must have done this. It's scrolly and undefined. He kept his settings simple. Very effective. I've still got a few pieces of his. Kept them when the wife passed."

"Nan does volunteer work at the Lake County Museum now," Vik said. "And the Lincoln Prairie Historic Society."

"Good for her. That mother of hers"—the old man shook his head—"the wife and I never had any inclination to live anyone's lives but our own, but that woman insisted that she and her husband and Nan were all artists and the art guild was snobbish for not letting them join. Truth is, none of them had much talent. He was good at what he did, but he didn't even think of it as being artistic. Very functional, all of his settings. Simple, elegant, functional."

Marti wasn't sure why that did not describe something artistic. She decided not to ask.

"Remember Arlene Johns?" Vik asked.

"She's a potter," he said. "We handle her supply orders. Opening that shop like she did was real smart. Always a loner, that one. Married a loner; stayed a loner when he died. Never even traveled except to that hippy place in Indiana. I thought it was a shame at the time, but she seemed to get herself together after that. She was always in here, dabbling in this, dabbling in that, didn't know what she wanted to do with herself, and not a lot of talent for most of it; but she is an excellent potter. Of course now her family isn't impressed. To hear them tell it, her mother and her sister were the real artists."

Something about the way he spoke implied that he didn't agree.

"In any case, poor 'better late than never' Arlene finally found something she could do *and* make a living at. Smart girl."

Marti wondered what he might have to say about Lucy Carlisle. She wondered how she could introduce Lucy into the conversation. Too bad they didn't have a photo of her.

The old man scanned the photos and picked out a few more people he knew who weren't involved in the case, then said, "Why, here's Carrie and her sister. She painted from the heart. It did something to you, looking at her work."

He looked at Vik. "Why have you got these red circles here?" he asked.

"Those are people we couldn't identify," Vik explained.

He went through them again and added a few names. Marti wrote them down.

"Well now," the old man said. "I wonder whatever happened to Scotty."

Marti tried to get a closer look. Vik was in the way. He moved a little to the side so that she could see.

"You mean the young man who's circled?" Vik asked.

"Uh huh."

It was the young man with Arlene, the young man they thought might be John Doe #17.

"What can you tell us about him?" Vik asked.

The old man gave Vik such a perceptive look that Marti expected him to ask why. Instead, he said, "He wasn't from around here and didn't stay long that I remember; but I do recall him coming in here and ordering supplies. I can't imagine what he would be doing at an art guild exhibit and certainly not with Arlene Johns."

"This young man, Scotty," Vik said, "you wouldn't happen to know his last name?"

"Sorry."

"Did he stay here long."

"No. He only placed two orders and that's the only reason why I remember him. Not many folks needed supplies for developing film."

"Don't you need a darkroom for that?" Marti asked.

"Sure, but a closet, any dark space, will do."

"Do you know what happened to him?"

"Never gave it much thought. I doubt that he was here for more than a couple of weeks. From the looks of him, he was one of those hippy types, and they never stayed anyplace long anyway. I never saw any of his photographs. He might not have been any good."

"Does Lucy Carlisle still get supplies here?"

The old man's eyes narrowed. "Why on earth are you asking all of these questions? Why are the police so interested in members of the art guild and exhibits that took place years ago?"

"That's a good question," Vik said. "I guess you haven't seen today's paper. Arlene Johns was found dead last night."

"Arlene is dead? Too bad; she was too young to die." The old man spoke in a tone that said he was used to people dying and not surprised, even if Arlene was "young," at least to him. "And I suppose this is just a routine death investigation." He did not sound like he believed that. Neither Marti nor Vik answered.

"So we're on to Lucy Carlisle now," the old man said. "Lucy Senior or Lucy Junior?"

"Both of them," Vik said.

"I take it Lucy Junior is still a spinster."

Vik nodded.

"Don't tell anyone I said this, Lucy Junior being a Carlisle and all, but she can't paint worth a damn."

"We saw some of her work," Vik said. "It didn't look too bad."

"Garbage, all of it. Her mother was better, not great, but better."

"But she still exhibits her work," Vik said. "Somebody must like it."

"*Her* work," the old man said, emphasizing "her."

"Well, it is, isn't it?"

The old man just smiled.

"What the hell do you think he meant by that?" Vik asked when they got back in the car.

"Damned if I know," Marti said. "Maybe she just copies other people's stuff."

"Maybe."

Too bad they didn't know enough about art to figure out which artist Lucy could be copying. It probably wasn't important. If Nan were here, they could ask her.

Sharon stood on the balcony and looked out at the ocean. The wind had picked up and whipped the water into frothy waves. Earlier, for a few moments, while she was wading in the water up to her ankles, the ocean had seemed gentle, almost friendly. But now . . . she fought back a sense of panic that came every time she thought of being swallowed up by the water, carried away by the current, dragged under by her own fatigue—alone—with DeVonte too close to shore and too far away to hear her.

She was so isolated here, so alone. If a thief came and broke in, there would be no one to help her. No telephone, no television, no radio, no nothing; just sand, water, and sunshine. Paradise to some; hell to her. How ironic. When DeVonte had said condo, she'd thought hotel, tourists, room service. Instead, it was just the two of them. When the French couple left this morning, the woman had pointed to the sky and said something in French. Sharon had nodded and smiled, not understanding a word. The woman became agitated, grabbed her arm, pointed, made windmill movements with her arm. Still not understanding, Sharon became serious, as if she did, and said yes until the woman nodded and ran to a waiting cab.

She had gone looking for the man who'd helped save her, but she couldn't find him. Then she walked down the road for maybe a quarter of a mile in each direction without seeing anyone or anything except palm trees and clearings where more condos would be built or foundations had been poured. If anyone had told her that a Caribbean island could be so sparsely populated, she would not have believed them. That would change soon. There was construction along the road. But, for now, she was alone.

The wind gusted and the surf bounced against the shore with a splash. She could almost feel the water, pulling her down, covering her. She could almost taste its saltiness. She turned away and went inside. There was an alarm clock. It was getting late. DeVonte had been gone for hours in his search for a boat. It felt odd not to miss him, strange to be glad he was gone.

Why had she done this? Who had she married? She knew so little about DeVonte; and if she had expected to find out anything more while she was here, so far she had not. This place was as bereft of personal effects as a hotel suite. There wasn't even a monogrammed towel. No photos, no papers, no mail, nothing. DeVonte could pack what little he had brought with him and leave without anyone knowing he had been here. Everything about the apartment was neutral. Gray carpet, parchment-and-mauve upholstery, ivory walls. It was cold, like the ocean. When DeVonte wasn't here, it was almost as if he didn't exist. This was wrong. Everything about it was wrong. She had married a stranger who loved flying and swimming and boating more than he loved her, a man who had watched her almost drown today, who would insist that she return to the water tomorrow.

He had been angry with her as he and that man had pulled her from the water. Angry? Why? Because she wasn't a strong swimmer? Because she was out of shape—at least by his standards? He had been truly angry. She could tell. He knew she could not swim as well as he could before he'd called to her to come that far out in the water. Instead of coming closer, he kept moving away. Why? Why? He knew that she could not swim out to where he was and back. He knew she would try to please him. He knew that. He knew. Why had he called to her? Why had he insisted? She sank down on the sofa. The wind should have carried her voice when she called to him for help, but he had not even turned around. Why not? The old man had heard her.

Back at the precinct, Marti was grateful for the peace and quiet. Vik sat at his desk, as silent as she was and just as thoughtful, with his head inclined and the tips of his steepled fingers pressing into his chin.

Eventually, she said, "So we've got Arlene, Nan, and Lucy. There is no common bond among these women except that their mothers were, or thought they were, artists, depending on who you ask; and these three wanted to be artists, too."

"People don't die or get killed because of art, at least not amateurs," Vik said. "How can paint smeared on canvas be that important?"

"It was these women's worlds, their lives, what their dinner table conversations were probably about when they were growing up, and apparently what their mothers expected of them."

That was an interesting idea. What had Momma expected of her? She thought about that for a few minutes. A good marriage maybe. Most likely a better job than cleaning other people's houses or train cars. There wasn't much talk of college then, except when she went to church. She did go to college. She did make two good marriages. What did Momma think of her job? She accepted it, like everyone else, but did she approve? How important was Momma's approval? Marti got up and went to the coffeepot. Empty. She was a cop. This was her job. This was what she wanted to do, whether anyone else accepted it or approved of it or not. On the face of it, making their own choices hadn't seemed to be that easy for Arlene or Nan or Lucy.

"We need coffee, Vik," she said.

"I'll go over to Dunkin' Donuts and get some." He grabbed his jacket, looking as stymied as she felt, and probably just as eager to escape thoughts similar to hers that just went in circles.

She put her empty mug down on her desk with a loud thump. Arlene, Nan, and Lucy. She could not put herself in their places, could not imagine a need to please someone else so much that it would drive her to murder. She tried to remember how things were in the seventies. Hippies came to mind right away, then Hari Krishna followers in long robes with shaven heads, then John Doe #17. She hadn't had many white friends then, didn't have any insights as to what drove them to these extremes. She understood Black Power, but the concept seemed totally different, born of a different environment and culture and problems. If these deaths were in any way connected with these women, it came from their environment as much as Black Power and riots came from hers.

What did she know about the way these women lived? Not enough. But people didn't just kill. Only sociopaths just killed; and even then, if she looked, she could find, if not reasons, at least the progression from thought to intent to action. These were three ordinary women. But somewhere, in their homes, in their lives, were there the elements to create that same sociopathic progression?

She did know that they had mothers who wanted to live beyond their own lives by living through their daughters, mothers who needed to control. She had seen so much evidence of how that need to control ruined lives. Did she try to control? She didn't think she was that kind of mother. But Joanna was controlling or tried to be. Until now, Marti thought it was because, deep inside, Joanna knew how little control she really had. But was that it? Did Joanna understand that, or did she believe she could control more than she could? Did her need to control go beyond trying to do everything possible to keep her mother alive because she had not been able to do that for her father?

Marti picked up her coffee mug, remembered that it was empty, and put it down. She would have to talk with Momma. Momma would help her make Joanna see the futility of trying to control other people. Again the three women came to mind: Arlene, Nan, and Lucy. What had their conventional lifestyle been like thirty or more years ago? Alternative lifestyles, abandoning their families without a backward glance, were more than a way of rebelling, of being nonconformist or just defiant—they were the ultimate rejection of everything family and home represented. What drove people to that? What sent them to communes? Only Arlene and Lucy had chosen the commune in Indiana. Their visits were years apart, at opposite ends of the same decade. Arlene stayed away for a few months. Apparently, she was able to separate herself from her mother's ambitions for her and had realized she could not be who her mother wanted her to be, since ultimately she did become her own person, or so it seemed.

Lucy stayed away for about a year. It must have been harder for her. And after her mother killed herself, she showed her mother's work. Why? Did she want people to remember her mother's work? Or remember that her mother had taken her own life? Lucy donated her mother's art to the library. But why a still life when her mother's best work was landscapes? Did Lucy want people to see that her mother was not as good an artist as they thought? Why? Because Lucy wasn't that good? Lucy was still painting. What did that mean? Or was she? Was the work on her walls copied from someone else? Or stolen?

The door opened. Vik came in with a paper bag in one hand and a shopping bag in the other.

"Coffee," he said, putting a large plastic foam cup on each

of their desks. He produced a box of doughnuts from the shopping bag—jelly filled and chocolate covered and others stuffed with pudding and creme.

Marti bit into one, savoring the strawberry jam, and tried to remember the last time she had eaten. After she ate the doughnut, she wiped her mouth with a napkin, took a swallow of the coffee, and said, "What if those paintings we saw on Lucy's wall were stolen?"

"You think so?" he said, not surprised.

"You're the only one of us who came close to knowing her. Does that sound like something she would do?"

Vik ate a few doughnuts while he thought about that. "I can't say," he admitted. "I didn't know her that well, but I never heard so much as a rumor to that effect, and they did hang her stuff up at the high school. Seems like someone would have known."

"But you said her painting wasn't any good."

"Not then it wasn't. It was hung there because of her mother. Stayed there too, until the high school split into two campuses, East and West. That's when it disappeared."

So Lucy's mother had enough influence to get her daughter's lousy paintings publicly displayed. Not a major feat in a town the size that Lincoln Prairie must have been back then, with only one high school, but interesting nevertheless, indicative of how important it was to Lucy's mother that Lucy also be an artist, whether she was or not.

"I'm beginning to think that Lucy would do anything to please her mother, Vik." And maybe to get even with her, too.

"That's not so far-fetched, MacAlister. Sounds weird now, with kids the way they are today, but back then . . . I became a cop like my dad."

"But if Lucy couldn't paint . . ."

"Her work did improve after she went to that commune. And even if I don't like much of what she did, I will concede that there probably are people who think it's okay, if not at genius level."

"After the year at the commune," Marti said. "She improved after the commune."

"That's a long time to just sit around and paint, Marti. You probably have to get better."

"What if Lucy didn't? What if she had to have something to show for that year spent there to avert her mother's wrath and disappointment and plain embarrassment because she'd gone there in the first place? What if Lucy just wasn't an artist? What if she just couldn't paint? I can't. You can't. Lots of people can't. How many artists do we know of who had children follow in their footsteps?"

Vik laughed. It was short and without humor. "How many artists do we know, Marti? Name five."

"Van Gogh, Gauguin, Jacob Laurence, Horace Pippin, and Grandma Moses."

"Okay," he conceded. "Now name their kids."

Marti didn't even know if they had any. "My point exactly," she said.

"So kids don't always follow in their parent's footsteps."

"Agreed," said Marti. "But Arlene, Nan, and Lucy were expected to."

"And Lucy succeeded."

"But did she? The stuff on her walls . . ." She stopped then said, "Vik, when I look at a van Gogh, I know that's what it is. I know he's the artist. Same thing with Laurence."

"And?"

"It's because of the way they paint. It's like a signature. How does someone who can't paint at all suddenly become able to paint in so many different styles?"

"When I looked at it, I thought it was just all different because she was flighty."

"I don't know," Marti admitted. "I suppose it's possible that she tried different things until she found something she liked. But there is still the question of how she became good enough to do that many different things that well. Could it have happened in one year at a commune?"

"Or did she steal them?" Vik finished.

Neither of them answered. Finally Vik said, "I think we need to talk to Lucy again."

The phone rang while Marti was finishing off her coffee. It was the librarian calling from Michigan City.

"Did you find out anything about the commune?" Marti asked.

"No. I'm sorry. It seems that, for the most part, we ignored it."

Marti tossed her cup toward Vik's wastebasket and missed. She had been hoping the commune lead would pan out.

"The only thing I could find was a newspaper article about a drowning. It seems a resident of an artist colony located in the county accidentally drowned in Lake Michigan, the third of June, nineteen-eighty."

"Do you have a name?"

"Just Starr, with two r's, no last name."

"Any pictures?"

"No. In fact, this is one paragraph long—three sentences—and was on the eighth page of a ten-page weekly newspaper."

"Anyone else's name? A police officer, the person who found the body?"

"No. I'm sorry I can't be of more help."

"Oh, but you have been," Marti assured her. Or at least the librarian's information might become helpful if the name Starr meant anything to anyone, or if she could ferret out a coroner's report or a police report.

Marti felt uneasy as they drove over to talk to Lucy Carlisle. Killing someone was a long way from stealing from them, she reminded herself. And just because a person would do one, it did not mean she would do the other. Arlene's death was an angry act, one that required strength. Lucy had neither the height nor the weight to overpower anyone. Now there was another death, one that was directly related to the commune.

Starr. Didn't anyone who stayed at that place have a last name?

"Vik, Lucy was at the commune when this Starr drowned. And I believe she was there when Scotty was. One way or another, she's the key to all of this. Whether she did any of it or not."

Vik agreed. "I think so too."

She heard a familiar sadness in his voice. He didn't like it when his recollections of the past were infringed upon by reality. Lord only knew how this was impacting his high school memories. At least he and Lucy had not been in the same class.

Her stomach grumbled and she wished she had taken the time to eat another doughnut. It had been a long day. With any luck, it was almost over. With their luck, it could be just beginning. She glanced at Vik. He sat beside her, scowling.

"Damn it, Vik," she said, unable to shake her unease, "I keep expecting another body to turn up, especially with Nan Conser gone missing."

He sighed. "Arsenic is a woman's weapon. But cutting off their arms? That's more like something a man would do. Did McIntosh ever come up with what was used?"

"Not that he's said."

"That probably means it was something ordinary. He likes drama."

Marti didn't intrude when Vik fell silent. Instead, she thought about Lucy's house. If Lucy had not created, but copied, or stolen, the artwork she displayed as her own, she had missed her vocation. She would have made an excellent interior decorator. Everything, even the cats, was perfect. But, given her mother, and the attitude that seemed so prevalent in the art guild, at least in the seventies, what Lucy was good at would not have been considered artistic at all.

"What if this Scotty is alive and well and killing people?" She gripped the steering wheel. Something just didn't feel right. "What if he's the killer and Lucy is the thief?"

"Lucy is expecting us, isn't she?" Vik asked.

174

"I didn't say what time."

"No, but you've called to ask about the commune, called to ask about this Scotty."

"If that's got her guard up, she'll know for sure that we're onto something."

The lights were on, upstairs and down, at Lucy's house. When they reached the front door, Lucy opened it before they could ring the bell. "I've been waiting for you," she said.

They followed her to the kitchen. Instead of sitting down at the table with them, Lucy stood there, wringing her hands.

"Is something wrong, Lucy?" Vik asked. His voice was soft, filled with concern.

"They're going to take my house," she said. "Not all of it, just eight or ten feet on the east side."

"That won't be so bad," Vik said. "You'll lose that old shed and the burning bushes, but they can be replaced. I'm sure they'll pay to put in mature bushes."

Lucy Carlisle shook her head. "You don't understand," she said. "Why don't you show me those pictures."

"Another name has come up," Marti said. "Starr."

"Too bad she couldn't swim," Lucy said.

"You were there when she drowned." It was a guess, but the expression on Lucy's face confirmed it.

Marti handed her the photographs and she sat down.

"My, my," she said, "these do go a long way back." She studied each one as if she was memorizing them or, perhaps, remembering.

"This was so very long ago," she said. Her voice sounded wistful. "There's Arlene. Our mothers brought art to this community. They were artists themselves. Such a pity that our ability could never quite measure up. They would have given anything to have given birth to another Georgia O'Keeffe or Mary Cassatt, but it just didn't happen."

When Lucy came to the photograph of Arlene with the man now identified as Scotty, she looked at it for a long time.

"That's the young man I spoke to you about," Marti said, "Scotty."

Lucy stared at the picture for a few more seconds, then said, "Would you excuse me for a minute? I'll be right back. I want to show you something that might help."

Marti looked at Vik. He shrugged. Maybe Lucy did have the key to all of this. From the looks of it, Lucy did know who Scotty was, and she certainly knew about Starr. Marti was becoming more and more convinced that Lucy could be their killer. Her 9-mm service revolver was in her purse. She put the purse on her lap, opened it, and put her hand inside. Vik unsnapped his underarm holster.

When Lucy returned a few minutes later, she had a small-caliber gun in her hand.

Marti stared at the weapon. She didn't speak. Her hand tightened on the grip of her gun. Could she get it out and fire first? Lucy stood well away from them. There was no way to go for Lucy's gun and reach it before Lucy had a chance to fire. Marti watched Lucy's eyes. She wasn't ready to shoot yet. Maybe they could talk her out of it.

"You know," Lucy said.

What did Lucy think they knew?

"Everyone will know as soon as they take down the shed."

The shed. Again.

"Nan," Marti said.

"What about her? Do you want to know if she's dead, too, like Arlene?" She laughed, but it was harsh and brittle. "Arlene should not have told you. I warned her when she called me, laughing and gloating. She had no business telling you what Scotty told her about me when I was at that commune. It was no business of hers when Scotty came here trying to find out where Jade was and looking for her pathetic abstracts. Artists. Hah! Jade had no sense of perspective. And Scotty, he couldn't even take decent pictures."

"Lucy," Vik said, "we need to talk. You need to think about this, now."

176

She laughed again. "Talk. Think. What else do you think I've been doing since they started talking about taking my property? All that talk and now they tell me they don't even need my permission to tear down my shed."

The shed. What was in it? The missing remains?

"Lucy," Vik said, "you know me, Matt Jessenovik. Gus's kid. We went to school together. You know my wife, Mildred. This is Lincoln Prairie. We've lived here all our lives. Everyone knows our families. Everyone knows us. We can work this out, I promise."

Lucy shook her head. Marti focused on her eyes and tensed. Lucy wasn't wavering. Lucy was getting ready to shoot. Timing. Get out of the chair. Hit the floor. Aim her gun. Vik had to be thinking the same thing.

"I tried," Lucy said, "I really did try." With that she raised the gun to her temple and fired.

14

Marti stayed at Lucy's house long after the body was removed. According to Lucy's note, she had killed the others. They would begin checking out the shed at daybreak.

"Bizarre," Vik said, for at least the fifth time. "Her note just doesn't make sense. None of them could paint as well as she could, but everyone thought their work was better than hers. So she stole their work and passed it off as her own to please her mother. First she pushed that girl into the lake; then she killed our first two victims because they found out who she was and where she lived and came to get their work. Because they were both transients and alienated from their families, she didn't expect anyone to come looking for them, but two people did, each as alone as the first two." He shook his head. "It's hard to believe that not one missing person's report was filed for any of them."

They still didn't have much by way of names. Maybe tomorrow they would know more after they took a look in, or under, the shed. Marti thought about the arms with hands. "You did say you thought whoever did it was sending a message."

"That note sounds like a message?"

"No, the dismembered arms."

"What were they supposed to do? Point to how good she was."

"That might not be so far off," Marti said. "It sounds like

Lucy believed her work was much better; and even though she claimed what they did as her own, the result was that they vicariously received recognition that they didn't deserve."

"Everyone thought that what Lucy did was awful, Marti, and if those paintings she had stored in the closet are any indication, they were right. I could do better with paint-by-number kits. Did she honestly believe they would make her famous after she was dead just because her mother's work got more attention after she killed herself?"

"A lot of artists didn't become famous until after they died. Why not Lucy?"

"She overlooked one thing, Marti. Nobody likes what she did for a reason. It's garbage. Dead artists become famous because they are good."

"But, Vik, she believed she was." Marti was sure Lucy needed to believe that because she was competing with her mother. What Marti didn't understand was this competition between mother and daughter. She thought maybe she could glimpse it in Lisa's relationship with Sharon, but she couldn't see it in her relationship with Joanna. She just hoped she wasn't turning a blind eye to it.

"I don't know, Marti. Just when you think you've seen everything, something like this comes along."

"We've got a killer, a motive however strange, and we've still got a lot of unanswered questions," Marti reminded him. Would they ever find out the identities of those arms with hands? And even with Lucy's note, now that she was dead, would they be able to prove conclusively that she was, in fact, the killer? And where was Nan?

There was a message from Momma when Marti got back to the precinct. Lisa had left a note saying she was flying to Nassau. Sharon had married someone named DeVonte Lutrell, and Lisa would be joining them on their honeymoon. Marti wondered whose idea that was since it didn't sound like something Sharon would come up with. Marti called the airline. The flight had taken off on time and Lisa had checked in. Marti bit back her annoyance. Sharon could have called her, could have let her know where she was staying. Well, at least Lisa would make sure Sharon knew how sick Rayveena was. That was probably why Lisa took off so fast—Momma was planning to take her to visit Rayveena tomorrow. It was either that or that French test that was coming up.

Marti was completing the day's reports when Cowboy and Slim came in. As usual, Slim smelled as if he had showered in Obsession for Men. For once, the scent, although overpowering, wasn't annoying. This was the first time she had seen him all week. She supposed that was why.

"Have you two turned on those computers yet?" Cowboy asked as he checked the coffeepot.

"Damned nuisances," Vik grumbled. "Of course we have."

Marti was beginning to understand why her kids spent so much time on their computer. Even though she was getting used to it, she was still hoping that Lupe would have time to replicate their most frequently used reports. There was a memo from the lieutenant suggesting that they keep him abreast of things by E-mail, another ploy to entice them to the keyboard.

While Cowboy made coffee, Slim busied himself with his notes.

Slim was keeping his distance, and Marti was glad that his remarks about newlywed/married women and his references to PMS, "that time of the month" and more recently, pregnancy—which wasn't going to happen—had stopped, at least temporarily, but they hadn't had much to say to each other lately, and she missed the camaraderie. She was willing to bet that Slim was more than a little concerned that she would call him by his given name, Amos, which he didn't seem to like said loud enough for someone to overhear. He had been Slim ever since he came on the force.

When the telephone rang, she let Vik answer.

"For you," he said.

It was Momma. "I'm worried about Lisa."

"I haven't had time to get worried. But you're right. Have you heard from her?"

"Nothing. And it's not like her not to call. She promised she would as soon as she got there, and nothing yet, not a word. And she's on an island with Sharon and some man that none of us know."

"I'll see what I can do."

This was not good. Vik was looking at her with a puzzled expression on his face when she hung up.

"Hey, Slim," she said, "what's the easiest way to track a teenager who you think is in the Bahamas?"

A frown creased his bronze brow. "Lisa?" he guessed correctly.

"Yes. Sharon's over there somewhere on vacation and apparently made arrangements for Lisa to join her. It sounds like there's a man involved who may or may not be Sharon's new husband. I'd like to be sure of what's going on."

Dimples flashed as Slim gave her his slow, smooth-as-caramel smile. "I'll take care of that for you, right now."

To her surprise, it only took him about ten minutes to get the flight information, credit card info, and also find out that Sharon had made reservations for two, herself and a DeVonte Lutrell, their departure and return dates, and their itinerary.

Marti scanned Slim's notes. DeVonte Lutrell. That had to be the man she had seen in Sharon's apartment, the man who exposed himself to strange women. She had better check him out now that she knew his name.

Aloud she asked, "Why did she get a one-way ticket for Lisa?"

"A hurricane is heading that way," Slim told her. "Maybe they weren't booking flights out."

"Then why in the hell book them in? Where is this hurricane?" She didn't pay much attention to the weather unless it was local.

"I don't think it's hit yet, but it might. Then again, it might go someplace else. Fickle, hurricanes, like . . ." He didn't finish that sentence. "It looks like they're going to wait it out, based on the return tickets, Sharon's planning on staying a week with this DeVonte Lutrell. I'm running a make on him."

"Thanks, Slim, I appreciate the help."

"Look, Marti, I know Lisa hasn't run away, but I've got a lot of connections for tracking down runaway teens. I can tap into them anytime. I guarantee it'll be faster than anything you can do. With kids you usually don't have much time. They bounce around faster than basketballs and then find a way to go to ground. So whatever you need, let me know."

"Thanks," she said again, "I appreciate it."

"Don't worry; you owe me," Slim said, with a smile.

Because she knew how aggressive he was when he had a case involving a teen, she knew he wasn't just making the offer to buy her silence about his name. "I can handle that."

When the report came in on DeVonte Lutrell, it wasn't as bad as she'd feared, but it wasn't reassuring either. She would prefer that Sharon go out of the country with a man who didn't have any police record. The assault-and-battery priors worried her. They weren't recent, but all three of them were against women. She called Ben.

"Well," he said, "we didn't have much of a honeymoon. Maybe a couple of days on a tropical island would make up for that."

"You think we should go there?"

"As soon as possible. Tonight if we can."

"Me, too," she said. "I'll see what I can do."

With Slim's help, she made reservations for two on a flight to Nassau that would depart at midnight and a return flight for five tomorrow afternoon, if—the person making the reservation said—the storm stayed on track and didn't hit the island before then. That wasn't much time.

Slim came over with some handwritten notes. "Now Sharon and this Lutrell flew to Fort Lauderdale, stayed overnight at this hotel, and took a six-hour cruise to Freeport. They didn't make any hotel arrangements there. Maybe he's got a time share. Lisa's reservation is for a direct flight to Nassau. Maybe that's because of the storm. Maybe it was the only flight available. I don't know. Anyway, if Lisa has met up with this guy, he must be planning to take them both to Freeport, but I haven't a clue as to how. An island-hoping cruise ship maybe, maybe another flight. There's nothing booked on their credit cards."

The thought of Sharon, and now Lisa, on an island with the man she had seen in Sharon's apartment made her more than a little uneasy. She told Slim about the incident.

"Was he built?" Slim asked.

"I didn't notice." She had been too taken aback to note that kind of detail, but she would remember his face.

"Most exhibitionists aren't dangerous. And Sharon can take care of herself. But he's not someone I'd want my daughter to be around. I'd get Lisa and bring her back pronto, no matter what any of them says. They might be ready to come back anyway. If that storm hits, this will be the vacation from hell. Call in tomorrow. I'll check on a marriage license first thing in the morning."

Marti thought about Sharon, afraid of heights, afraid of flying, afraid of deep water. Going off alone to an island to sit and brood or maybe drink to forget was one thing; going there with a man was quite another. This DeVonte Lutrell would expect her to do more than cry in her beer, whether they were married or not. He would expect to have a good time. It was hard to imagine Sharon having a good time on an island; she didn't even like to sit in the sun.

"What's the matter?" Vik asked.

"I don't know," she admitted. "None of this sounds like Sharon. None of this sounds good."

"Well, just don't get stuck in that storm. I need you back here."

"We've still got a few loose ends," Marti pointed out.

"I'll take care of things here," Vik said, "just get in and out of the place safely. I never was one for leaving the country. And remember, if they shut down the airport and that storm hits, you could be stuck there for days." He opened a manila folder, flipped through his notes, and looked at his new computer. "Maybe I should go with you."

"Just keep looking for Nan Conser."

Lisa sat in the small shack near the restaurant that was almost on the water's edge. It was filled with small boats and sails and masts and smelled of seaweed. She knew she would not be safe here if the storm came, but she also knew that nobody would look for her here. She would be safe for the night, and in the morning she would find a police station. They would have to help her find Sharon. They could check the hotels and motels in Freeport much faster and easier than she could. If she could find them. She had never been anyplace where the police weren't everywhere. Maybe if she went to one of the casinos. Twice she had tried to call home, but had not been able to get through. How could anyone live in a place where telephone service was so unreliable?

The shack creaked and swayed as the wind whistled through the cracks between the planks of wood. Any other time, she would have been afraid. Now she just felt grateful for a place to hide. She grabbed an armful of sails and climbed into one of the boats. She didn't want to go to sleep, but she didn't think she could stay awake much longer. As long as the storm didn't come, she would be all right until morning. The wind blew harder, and she could hear the crash of the waves. She got up, peered outside. The tide did not seem to be any closer. This hut was at least fifty feet from the water's edge. She returned to the boat. The sails smelled of salt, but not fish. She huddled beneath them.

It was no longer possible to rent the boat. The storm was too close. DeVonte talked with a pilot of a small airplane and convinced him that it was safe to remain in Nassau until morning.

184

The storm had stalled and was not expected to hit until the following night. Unless its direction changed, as DeVonte hoped, it might be a glancing blow. He scoured the island as best he could and wished he was as familiar with Nassau as he was with Freeport. He had Sharon's photo of Lisa but could not make himself conspicuous by showing it. Besides, it wasn't the best resemblance. Instead, he got a map and wandered around, following a grid he laid out, from casinos and college campus to shanties near and far from the ocean. He looked for a girl in a baseball cap and sunglasses even as he wondered if she had disguised herself again. He would not be outsmarted by a teenaged girl. He would not. But, in the end, he had to admit that he *had* been outsmarted. Furious, he gave up and went to the airport. The prop job that seated four was gone. There was one plane beside a hangar. A man was sleeping beneath it.

"Hey, man."

The man jumped up as DeVonte touched his shoulder.

"What you want?" he asked.

"Are you the pilot? Can you fly this?"

The man nodded.

"Good, then take me to Freeport."

"Tonight?"

"Yes, tonight," DeVonte said.

"Are you crazy? I cannot fly out of here tonight. The storm is out there. Who knows when it will hit? Have you ever been in a hurricane, man?"

"The storm isn't anywhere near here. It won't be here for hours."

"Oh, and someone has made you god that you know that? Nobody tells these storms when to come. Nobody knows when they will leave. I am here for the night, man, and here I stay."

"In the morning then," DeVonte said, "if the storm is not here."

"You come back then and see. I promise nothing, but I will not cross that water tonight."

Nothing DeVonte said, nothing he offered him, changed the man's mind.

DeVonte headed for the nearest casino. Damn. He had to get back to Freeport. The handyman was in the storage area. There was no basement, and he hadn't had the time to leave him anywhere else. God, but it had felt good, smashing his skull with that two-by-four. If it hadn't been for him, Sharon would be dead. He would have told Lisa something different, that she was sick maybe, and the girl would have gone with him. This would be over and done with. Instead, he had both of them to get rid of. He should have known Sharon would be nothing but trouble. If only she hadn't been such a pushover. He always had a hard time turning away from an easy mark. And there was a lot of money involved once she—and Lisa—were dead.

Marti loved to fly at night, even if getting on the plane was a hassle. She had to pin her badge to her holster before she packed her weapon so that when it went through the metal detector, they would know she was a peace officer. Then she had to declare it and show her registration and permit. By the time they let her through the gate, the plane was almost ready to take off.

They were in the first-class section, and she insisted on the seat by the window. She leaned her forehead against the glass as she looked down at the lights and then the curve of the shoreline as they headed across the lake. "Lord, I love the beauty of your house, the tenting place of your glory," she said softly.

Ben chuckled. "This has to be the first time I've flown with anyone who thought flying was a religious experience."

"It is," she said. "It's like being able to see the world with God's eyes."

He squeezed her hand. "I love you."

"Me, too," she said, then determined to amend that off-handed phrase she repeated far too often, "I love you, too."

"Be nice, maybe, if we could stay here for a week," Ben said.

"Maybe," Marti considered. She thought of their cabin in Wisconsin. No sand, no beach, no banana trees or palmettos. Their place: woods, a lake, a canoe, campfires, kids, and, in the winter, snow. "I think I like our place better."

"I'm glad," Ben said. "Me, too."

She put her head on his shoulder and closed her eyes. It might be a long time before she had another chance to get some sleep.

When they arrived at the Nassau Police Station, it was filled with purposeful activity. A storm was coming. Everyone was focused on that. Evacuation plans were being put into effect, shelters being made ready—just in case. The storm was poised to attack, stalled across the water, gaining strength, but it could change direction. By the time a short, light-skinned officer with a paunch motioned them into a small room, they had waited the better part of an hour.

"Well now," the Bahamian officer said, "it's always a pleasure to meet an officer of the law from the States. How can I help you?"

Marti wondered how she would feel if she had to wear his uniform all day. Although the fabric seemed soft enough, the color and the tight cut of the coat looked uncomfortable. Then she wondered if female officers wore the same uniform or even if there were female officers. She didn't ask. It would be interesting to entertain everyone back home with the history of the Bahamian police force, but she did not have the time. She took out the eight-by-ten photos of Sharon and Lisa that she had been carrying in her purse, along with some three-by-fives of Lisa. The three-by-fives were school photos taken two years ago, but they were a reasonable likeness.

"I need to find my friend and her daughter," she said. "As

far as I know, they are either here on this island or in Freeport. Her daughter flew in to Nassau today, so I thought we should start here."

She had found out that taking a small plane or a boat to another island might not be that much of a problem during the day. It was almost four in the morning now, and she would not be able to pursue that possibility until after daybreak.

"In your country they are missing?" the officer asked.

"No," Marti said, "we just need to find them as quickly as possible. My friend's mother is dying."

There had been another call from the hospital. Rayveena was not doing well. Momma had to come home and watch the children so she could not stay the night. Rayveena had asked for Sharon, but that was not why Marti had come. She had come because of DeVonte Lutrell. She pulled out another picture, a mug shot. "I believe they are with this man."

"And? You do not trust him?"

Smart cop, Marti thought, *one who is not afraid to play hunches.*

"We don't know him," she said. "He has an arrest record for assaulting women."

The officer looked at the pictures. "Then I would be worried also. Now there is not a lot I can do. But, yes, I will be certain that these photographs are distributed along with descriptions of the woman and this man. We will all be busy preparing for the storm. I will have descriptions sent to the storm shelters as well. Should the storm hit, there will be many who are missing, which is not good; but also many eyes watching for them and many praying for their safe return. Where are you staying?"

They had not checked into a hotel yet. He suggested one that was part of a casino.

"And when will you be leaving?"

"Our flight leaves at five o'clock tomorrow afternoon."

"That is good. I do not know what the storm will do. The weatherman thinks he can predict, but God decides these things. In any case it could be several days before you leave the island and much hardship before you could go. I will do all that I can."

As they left, Marti watched the concentrated activity around her and wondered how much time anyone would have to look for an American with her daughter—and, she reminded herself, DeVonte Lutrell.

Marti walked with Ben to the water's edge. They both agreed that they could not leave here without at least a quick swim. There was something wild about the swaying palm trees behind her and the cloudy, starless sky overhead. Wind-tossed and foamy, the sea churned as if it were fermenting. When she waded in, it was cold.

"Come on," she said, diving in when it reached her shoulders and swimming parallel to the shore.

Ben joined her, swimming beside her. After a few minutes, they floated on their backs, holding hands, letting the Atlantic rock them with an insistent pull first toward, then away from the shore. She had never swum in saltwater before. It was different, more buoyant. *Seductive,* she thought, as she felt the pull away from land. If she let it, it would take her far out to sea, like a boat with the wind filling its sails.

"Time to go in," she said. "I feel like floating forever." Relaxed, she turned and began swimming with long, easy strokes toward shore.

"Now what?" Ben asked as they sat on the sand. The light on the horizon announced the coming of day. She had never watched the sun come up like this before. He rubbed her back with a thick towel, then put another over her shoulders. "Wind's picking up."

"I don't know what to do now," she admitted. "If it weren't for Lutrell's police record, I wouldn't be as worried."

"He's a batterer, right? Not a killer?"

"There's always that fine line. It just makes me uneasy. We didn't have to come here; nobody sent out an SOS. They must be okay. I wish it wasn't so difficult to call home." She had tried without success several times before they left the airport. It had taken the better part of an hour to get a call through after they left the police station, and then there had been no word from Sharon or Lisa. "Maybe we should have just waited to hear from them. I'm sure they are both okay."

"Not come here?" Ben said. "And miss this?" He kissed her.

Sharon could not get to sleep. She did not want to sleep. She wanted to go home. There was something eerie about the way the wind was almost singing as it whipped around the corners of the building. *Like a siren's song,* she thought, and shivered. With the French family gone and the handyman nowhere to be found, she was here alone. There was nothing but poured foundations, shells of buildings, wooden frames like ghosts. She fixed a rum and Coke, then decided not to drink it. It would make her sleepy. As much as she wanted to sleep through this, she felt too alone. Why wasn't DeVonte back yet?

She wanted to turn on all of the lights, put on a CD, and turn up the music full blast. She wanted to hear the sound of an announcer on the radio or watch some mindless talk show. She wanted someone, anyone, just one other human being. Even with the doors locked, she was afraid here all alone. Afraid. She had been afraid ever since they'd gotten on that airplane, afraid almost since she'd gotten married. Was that what he wanted? Was that why he wasn't here? Did he enjoy scaring and then comforting her? Did he like being the strong one? If he did, this was taking it too far. She had almost drowned this morning. It wasn't a game anymore.

15

Lisa awakened to the screams of many seagulls. She remembered at once where she was. Daylight seeped in through the cracks in the boards, and the the odor of salt overwhelmed her. She wanted to vomit. Instead, she threw off the sails that covered her, made sure she had everything she'd come in with, and pushed open the door to the boat shack. Sleek, beady-eyed seagulls looked at her without scattering. Several fought over fish. Others wheeled and screeched overhead. The tide had come in. The water wasn't more than fifteen feet from the shack. The waves were pounding the sand and retreating with a loud, scrabbling sound. The sky was overcast, as if it was going to rain. The wind had picked up, and, although it wasn't cold, it was brisk. Palm trees swayed and bowed as if they were dancing.

Her bladder felt as if it was about to burst. There were no facilities, so she went into the bushes. When she emerged, she stared at the ocean for a minute, wishing for a sink so she could wash her hands, then went to the water's edge and tried to skirt the waves without getting her athletic shoes wet and dip her hands in at the same time. Now if she had just brought her toothbrush. She pushed back the visor of her cap and looked around.

She walked to the rutted dirt road and decided to go in the direction opposite the ocean. She did not see anyone as she walked. It seemed several miles before she came to a small store with the windows covered with plywood and a cluster of stalls, locked with the doors boarded up. She could not find a pay phone.

After about half an hour, she saw buildings in the distance, outlined against the sky. Another hour and there were people. Tired people, hurrying people, women with babies in their arms, men and boys on bicycles. The storm was coming. She had to find Sharon; but if what DeVonte had said was true, Sharon wasn't even on this island, she was in Freeport. How could anyone here help her get to Freeport? Even with all of these people moving inland and the stores boarded up, she still didn't see a police officer. She did not even see a telephone.

As much as she disliked him, she would have to find DeVonte, or maybe let him think he found her. He was the only one who knew where Sharon was, who knew if she would be safe if the storm struck. Was DeVonte still looking for her or had he left last night without her? She was willing to bet he was too macho to stop looking for her. When she reached the city, she went to the airport. Sure enough, there he was. She went over to a food stand and bought a doughnut and some coffee and spoke loud enough to catch his attention. When he looked her way, she nodded and waited.

"Where were you?" he asked.

"Checking out the island."

·"Didn't it occur to you . . ."

"It occurred to me that it's almost impossible to have fun with adults."

"And your mother? And the flight we have to take now to join her? The flight we must take at once, if I can talk the pilot into it."

She shrugged. Those were his problems. He would find a way if he wanted to.

"I can't leave until I call home."

"There is not time for . . ."

"Then leave without me. I can stay here until there's a flight back."

Anger flashed in his eyes as he looked at her. How many times had Joanna told her to never let anyone know she was intimidated by them, especially not a boy. She stood her ground.

"Over there," he said. "But you'll have a hell of a time getting through to the States."

She did after six attempts. It only took fifteen minutes.

"Lisa?"

"Momma."

DeVonte stood close enough to hear her end of the conversation, but that was okay. She used their code question right away. "Did you go with Joanna to that movie last night?" Now Momma would know that she wanted to come home but couldn't say so. She had hated that until now, told lies about where she was going and who she was with so they couldn't come get her. Never again.

"Lisa, are you with that man Sharon married?"

"I told Joanna you wouldn't like it."

"Is Sharon there?"

"No, I haven't seen it yet."

DeVonte glared at her. "We don't have time."

"Yes, I'm staying here for a few days." That meant no, she was leaving the island.

"Is he dangerous?"

"Maybe. I don't know if I'll go swimming today. Maybe when we get to Freeport. A storm is coming."

"Marti and Ben are there." Momma told her where Marti was staying, but Lisa knew she couldn't go there now, couldn't call.

"Tell Joanna I'll see her when I get back. I'll bring her some pretzels, or peanuts, whatever they're serving this morning."

She hoped Momma understood that meant she would be getting on a plane.

DeVonte grabbed the phone. "We have to go." He held the receiver to her ear. "Bye, Momma, I've got to go. I really do have to go."

The plane was so small that she debated getting in.

"It's over there." The pilot gestured toward the clouds gathering in the sky behind them. "It moves very slowly. It is not in a hurry. It may just touch the islands. We can get to Freeport easily, but I will not be able to return." He spoke to DeVonte. "You will see that I have accommodations at the casino until this is over and that my plane is inside a hangar, where it will not be damaged. It will cost much money."

DeVonte agreed.

It occurred to Lisa that they were doing the man a favor, that without them, his plane would be exposed to the storm. Like several others, it was just sitting on a runway, leeward of a hangar that was already occupied. All of the hangars were shut tight.

"We will go now," the man said.

Lisa climbed into the airplane. There were four seats. DeVonte sat up front. Although she avoided going to church as much as possible, she did believe in God. As the engines started, and the propellers turned, and the plane trembled, she prayed. The plane gathered speed, left the runway, and as she saw the water approach, dipped down, nose first. DeVonte cursed. She kept praying. The nose went up and they were airborne.

She didn't want to look out the window. She wanted to keep her eyes closed. What she really wanted to do was go to sleep so that when they crashed, she wouldn't know anything, wouldn't feel it when they hit the water, going straight down at hundreds of miles an hour. She had never flown until yesterday, didn't know what it was like to fly in anything this small, and couldn't tell if the drone of the engine and the way first one wing and then the other dipped and pointed toward the water were good or bad, right or wrong. She watched, first sky, then water, then sky again. Nobody spoke. After what seemed like forever, an island came into view. The plane bounced up and down several times as it landed and seemed to to be moving too fast to stop, but it did, and right side up, and with nobody hurt. She prayed again and said thank you.

DeVonte stood near the road with his hand on Lisa's arm. She was not getting away from him again. As it was, he didn't see a van or taxi and he had no idea of how they would get to the condo, or if they would get there before it began to rain. The pilot had lied. They both knew that the hurricane was on a direct path to Freeport, and would hit Nassau with a less severe blow. The pilot had wanted his plane inside, where perhaps it would receive less damage. DeVonte had wanted to be on this island, not in Nassau. They both had something to gain. They both took the risk of beating the storm.

"We have to hurry," he said. "We'll have to walk until we see a bus or a cab." The storm would hit the beach where the condo was first and hit it full force. The building should be able to withstand the rain and the wind, but there would be flooding. The body in the storage area would not stay there long once the water began coming in. Everyone, except him, would be swept out to sea.

"How far do we have to walk?" Lisa asked.

"The condo is on the other side of the island. But we may be able to buy bicycles if nothing else. When we are closer, there's a lake and we can take the taxi boat." The storm wouldn't affect that, not right away.

He walked fast, surprised when Lisa kept up and did not complain. He looked up at the clouds. The rain would come soon, and along with that, the wind.

Sharon awakened to the sound of the wind. It made a whistling noise at the rear of the building where the bedroom was, but a louder, howling sound when she walked to the sliding doors that led to the balcony. Outside, gray clouds scudded across the sky, driven by the wind. In the distance, the clouds were much darker. The storm was coming. She was alone. She wasn't sure what she should do. If it was a tornado, she would go to the central part of the lowest place in the building, but here, the water might rise.

She went into the kitchen, made a pot of coffee, and found a thermos. Then she made sandwiches and put them into a bag. That done, she fixed hot cereal and toast for breakfast. After she ate, she got out a flashlight, some matches, and candles. She wrapped them in a comforter. Then she sat down to wait.

Marti awakened to the aroma of hot coffee and fried bacon. It took her a minute to remember where she was. Too bad there would be no more time to swim. Then she thought of Lisa and Sharon. When she opened her eyes, Ben was standing by the window. It looked like it was raining. There was a tray on the table with breakfast. She pushed the sheet away and sat up.

"We don't have time,"

"We've got plenty of time," Ben said.

She looked at the clock. "It's after ten. We've got to find Lisa."

"Here, eat," Ben said. He put the tray on the bed beside her. The eggs weren't scrambled as hard as she liked them, but she was hungry.

"You shouldn't have let me sleep in. We've wasted too much time."

"You were running on adrenaline," he said, "and that swim was just what you needed to help you relax. I was out detecting."

"Oh?" He didn't look pleased by whatever he had found out. "Lisa," she asked, "you couldn't find her?"

"I got through to Momma. Lisa called home this morning about seven. She said she was with Sharon's husband—who apparently was listening—and that she hadn't seen Sharon yet."

Marti's stomach lurched. She put down a forkful of grits.

"Momma thought she was getting ready to fly out of here,

so I went to the airport and checked. A young girl and a middle-aged man fitting their descriptions took off for Freeport in a small plane about an hour before I got there. I got them to call Freeport, and the plane did land safely."

"Good, we can go there. It's a smaller island, and it'll be easier to find them."

"We can't go anywhere," Ben said. "The hurricane is already hitting this island, although we won't get the brunt of it. Everything is battened down."

"We can't leave?"

"No."

"We can't do anything?"

"No, not until the storm passes. The phone lines are down now. I have got a pilot who will fly us there as soon as the weather clears."

"I should have had them call the police in Freeport instead of waiting to go there."

"Lisa wasn't in Freeport when we went to the police station; and as for Sharon, what could we have told them? We don't know where she is."

"Ben . . ." She had to do something, but what?

Lisa jogged beside DeVonte. It was raining, not hard, but steady. The wind blew it against her face. She didn't have a raincoat or even a rain scarf. Her clothes were wet. She was cold. She wondered where the people had gone. The streets were deserted; the stores boarded up. She wanted to ask how much farther it was to the condo but said nothing. They had passed the casino and an empty, shuttered marketplace that took up at least a block. Was this the island's equivalent to the mall? Wait until she told Joanna.

A car drove past. DeVonte tried to stop the driver. The car was filled with people. They had doubled up by sitting on laps. The man looked at DeVonte and shook his fist. The car didn't slow down. DeVonte walked faster.

"We've got to get to the water taxi," he said.

"Is it near here?"

"No."

They went past a church. Lisa thought about seeking shelter there, but she didn't think she could stay there without knowing Sharon was okay. Across the street there were a few houses, but mostly just scrub and stunted trees. A sign advertised a park that had gone to weed. Another advertised horseback riding. The road seemed to go on forever. Her legs felt as if she had been walking for hours. Maybe she had been. It was getting dark, like night.

"Is your condo near the ocean?"

"Umm."

"How close."

"Too close," he said.

"If there's a tidal wave, will it get washed away?"

"This is a hurricane, not a typhoon, not an earthquake."

When he didn't say anything else, she figured the answer must be no.

They passed what had to be a motel, although there were no signs.

"We can stop here," she said.

"No! We have to get to your mother. She's alone. You know how scared she is."

Sharon. He was right. Sharon would know what to do in a storm, but she would be so afraid. This might be the only time in her life when Sharon would need her, and he was taking her there. The wind was blowing toward them now, so strong that they had to fight against it to move forward. Even the thick-trunked palm trees were bending. If the condo wasn't near here—if they didn't reach this water taxi—where would they find shelter from the storm?

Lisa felt afraid, too. This place was desolate. There was nobody out here but the two of them. No cars, nothing. They passed two more groups of plywood-protected stores before the pavement became a dirt path. She was soaked to the skin and shivering. Her hair was wet and clung to her forehead, her face. The rain looked like one gray sheet that shifted directions from vertical to almost horizontal.

"Almost there," DeVonte said.

Almost where? she wondered. Wherever this boat taxi docked? Who would take them across the lake in this? How would they cross the lake? How would they get to Sharon? Where could they go if they couldn't reach the condo? There was some type of building across from them. A big building, a manufacturing plant maybe, a refinery, something.

"Let's go there," she yelled above the wind. She pointed.

"Shut up," he said. "Nobody's there."

He pulled her along as he turned up a narrow path that led to a one-story building. There was no need to wonder if anyone was home. Plywood had been nailed to the windows. The dirt had become mud that sucked at her athletic shoes as they walked. As they passed the building, the water came into view. Not the ocean, much smaller. She followed him to the dock, but there was no boat. Nothing. The water was choppy and surrounded by land. There was a long, two-story pink building across from where they stood, with three small boats that might seat ten or fifteen people tied up at short, wide docks. She didn't know how far it was to the other side, but the lake wasn't any bigger than Fox Lake back home. There had to be a way to walk around it. The pink building was dark. Did that mean everyone was gone or that the electricity was out? If Sharon was alone in this storm and in the dark. . . .

DeVonte cursed. Now he would have to walk around the lake. Why hadn't Sharon just drowned yesterday? Who would know? He remembered how it had felt when he put his hands around the handyman's neck and squeezed until the man stopped struggling. He wished he could choke him again. If he could just reach Sharon before the eye of the storm passed, he would have that lull to get her body and Lisa's into the ocean, the handyman as well. Then he could just wait out the storm. There were plenty of emergency supplies. "Damn!" This was supposed to be easy. Until now, it had been. He wiped at the rain that streamed down his face.

Storms, he loved storms, especially terrible storms like this one. The trees bent to its will, the ocean rose and heaved. Boats were flung across the sand and those huts, those shacks, those stalls where he had lived and worked all those years were destroyed. It would takes weeks, even months, before they rose again. Here, on the dock, the wind blew so hard that he had to brace himself. It whipped around him like the scourge of God and it was. It would pluck the trees clean and flatten everything in its path. He lifted his face to the rain and laughed.

"Yes! Yes!" he shouted. "Come, Jah! Come!"

He laughed again, then looked down at the girl. For a moment he had forgotten she was there. She was looking at him as if she thought he was mad. This one was not like her mother. She didn't scare easily; and when she was afraid, she did not let it get the best of her. It would not be easy to kill her. She would fight back . . . if she was expecting his attack.

He looked across the water at the motel. There were no lights there. Good. That meant there was no electricity at the condo either. The French couple in the first-floor apartment had packed up and left. By the time he reached Sharon, she would be distraught. He didn't need this one with him when he got there. He had to get rid of Lisa now. The thought pleased him.

"Is that a light?" he asked.

"Where?"

"On that boat, the one at the far end. A lantern maybe."

He stepped back, so that he was behind her. "If we could just get his attention. The water isn't that bad here. The boat could cross."

She took a step closer to the edge of the dock. Before she could speak, or turn, he ran toward her, hitting her back with both hands, knocking her into the water. He stood there long enough to watch her go under twice, then hurried away.

Marti paced from the window to the bed to the chair, sat down, got up, and paced again. The room was small. She was getting claustrophobic. No. She was scared to death, scared for Lisa and Sharon, afraid of this DeVonte because she didn't know who he was. And helpless. That was the worst of it. There was nothing she could do but wait it out.

"I've seen these storms on TV," she said. "Even when they're in the States, sometimes it takes days for the water to go down, days before they find people who are missing. Lisa and Sharon aren't even islanders. Who knows they're there? Who cares? Tourists come and go every day. How do they even keep track of them? They don't. Those cruise ships from Fort Lauderdale pull in and out every day. I'm surprised you were even able to track Lisa and that DeVonte to that airplane." She sat down on the bed. "Thank God they at least made it to Freeport. What if they just said that so we'd stay calm? What if they don't really know if the plane landed at all? How did they get the information so fast? Are you sure they didn't just say that?"

She began pacing again. Even Ben, who was always so calm, was having a hard time just sitting there. He went to the window. She stood beside him. They were on the second floor of a four-story building that covered a city block. They were right on the beach with a view of the ocean. The sand had stretched about 150 feet away early this morning. The distance to the water did not seem that great now, but that could be her imagination. The palm trees were swaying in a rhythm that nature had not intended, some almost bowed to the ground. Palm fronds were scattered everywhere and blowing about like crazed fans. They probably shouldn't be standing so close to glass windows, in case they broke, but the fury of the storm was having an almost hypnotic effect on both of them.

"You hardly touched your breakfast," Ben said. "Let's go downstairs, see if we can find some magazines or newspapers, maybe just kill a little time in the casino, have lunch."

"Theo and Joanna and Momma and Mike must be worried," she said.

"I talked to them when I called. They know we're in a safe place, and we're not going to get the brunt of the storm."

"Are we in a safe place?" she asked. "I wish we weren't so close to the water."

"The worst we could get is a little flooding," he said.

Marti shuddered. "Leave it to Sharon. I just wish we were all home."

When they went downstairs, Marti realized how well insulated the building must be, at least the part of it where the action was. It was as if there were no storm gathering strength outside. She couldn't hear the wind or the rain. There wasn't even any Muzak. There was very little lighting in the casino that didn't come from the slot machines and almost no conversation. They looked into the rooms with the gaming tables but didn't go there. The gambling rooms were filled, but everyone was quiet, intent on their game, intent on winning. Nobody seemed to be having any fun.

"Boring," Marti said, understanding that word, so often used by her kids, for the first time.

Ben was restless, too.

When they tried to use the phone, the line was dead. "There has to be an emergency system." She went to the concierge, then the manager, showing both her badge.

"I'm a peace officer," she said. "I have to contact someone in the States. There has to be some mode of communication here."

The manager was an elderly man, as tall as she was, with skin as smooth as polished mahogany. "There is a storm, madam." He spoke with a British accent. "This is an island. We are alone." He seemed unperturbed by this.

She insisted. "There has to be a way."

"Perhaps as an officer of the law you know something that

I don't, and there is some emergency system that I am not aware of. However, the only people who would know that are the police, and you are not going to be able to go where they are until the rain stops, and then only if there is no major flooding."

"And you're just here? You can't talk with anybody? Suppose somebody robbed this place."

He looked about, held out his hands, palms up. "And where would they run with the money? I do assure you that we have sufficient security to handle any emergency. In fact, since you are a peace officer, you might want to see someone about getting a flashlight, just in case your assistance is needed."

"Two," she said. "My husband is a fireman and a paramedic."

The manager turned to Ben with a wide smile. "Does that mean you could assist with emergency first aid, sir?"

"Yes. Will that get us a telephone line out of here?"

"I'm sorry. We really are alone."

He motioned to a uniformed security guard, and within five minutes, Marti and Ben were each armed with a six-battery flashlight and extra batteries.

"People tend to panic when the lights go out," the manager said.

Ben said, "You've been through these storms before."

"Yes, sir, many times." He looked at Marti with raised eyebrows. "And, madam, the storm, she is in charge now. As difficult as it may sound to you Americans, we sit now and wait it out. If we are lucky, she will not be too unkind."

As the manager walked away, Ben said, "And, madam peace officer, since it seems we will be in residence here until said storm passes, may I inquire to what madam would like to do now?"

Marti laughed. He was right. They were stuck, and they were going to have to make the best of it. All she could do now was worry.

They found a restaurant in the interior of the building. No windows, not a lot of light, chandeliers, and gospel music. It was crowded. They had to wait ten minutes for a table.

"Looks like we picked the right place to stay," Ben said. He nodded toward several tables where uniformed cruise ship's staff were eating. "And I saw some pilots and stewardesses leaving this morning."

"That was a smart idea."

"Does that mean you wouldn't like being alone on a deserted island with me either?"

She squeezed his arm. "I would enjoy being on this crowded and storm-battered island with you if Lisa and Sharon weren't out there somewhere. Lisa might have picked up enough survival skills from Joanna to able to take care of herself, but Sharon with Mr. Wonderful? I don't know."

The waitress motioned them to a table. Marti listened to the rhythms of the islands in the voices of the ship's crew sitting at the next table. The menu was limited. They were out of what she ordered. Ben decided on the conch soup. She had a hamburger. While she was waiting, she eavesdropped. None of the ship's crew seemed concerned about the storm. She hoped that indicated past experience and wasn't just the influence of the rum in their Bahama Mamas. Their laughter, and the chandeliers, and the gospel music made her think of the *Titanic*. No, she reassured herself, hotels didn't sink.

Lisa held her breath and went below the surface. She didn't come up until she had to. He was watching. Another deep breath and she went under again. This time she stayed under the water until she thought her lungs would burst. When she came up, she was gasping. She flailed about, as if she was in trouble. She even reached out one arm to DeVonte. When she had caught her breath enough to take another deep one, she did and dropped below the surface of the water again. When she came up, he was gone. When her eyes adjusted to the darkness, she could see him hurrying away.

The water wasn't much colder than the rain had been. She could feel the water shift one way, then the other, but there was little current. She wasn't that far from the pier either. Her back hurt where he had shoved her. When she tried to swim, she got a sharp pain in her chest. She yielded to the buoyancy of the water and bobbed about for a minute. It pushed her one way, pulled her another, going with and then against the wind. Her chest hurt. She could make out the pier, the land that surrounded the lake. She wasn't sure how far she could swim or where she could come ashore.

Marti decided she preferred the lounge, where not even the sounds of the storm could penetrate, to their room, where she had to watch the storm's steady advance and slow destruction. The manager, when pressed, gave her half a dozen magazines and a week's back copies of the island's daily newspaper. The waitress brought a fresh pot of hot coffee. Marti passed both sports magazines to Ben and settled back to catch up on the local news.

Not much happened on the islands. Prices at the supermarket were higher than they were in Lincoln Prairie. Births were listed and weddings, but not divorces or traffic violations. There were a lot of churches and many services. Those inclined could attend several times a day. The article on the death of a ship's steward was the exception. Marti read it twice.

"Ben, someone got killed on the ship Sharon came over here on. One of the ship's stewards. The found him in a cabin when they were cleaning up before making the trip back to the States."

Ben grinned at her but didn't comment.

"Once a cop . . . ," she said.

He nodded.

She picked up a copy of *Good Housekeeping* that was two

years old. This was going to be a long day. "How about a game of poker?"

"Poke her?" Ben said. "With what?"

She grinned, then shook her head.

"Well then, I guess I'll go get a deck of cards."

She leaned back in the upholstered booth while he was gone and closed her eyes. Had Lisa and this DeVonte Lutrell arrived safely at Freeport this morning? Or had someone told Ben that to keep them from worrying until after the storm passed. How long did it take a hurricane to pass over an island? How long would it be before they could get to Freeport, before they could go home? Bored, she began listening to the men in the booth next to hers.

"Yah, man, that Louis, always so smug, that one, always knowing so much and telling so little and grinning so wide." His voice was high-pitched and thin, annoying. "Well, all of that listening and watching has gotten him nothing more than his neck broke."

"I heard it was a rope," another man said. "Whoever it was hung him."

"No, no," said another. "My brother is a janitor at the police station. Whoever it was came up behind him and used a wire. And no fingerprints either. Wiped the place clean."

"Well, whatever it was," the man with the high-pitched voice said, "I am thinking that this is not such a safe occupation to be in anymore. I am thinking about working someplace else instead."

"Oh, man, we have always had people missing from the boats. They want to be missing. Or they are found and we are not told."

"Yes," the high voice said, "but how often is one of us killed? And not in the street for our money, but on the boat because somebody wants us dead."

Marti knew they were talking about the steward's death that she had read about in the newspaper. She didn't know what

206

the reference to people missing from the boats meant, but she was interested. Once a cop . . .

As Sharon watched from the window, a tall palm tree, now standing alone, swayed back and forth, its fronds scraping the window. The wind was going to blow it over, just as it had the others, and she should be standing away from the window when it did, but she was mesmerized by the way it went back and forth, bending like a ballet dancer practicing pliés. Watching it, she could ignore the wind, ignore the sailboat that had been carried from the water's edge to the yard below, ignore the relentless howl, and all of the rapping, flapping, banging noises that must mean this building would soon break apart.

As she watched, the palm tree came out of the ground. It was as if an invisible hand grasped it around the trunk and ever so slowly pulled it free. Just as gently, the hand laid it across the balcony. When the sliding door shattered, and the wind and the rain rushed in, Sharon grabbed the rolled comforter and the overnight bag she had put by the door and ran downstairs.

Lisa huddled in the water, beneath the dock, holding on to one of the pilings. She couldn't swim, her chest hurt too bad, but the water was rising. In an odd way, she felt safe, sheltered by the wood above her head. The wind didn't seem as loud or as close. Here, near the edge of the lake, the water rocked her back and forth; but it seemed calmer than it was farther out. If the water was colder, she would be at risk of whatever that thermia thing was, but she didn't feel that cold, although she wasn't warm either. Why wasn't she cold? Maybe she should be. Her arms were tired, but she could hold on. She would have to. Her chest hurt, but the pain was more of an ache now. When she'd swum over here, it had felt as if someone was jabbing her with a sword. The water was inching up toward the pier. Before long it would be high enough, and she could pull herself out. DeVonte had tried to kill her. But why? What kind of madman had Sharon married? Why bring her here to kill her? Because Sharon was dead? Because he had already killed her?

Sharon ran to the storage room. It was in the center of the building; she would be safe from the storm, from the wind— until the water came, if it did. She unfolded a lawn chair, unrolled the down comforter, and used her change of clothes as a pillow. The wind wasn't as loud here, but the ocean was. She could hear the waves crashing and pounding against the shore. She thought about the water sucking her under, pulling her out to sea. She would rather be upstairs, take her chances with the wind. She put her head under the comforter and her hands over her ears, but the sound of the water would not go away. When she couldn't stand it any longer, she switched on the flashlight and began gathering up her things. At first she wondered who had left a pile of clothes in the corner. Then she saw two shoes and then, looking up, his face.

Screaming, she dropped the flashlight and ran. The wind caught her as she rushed out the front door and flung her against the bannister. She fell, scraping her knees, picked herself up, and the wind knocked her down again. She felt the bannister shake as she held on the railing. She had to go back inside—where he was.

16

Marti waved to Ben when he returned with a deck of playing cards. He had a cribbage board, too. She had joined the stewards at their booth. Ben pulled up a chair.

"Why are you here," Marti asked, "if your ship docks in Freeport?"

"Our ship is out with another crew. We take turns. Would you like to be in Freeport right now? It is bad enough right here."

"And," she said, "you think you might have seen the man I described?"

"I would need to see a picture," the round-faced man said. "The only reason I think it is possible is because this person you describe, if he is who I think he is, is what we consider a gambler. Someone who goes back and forth between Fort Lauderdale and Freeport maybe every month or two, and sometimes, two, three times a week for a couple of weeks."

The man with the high-pitched voice said, "People think that because so many travel with us every day we don't know one from the other. What they don't realize is that we only make certain trips, not every trip. If someone happens to book on one of our regular trips more than a few times, yes, then they are familiar to us."

"The reason that we try to watch for them," the round-faced man said, "is that we don't want them bringing drugs or contraband to the island. Once we see that someone travels with us a lot, then we pay more attention to what they are carrying and what they are taking back to the States. Sometimes they are detained; and if anything is found, there is a reward."

Marti hadn't spent enough time thinking about Caribbean cruises to consider any of this. It would not have occurred to her that these men were doing anything more than serving drinks or food or working in the casino. She would see that they looked at a picture of this DeVonte Lutrell as soon as possible. Meanwhile, she had brought snapshots of Lisa and Sharon.

The men passed the photos around, but shook their heads. After they left, Ben began shuffling the cards.

"I can use that," she told him.

"Use what?"

"That business about carrying drugs. If I tell the local police that's possible with Lutrell, they'll take a much closer look at him, maybe even put some effort into finding him."

Ben paused, midshuffle. "It really isn't too important, is it, when someone is missing."

She shook her head. "Missing is only the definition of the person who is doing the looking. Whoever they are looking for might not consider themselves missing at all; or if they do, they might want to be."

"And that's how the police look at it, too."

"It's easy to make yourself hard to find. And in the case of foul play, look at the arms-with-hands victims. We still don't know who they are. If someone doesn't want you to be found, that's not that hard either." She thought about the two women missing from the ship this crew worked on. And, they had told her, more women, maybe a half dozen in all, were missing from other ships. "What are we going to do if we can't find Sharon and Lisa? What if they're missing, too, like the others." For the first time she wondered what she would do if she had to go home without them, or worse, if she would never see them again.

By the time Lisa was able to pull herself out of the water, the rain had stopped and the wind had died down. The sky was a strange shade of yellow, and in the distance, green. The quiet, after so much noise, was eerie. She was afraid. It was as if the storm had not passed, but was waiting, like a monster, to strike again. Her shoulder and her chest hurt so bad that she had to walk slowly without moving her arms. She had had to kick off her athletic shoes to swim to the dock. Mud squished between her toes as she made her way past the boarded-up building and back to the road. Nobody was out. She looked up at a stand of palm trees, stunned. It was as if an invisible hand had stripped off the leaves and left the trunks standing. Debris was everywhere. And there was the quiet, the terrible sound that was no sound at all. Not even a birdcall, not even a gull flying overhead. The lack of noise was more terrifying than the howl of the wind.

She didn't know where DeVonte was. She hoped he thought she was dead. She didn't think he had waited around very long to see if she would make it out of the lake. For some reason he had decided to return to the condo, at least that was where they had been heading. If it was just so that he could throw her in the lake to drown, he could have done something like that in Nassau. Why hadn't he? Because it was easier to kill her here? Or because of Sharon? Was Sharon still alive? Or had he killed her, too?

She walked toward the other side of the lake. The air was damp, clammy, not hot, not cold. She didn't look up at the sky. She hadn't ever seen a sky that color before. She didn't know what it meant. Instead, she looked down, avoiding the boards with nails, and sharp-edged strips of tin; stepping over tree trunks and branches and soggy clumps of clothing and the feathered remains of dead birds. She lost all sense of time. Eventually, she could see a road ahead. When she got there, she would have to decide, left or right.

Sharon huddled in the closet. She hid behind the clothes, under a pile of blankets, and listened as someone walked about the house. Was it DeVonte? Would he find her? Maybe he was dead. Maybe whoever had killed that man had killed DeVonte. Maybe that was why he never came back. What if whoever it was knew she was here and had returned to kill her, too?

She stifled a sob. God, what a nightmare this was. Would it ever end? Would she be alive when it did? The footsteps came closer. The door opened. She stayed still beneath the blankets, not daring to move. The door closed. Whoever it was walked away. The front door slammed. She could hear footsteps receding. He was gone. Or was it a trick? She didn't move.

She wasn't sure when she noticed the quiet. One moment the rain was beating down on the roof, the next moment it was not, or at least it seemed that way. She pushed the blankets off of her head and listened, but the wind had died down, too. The storm had passed. She could leave now, walk down the road to that motel and get help. As soon as she stepped out of the closet, he was there. She screamed then looked again.

"DeVonte!" She fell into his arms, crying. "Oh, thank God you're here. I was so afraid."

She kissed his face, his lips. "What do we do now? How do we get out of here? That man, DeVonte, that man who helped me, he's dead. Someone killed him. I thought whoever it was had killed you, too. I thought he was coming back for me."

She hugged him, grateful for his arms around her. She wasn't alone anymore, and the storm, the storm was over.

Part of the palm tree was in the living room. Glass from the balcony door was scattered across the carpet. The drapes hung wet and limp. *No wind,* she thought, *no wind.* "Thank God you're here. Where were you? How did you get here? It's so awful outside. You came back for me, didn't you?"

He nodded.

She went to the window. The sky was a peculiar color—yellowish green. She turned to DeVonte. "It is gone, isn't it? It's not coming back?"

Looking down, she saw the small pleasure boats, sails broken, cabins smashed, lying at odd angles along the beach, as if some giant child had tired of playing with them.

"Surreal, isn't it?" she asked.

He just stood there, dripping wet, looking exhausted. She ran to him. "Oh, baby, here, sit down." She led him to the sofa. "There's no electricity, no nothing, but here, I've got a thermos. The coffee must still be warm."

She rushed into the kitchen, found a cup. "There's no damage here at all, except for that palm tree. You should have seen it come out of the ground. My God, I've never seen anything like it. Here." She pressed the cup into his hands. "Drink, drink, you'll feel better."

She ran and got the comforter and dragged it over. She put it over him, got under herself, and huddled against him. "Oh, DeVonte, thank God you're back."

DeVonte was cold and tired as hell. He didn't want to move. He was getting cramps in his toes. His legs felt as if he had walked a hundred miles. The coffee was good, warm but good. He hadn't eaten since early this morning.

"Is there any food?" he asked.

"Sandwiches. I forgot. They should still be okay to eat."

He smiled as he watched her rush back and forth. He smiled at how grateful she was. He had dragged the maintenance man to the water's edge, waded in with him, then pushed him and watched as he floated away. The water wasn't more than twenty feet from the door. The eye of the storm was passing over. The storm would return; the ocean would surge and flood at least the first floor.

He smiled as Sharon handed him a packet of sandwiches.

213

He bit into one. "No mustard?" He watched as she rushed to the kitchen. Poor Sharon, by the time the wind and the rain came again, she would be dead.

Marti couldn't concentrate on the cribbage game. Ben wasn't attentive either.

"So," she said, "what's bothering you?"

"Oh, a missing girl, her missing mother, a dead steward, a few other women who are missing. The same things that are worrying you."

She tossed in her hand.

Ben scooped up the cards and put the cribbage pegs in the compartment on the underside of the board. "Those guys from the ship haven't gone anywhere," he said. "Let's find them."

The crew members were still in the dining room. They waved and grinned as Marti and Ben joined them.

"There is something else we can tell you?" the round-faced man asked.

"Tell me about the missing women," Marti said. "How did you find out about them?"

"Oh, when we got to Fort Lauderdale a couple of weeks ago, the police came to the ship. They had pictures for us to look at. I didn't remember either of the women who had boarded our ship."

"What happened to them?" Marti asked.

The man shrugged. "Nobody knows. They are gone."

"Disappeared," one of the other men offered.

"They came to the island on a daytrip," the man with the high voice said. "They boarded to go back to the States but never got there."

"Do you know anything else about them? What did they look like?"

"Not bad for their age," the round-faced man said. "Typical seekers."

"Seekers?"

"Yah. They are older, come on board with a younger man, enjoy the casino, the island, go home to their husband."

"Were these two women married?" Marti asked.

. "Oh yes, and I take it they left a bundle somewhere, either at the slot machines or in some other man's pocket. At least that's what Louis said."

"Louis," Marti said, "the steward who was just found dead?"

"Yes," the high-pitched voice said, "Louis the thinker. I think this time he thought too much about something he should not have thought about at all." His laugh was more like a cackle.

The men around the table laughed, too.

"Did you notice many gamblers on this cruise where Louis died? Maybe one who had been there before?"

"Oh yes, there were several who had sailed with us more than once."

"Was the man I described to you one of them?"

"Yes," the round-faced man said, "he was."

"Was he on board when either of the two women went missing?"

"That," the round-faced man said, "I could not tell you. Too bad Louis isn't here. I bet he would know."

When they returned to the booth in the lounge, Ben sat across from her and said, "Sharon doesn't fit the gambler's profile, does she?"

"That depends on how you look at it. Those women were marks because they were vulnerable, not necessarily because they were old."

"But Sharon doesn't have any money."

"I know," Marti said. She thought about that. Like her, Sharon had a pension plan, a 401K, none of which she could access now, and her life insurance. "Not alive, Ben," she said. "Not alive."

"So he married her." Ben leaned back, then said, "Wait a

minute, Marti. We're making this up as we go along, and it's getting pretty far-fetched. Maybe we just have too much time on our hands."

"I know," she admitted. "It's just that this Louis was killed while Sharon was on board that ship. And other women on that ship have disappeared. I'm just so worried about her and Lisa. What if something happens to them?" Bringing Lisa over was something else that she didn't understand. And with a one-way ticket. "Something isn't right Ben, I just know it."

He covered her hand with his. "We know that Sharon doesn't make smart choices when it comes to men. This time she wasn't just secretive, she was impulsive. Maybe she sent for Lisa on impulse, too." He was silent for a moment and looked worried. "If anything happens to Lisa, where is she? Do you think they lied when they said the plane landed okay?"

"Who knows," Marti said. She felt so useless. "Who knows. But I'll tell you one thing, as soon as this storm is over, we're going to Freeport. We are going to find Lisa and Sharon alive and well. And before I'm finished, I'll know everything there is to know about this DeVonte Lutrell, whether Sharon likes it or not."

She scooted out of her bench and onto Ben's and rested her head on his shoulder. "Let's go upstairs for a while," she said.

When Lisa reached the end of the road just past the lake, she knew that the pink motel was to her left even though she couldn't see it. The ocean was straight ahead. Trees were mid-trunk in the water and a boat shack was half-submerged. Unlike the wind, which was calm, the ocean raged. Waves crashed against the shore. One of the trees toppled over. She shivered, as much from cold as fear. Her chest still hurt, and whenever she stopped walking and rested for more than a few minutes, she got so cold her teeth began chattering. She felt chilled to the bone, an inner cold that required more than just a sweater or a jacket. A long soak in a hot tub was going to feel very good and then a bed piled high with blankets.

There was nothing but construction to her right, but there was a bend in the road. She decided to walk at least that far to see what was beyond it. The sky was getting dark again as if it was going to rain, and the wind was picking up, perhaps because she was so close to the ocean. She had gotten used to the quiet, the deserted road with nothing but uprooted trees and low scrub, but she had never been so alone in her life. She wanted to yell just to hear her own voice. She wanted to hear someone answer.

There was more construction beyond where the road turned, but maybe half a mile away, there was a two-story apartment building, painted pink. There were no other buildings. There was no other place that she could see where DeVonte could have been going. There was no sign that anyone was there, no cars parked outside, just overturned boats floating in what had been the yard. She walked as fast as she could, grateful now for the mud because even though it slowed her down, it kept the soles of her feet from getting sore.

It began raining as she walked, not gently, but a fierce rain that pelted her face and stung. Once she got to the building, she might be trapped there. Could the water rise high enough to cover the roof? Was it powerful enough to undermine the foundation and cause the building to cave in? She walked faster, ignoring the pain in her chest as long as she could, then slowed down to accommodate it.

Sharon shivered. Even with DeVonte's arms around her, she was afraid as they sat on the sofa in the living room and watched as the storm returned. The wind picked up all at once, soft as a whisper one minute, loud as an oncoming train the next. The tree trunk began to sway as it hung over the balcony railing. The branches rustled as they brushed against the carpet. The rain blew in through the broken patio door.

"Should we leave?" she asked.

"And go where?"

217

The last time she looked, the water was beginning to cover the steps. Soon it would be up to the door. Then what? Would the water come upstairs? She was afraid to ask. Would they be trapped here? Die here? She didn't want to know.

She snuggled deeper into the blanket, hiding her face. DeVonte had eaten all of the sandwiches. Now that they were gone, she was hungry. She was thirsty, too, but she did not want to move.

"That man," she said. "He . . . his . . . face . . . his . . . tongue . . ."

"Got the shit choked out of him, nosy bastard."

He sounded angry. His language surprised her. He seldom swore.

"He's downstairs," she said. "If the water comes up here, will he . . ."

"I got rid of him," DeVonte said.

Got rid of him? How did he know the man was down there? Unless . . . no, this storm was making her crazy.

"Did you rent a boat?"

"No."

"You were gone a long time."

"Had to make a quick trip to Nassau. Got stuck there until this morning. Not easy finding someone willing to fly out of there with this coming."

How did he know that man was dead? He wasn't here when it happened. Or was he? She was asleep by the time DeVonte had left.

"What do we do now?" she asked.

"Wait," he said.

"For what."

"For the weather to change." As he spoke, his grip tightened on her arm.

"We just sit here?" she asked. Why did he get rid of the man? What did he mean? What did he do with him?

"No hurry."

For what? No hurry for what? There was a loud whap as

218

something hit the roof. He knew the man was down there. He had gotten rid of him. Why? The palm fronds waved in slow, then frenzied gyrations. Why? Unless . . . nosy bastard, the man had seen her in the water. He had saved her. She wanted to get up, see how high the ocean was, how close it was to the front door. Water. Saltwater. In her mouth, in her nose, her eyes. She shuddered again, remembered the gurgle of the water as she flailed below the surface. She could almost feel the pull of the ocean, hear the rushing sound in her ears, feel her throat constrict as she fought against swallowing, breathing. She huddled against DeVonte, remembered the back of his head, bobbing in the water, not turning as she called to him, not turning until the man came running from the building. If it wasn't for the man, she would be dead. Now the man had been . . . choked . . . to . . . death. How did DeVonte know that? Why had he gotten rid of him? *Because if it wasn't for that man, she would have drowned.* She gasped, looked at DeVonte.

"No," she said. "No."

His hold on her arm tightened.

Yes," he said. "Yes." And he smiled.

When Marti awoke, the rain had stopped. She didn't hear the wind anymore either. She jumped up, pulled her robe around her, and went to the window. "Ben! Wake up! I think it's gone. It looks like the sun is coming out."

Ben sat up and rubbed his eyes.

"Hurry up!" she said. "Get dressed and go find the man who told you he could get us to Freeport. Hurry! I'll pack and meet you at the airport."

Thirty minutes later she had packed, checked out, and found a taxi driver willing to risk the rain-flooded streets.

Ben saw her right away and came over. "The eye has passed over Freeport, now they're getting the rest of the storm. The pilot says it's moving fast; we might be able to leave in another hour or so."

He looked at her for a moment. "You're sure about this. We'll be in a ten-seater with two wing-mounted engines."

"Will it get us there?"

"Three guys run this operation, all retired pilots, worked for United Airlines, and it's not a prop job. They know their stuff."

"You don't like small planes," she said.

"No, I've been called out a few times after they went down."

Marti ignored that. She had to find Lisa. She had to make sure Sharon was okay. "Any phone lines yet?" she asked.

Ben shook his head.

"The pilot thinks we might be able to leave in an hour?"

"Or thereabouts."

"Good, we've got time for coffee."

"No, DeVonte," Sharon moaned. She had managed to get free of the blanket before he did, but now he was twisting her arm behind her back. Why hadn't she listened when Marti tried to teach her self-defense? "Why, baby?" she asked. "It's me and you out here. It'll always be me and you." He didn't even answer, just pushed her toward the door.

"We're going for another swim," he said. "Just me and you."

"No, God no. Not the water. Not again." She tried to get free. He gave her arm another twist. As they walked down the stairs, all she could remember was Marti telling her to hold her fingers straight out and poke him in the eyes.

The water was covering the steps. She stepped into it and slipped. She slid down until she was sitting on the floor with water up to her shoulders. DeVonte landed on top of her. He had let go of her arm. Her head was against the bannister. Water filled her mouth. The edge of the step pressed against her back. DeVonte's knee was pressing into her stomach. The water surged and pushed them back. DeVonte grunted, moved away. The pressure on her back eased. Her right hand was pinned beneath her. He stood, pulled her up, pushed her against the wall. She kept her hand down, fingers pointed.

"Don't hurt me," she said.

"No time."

"Let's just get out of here, please. Let's go home."

He grabbed her by the throat. She brought her hand up, thrust her fingers forward. He yelled and released her.

She screamed as she waded into the water, lost her balance, fell down. She felt his hand on her back and screamed again.

Lisa heard the screams above the wind and began running toward the pink house. She could hardly breathe for the pain, and wrapped her arms around her body like a brace. The water had reached the first-floor windows, and she could hear glass pop and shatter. Another scream and she was still too far away. The water was rushing across the road, swirling at her ankles, almost to her knees. A piece of wood whacked her on the shin. There was another scream.

"Sharon!" she yelled. "Is that you? Sharon!"

Her call was answered with a scream.

She had to hold her arms out to keep her balance as the water surged across the road and into the field. The pains in her chest were sharp and swift. She stopped, gasped, then pushing against the force of the water, she went on.

Sharon made it through the front door. Rain slapped against her face like a huge wet hand. DeVonte kept grabbing at her back. He almost gripped her shoulder.

"Godammit!" he swore. Water splashed.

She kept moving, holding the bannister as she went outside, sliding and tumbling until the water was over her head. Her feet touched ground. She fought her way to the surface. The ocean had rushed into and past the house. There were no trees, no hibiscus. Just the water. She would have to swim, but how far? The water was rushing toward the road that was on the other side of the house. A capsized boat banged against a first-floor balcony. Palm trees floated past. The current was swift. If she could get clear of the house, it would push her in the right direction.

"Sharon! Help me! I can't see."

She looked back. He was floundering in the water.

"Sharon. You blinded me, you bitch. I can't see."

She turned away. The water was rising higher. A log that had broken away from some pilings grazed her leg. Others moved fast with the current.

"Sharon!"

There was a loud groan. He didn't call her name again. When she looked back, all she could see were the logs as they battered the house.

"Sharon!"

The water was pushing her now. She swam with it.

"Sharon! Is that you?"

It wasn't DeVonte, but who . . .

She was getting closer to land. She tried to stand. Her feet touched bottom, but the water was moving too fast.

"Sharon!"

"I'm here!" she managed to yell. Who was it? Marti?

"Can you see the tree?"

She saw palm fronds. "Yes."

"Meet me at the tree!"

Lisa? It couldn't be.

When she reached the tree, Lisa was leaning against it, clutching her chest.

"What are you doing here? Are you okay?"

"Where is he?" Lisa asked.

"Back there." Sharon nodded toward the condo. "I think."

She sagged against the tree and pulled Lisa against her. The water rushed past.

"What do we do?" Sharon asked.

"Hell, I don't know," Lisa said. "Drown."

"No," Sharon said. "There is no way in hell . . ."

Lisa's breathing sounded harsh and ragged. "Are you okay?" Sharon asked.

"I don't think so."

Sharon hugged and rocked her. "How did you get here?"

"He sent for me."

"DeVonte?"

"Yes."

When Sharon tried to hold her tighter, Lisa cried out.

"Oh, I'm so sorry; I didn't mean to hurt you."

They stayed there, cold, wet, shivering. The tree swayed in the wind, but it did not yield to the water.

While Marti paced from the window to the rows of seats, Ben changed their reservations to a three o'clock flight that afternoon.

"Optimist," she said.

"No. Once the weather clears, they won't waste any time getting the tourists back in here."

They waited for three hours until the pilot got clearance for a flight to Freeport. A copilot climbed in beside him. As the plane lifted off, she looked down. She could see areas that were flooded, even roof damage and uprooted trees. Boats were beached in the sand.

"We hardly took a hit," the pilot said.

Marti looked out the window again and wondered what a "hit" would have done.

The plane glided along as if there was only one air current. The sky was a clear, cloudless blue. It was as if the storm had left a profound peace in its wake.

It was dark when they reached Freeport. Looking down, Marti could see a few small patches of lights.

"Electricity is out on most of the island," the pilot told them. "They didn't get the full brunt of the storm, but there is major damage. Don't expect to get any telephone calls through. I'm not sure what kind of accommodations you'll find, or how you'll be able to get around. We're going to sleep in the plane. We won't leave before eight in the morning."

There was a bump as they landed. Marti counted three small prop jobs off the runway and damaged. Another was upside down.

She thought of the dead steward. "Where are the cruise ships?"

"A long way from here. They reroute them, but they won't stay away long. The casino should be up and running. If you need a place to stay, go there, if you can get there. Oh, and stick to bottled water and cans of soda."

The airport terminal was small. Marti spotted a young woman sitting at a desk and inquired about the pilot who had flown Lisa and DeVonte here from Nassau.

The woman checked a logbook. "That airplane is still hangared here," she said. "The pilot is probably at the casino."

Getting to the casino was impossible. The water was so high when they reached the street that any car that tried to get through would flood out.

"Boat, maybe," Ben said. "I can paddle a canoe."

Marti considered taking off her shoes and wading through the water to get to the casino. Any other means of transportation seemed unlikely. Instead, they went back inside. Ben returned to the woman at the desk while Marti used the facilities. When she joined him, he was talking to someone on a ham radio.

"The casino," he said. "A guy named Rommel is the pilot who brought them in." He spoke into the headset. "And you think they were going to other end of the island?" He listened. "That's where the boat taxi is?" He listened again. "Oh, there's a lake, and that's how you get across." He wrote a few things down in the margins of a newspaper. After a few minutes, he thanked Rommel and signed off.

"They did get here," he told her.

Marti felt so relieved she thought her legs were going to give way. She sat down. "And?"

"This DeVonte Lutrell said he was going to take a boat taxi

across the lake. It's a small lake near the end of the island. There's one motel out there, a restaurant, a lot of new construction, and a condo." He went to a machine and brought back two cups of coffee. "Now, you relax. There are emergency generators at all of the important places, like the casino; and this young lady, Dominique Bastion, is going to help me see what I can find out using this."

The young lady displayed double dimples as she smiled first at Ben, then at Marti.

"Put your feet up, Marti. Get some rest."

"I'm not tired," she protested.

"No, you're wired; same difference."

She put her feet up and picked up the paper cup. "Cocoa?"

"Drink up, you need something decaf, but that will have to do."

Marti sipped the hot chocolate. Lisa was here—somewhere on this island. Was she okay? Had she found Sharon? Was the damage from the hurricane as bad here as it was in Nassau? She massaged the throbbing that was beginning at her temples. She did not know where to begin. Did they even have a system in place here for finding people? Where were the police? Marti closed her eyes and rested her head against the plastic-covered, thinly upholstered chair. She could not remember the last time she had felt so frustrated. No transportation, no street to walk down, just a river to ford, no way to phone home. And—she looked about the room—with the exception of whatever was in both of those vending machines, no food. Her stomach rumbled. No point in getting hungry, she admonished herself. No point at all in wanting something to eat. Her stomach grumbled again.

"They're at the hospital," Ben said.

Marti sat straight up. "Hospital? What hospital? Why? Who's at the hospital? Lisa? Sharon?"

"Slow down. It's okay. Relax. Lisa has a few cracked ribs. Sharon is with her."

"And Lutrell?"

"He's not there."

"Where is the hospital? How do we get there?"

"You rest," Ben said. "I'll take care of it."

"They're okay?"

"Yes, they're both okay."

"Thank God."

"The woman I spoke to said that she would get a message to Sharon."

Now if they could just figure out how to get there. She needed to see for herself that they were okay. Marti felt exhausted. The throbbing at her temples increased. She closed her eyes again. Ben was managing just fine without her. She would wait.

Sharon sat by the bed. There were three other patients in the room, all sleeping. She could tell that Lisa was getting groggy from the Demerol, but she was still awake.

"It's okay," she said. "We're safe. Sleep, Lisa. We're safe now."

"Marti," Lisa said. "Where . . ."

"She's somewhere on the island."

"She did come." Lisa closed her eyes and drifted off.

Sharon held on to Lisa's hand, even though Lisa didn't want her here. It was her fault that Lisa was calling for Marti, just as it was Rayveena's fault that when she got into trouble she went to Momma, Marti's mother, instead of her own kin. She hadn't meant for it to be this way. She had never intended to be anything like Rayveena, but she was. And now Rayveena was dying, and she was maintaining the legacy Rayveena had passed down. Lisa didn't want any part of her. Lisa wanted her best friend's mother to be her mother, too. That was her fault, not Lisa's.

She put her head on the bed and closed her eyes. Her clothes were still damp. Her hair was . . . as if she needed to worry about that now. No, she did need to think about that, think about anything but the water, and that dead man, and DeVonte. What had happened to him? The men who pulled them into the boat were going to take them to a shelter until they realized Lisa needed to be seen by a doctor. Was that where DeVonte was? In a shelter somewhere on the island? Was Lisa telling the truth? Did he push her into the lake deliberately or was it an accident? She thought of that dead man, put her hands to her face as if that could block out the picture that came into her mind. "Choked to death," that's what DeVonte had said. That is what he had done. How could she have slept with someone like that, thought she loved someone like that, married someone like that? What was wrong with her?

17

SEPTEMBER 21

It was daybreak when Marti and Ben left the small terminal. The pilot who brought them here had agreed to wait until they returned. Outside, the water had not receded. Two men rowed them to dry land. Marti stared in disbelief as they passed wooden houses that had collapsed, others that had been pushed together. There were homes without roofs, without windows. In the distance she could see the ocean. A freighter, torn from its moorings, was partially beached on the sand. Along the shore, boats had been tossed and reduced to kindling. People clad in shorts or with their pants legs rolled up walked through the destruction, bending and stooping.

Ben took her hand. "Dear God," he said, "it's like 'Nam." There were tears in his eyes.

As they passed a stand of trees that had been felled by the storm, children sitting on the trunks and the branches smiled and waved to them, as if they had been through this before.

"Will someone help them?" Marti asked. "They have no homes."

"Aid comes," Ben said. "The Red Cross mobilizes real fast."

The boat stopped at a makeshift dock. A ladder leaned against it. When Ben tried to pay the two men, they waved the money away.

"Is storm, man," one said. "We are all neighbors when the storm comes."

228

"But I'm leaving here," Ben said, "later today. You have to stay. Now take this."

"The hospital is right up there." The man pointed. "That building halfway up the hill." This time he accepted what Ben gave him.

Plywood spanned the muddy gap from makeshift dock to dry land. As they walked along the paved road that led to the hospital, Marti tried not to look behind her. Here it was just fallen trees and jagged strips of tin, pieces of wood, and other debris. She could almost pretend she was walking through a vacant lot in Chicago. When she looked at the flooded street below, at the chaotic collapse of houses and the flooded streets, it spoke of a nightmare she had never experienced. She hoped she never would.

By the time they reached the hospital, Marti could hear birds singing. The trees clustered nearest the building had not been damaged. The breeze was light and sunshine warm on her arms. She could almost pretend yesterday and last night had not happened. Almost.

"Ma! Ben!" Lisa held out her arms to them.

Ben reached her side first. He looked at the IV with a critical eye. "Are you feeling okay?"

"I want to go home. Please take me home with you. I don't ever want to see an island again."

Marti went over to Sharon and hugged her. "You okay?" she whispered into her hair.

"No." Sharon's shoulders shook. She began crying.

Ben came over. "Let me talk to the doctor, see if Lisa can leave." He patted Sharon's shoulder. "Are you going to be all right?"

Sharon sobbed.

From the bed Lisa said, "Calm down, Sharon. Everything's okay now." She didn't sound angry, but she spoke with adolescent impatience.

Marti wanted to know what had happened, how Lisa and

Sharon had found each other, where DeVonte was, but she didn't think this was the right time to ask. She led Sharon to a chair, gave her some Kleenex, and went to Lisa. She had to find out.

"What happened? Why are you here?"

Lisa looked at Sharon. "I'll tell you later." When we're alone, her expression implied. "Do you think I'm going to have to stay here? They're giving me stuff for the pain."

"Ben is a licensed RN. If you can be moved, I'm sure they'll release you to him."

Marti returned to Sharon. Her sobs had subsided. She sniffed and blew her nose, but said nothing.

"We can talk later," Marti said. "Right now I just want all of us out of here."

Sharon nodded but kept her head down. She didn't say anything about DeVonte Lutrell, so Marti didn't mention him either.

Ben returned a few minutes later. "Well," he said, "I don't know how to tell you this. . . ."

"Oh no," Lisa wailed. "I have to stay here."

Ben smiled. "No, but you might wish you did. We're going to get you to the water's edge in a wheelchair. Then you've got to get into a rowboat."

"What?"

"Everything at the bottom of this hill is flooded. You should see what it looks like out there."

"I was in it," Lisa said. "I know."

"What?"

Sharon's sobs got louder.

"Later," Lisa said.

Marti looked from Lisa, who looked sad and bewildered, to Sharon, who was sobbing uncontrollably. Maybe she didn't want either of them to tell her what had happened. Then again, she did want to know.

18

Marti missed roll call the following morning. She awakened to the sounds of her kids getting ready for school and hurried downstairs. Joanna was standing at the stove with her back to her. She didn't turn or speak. Theo and Mike jumped up from the table, rushed over, and took turns hugging her.

"Are you two all right?"

Their faces were solemn as they nodded. Momma told her Theo had had a nightmare the night she was gone. That hadn't happened in a long time.

"Did you see Ben before he took Momma and Sharon to Chicago?"

Another nod.

"I'm sorry. There was no way we could call when you were at home. We were lucky to get through at all." She had apologized at least five times.

"We know, Ma," Mike said.

Theo looked down at his shoes. He was still upset with her.

"It's not like it is here," she said. "We take a lot for granted."

She put her arms about their shoulders and pulled them to her. "I didn't know what it would be like there."

Both boys nodded.

Mike said, "We know."

Theo said, "It looked really scary when they showed the storm. The trees were knocked down, and the houses were gone."

She hugged him. "Everyone there was so brave. There was so much destruction. They must have lost so much, but nobody was crying. And," she said, "they had been through it before. They knew what to do. Nobody died."

"They didn't say that on the news," Theo said. This time, when he hugged her, he grinned and gave her a kiss.

She walked over to Joanna, whose back was rigid as she stirred something on the stove.

"Oatmeal," Marti said.

"We're not eating any," Mike and Theo said in unison. "We want cold cereal."

"This is good for you," Joanna told them.

Marti thought of the times Momma comforted herself by preparing food. "You were worried about Lisa, weren't you?"

"I was worried about you and Ben making it through that hurricane. I was mad at Lisa. Sharon, too. Just wait until Lisa's feeling better. Taking off like that and leaving a note! As for Sharon, what was she thinking of? Anyone besides herself?" She sprinkled more cinnamon on the oatmeal, which was thick and lumpy and sticking to the sides of the pan. "If they want to be part of this family, they are going to have to be more considerate, both of them."

"Do you want them to be part of this family?"

Joanna turned to her. "Lisa's like a sister to me, a dumb sister, but she'll be okay when I'm finished with her."

"And Sharon?"

"She is a dumb sister, too—but she's your sister, Ma, not mine. You handle it."

"Nice of you not to try to take on both of them yourself."

Joanna gave her that look that said, I know you're being a smart mouth, but it's okay.

"I looked in on Lisa," Marti said, "she's still sleeping. Momma's church sister said she would get here before you left for school and keep an eye on her."

"Good. She shouldn't be alone. She woke up half a dozen times last night, scared and crying."

"Neither of them has told me everything that happened, not yet anyway."

Joanna dropped the spoon in the oatmeal and turned off the burner. "I'm sure Lisa will tell me, whether I want her to or not."

When Joanna got this grumpy, she was more than a little upset.

"I didn't realize how worried you and Theo and Mike would be," Marti said. "I'm sorry."

Marti hugged Joanna, and Joanna clung to her. There were tears in Joanna's eyes when she let go.

When Marti got to the office, Vik jumped up and came over to her.

"You okay?"

"I'm fine," she said. She was as tired as usual, and the experiences of the past few days had aged her about ten years; but otherwise, she did feel okay.

He looked her up and down, then said, "Where were you during the hurricane?"

"In a casino."

"Win anything?"

"I didn't make any bets."

He checked her out again. "Had breakfast? My nephew went over there. He didn't like the food at all, said it just wasn't American."

"Breakfast sounds good," she admitted.

"Too bad. You got a call from Nan Conser, and we've got to go see the lieutenant."

"Nan! She's okay."

"She left this number for you."

It was a Chicago area code. Marti picked up the phone.

"Nan . . . what on earth . . ."

"Could you just come here, please. I need to talk to you, and I need to know what's going on."

While Marti took down the address and promised to get

there as soon as she could, Vik scooped up a couple of files, checked his in-basket, pulled out a report, and said, "Come on," when she hung up. "I'll fill you in."

She had to walk fast to keep up with him.

"They found the bodies buried inside the shed on Lucy's property. There was a dirt floor. They weren't buried deep. They found bits of clothing, leather that hadn't deteriorated too much, and some ID. They're still confirming the identification on the victims, and McIntosh is doing a postmortem on the remains."

"And all because of some paintings, pictures that you hang on the wall."

"Well, Lucy was a nutcase. You saw those crappy canvases that we took out of her closet. She was deranged. How else could anyone believe they could steal someone else's work to get attention, go out in a blaze of gunfire, and then have people discover what a genius they were?" He shoved the folders under his arm and headed down the hall. "Lucy couldn't paint cow dung with flies on it and make it look real. Five people dead," he said. "Stupid! Senseless and stupid!" He stopped and she almost bumped into him. "Just like your friend Sharon," he said. "You'd better keep an eye on her. She doesn't have any common sense either."

He was angry with her, too, or annoyed because he had been worried.

"Sorry," she said. "I had no idea what I was getting into when I flew to that island. But I was never in any danger. That casino was so insulated you couldn't even tell there was a storm outside unless you went to your room."

"Yeah? Well the next time, call."

"I couldn't."

"Don't give me that; you're a peace officer."

"That really didn't count for much, Jessenovik. I don't think that mattered to anyone at all."

* * *

When she knocked, then entered Lieutenant Dirkowitz's office, he was running his fingers through close-cropped blonde hair. He stopped with his hand still on his head.

"You okay?"

She nodded. Not him, too.

"Did you get in any swimming, Marti?"

"One swim before the storm hit."

"Oh yeah? Next time, we want souvenirs."

She grinned. "I'll try to remember that, sir."

"Solve any homicides while you were there?"

"No, but I found a few."

He ran his hand through his hair again. "Let them handle it."

"Yes, sir."

He waved them into chairs, then turned to Vik. "So, Jessenovik, how's the digging going? My mother was not pleased to hear of Lucy Carlisle's demise, but she did say that the senior Mrs. Carlisle was so controlling and such a perfectionist that it was no wonder Lucy Junior stole other people's paintings. I didn't ask her what she meant by that, so I hope it's not important to your case."

Marti settled in with a can of diet pop, while Vik brought her and the lieutenant current on where they were with the case.

"She buried everything with them except their paintings," Vik said. "She should have buried her paintings down there, too. Unfortunately, she's willed them to the historic society. I think they're planning a bonfire."

While Vik was talking, Marti got a glimpse of the lake from the lieutenant's window. Like the ocean, it stretched to the horizon where the light gray of the water met the pale blue of the sky. *Peaceful*, she thought, like she hoped the ocean at Freeport was now.

Vik flipped open a folder. "We think the first two arms with hands are James Scott Benton and Victoria Lynn Dale. Hopefully we'll find some next of kin. We've got some information on the commune from the Michigan City Library archives. As for the other two arms with hands, there's nothing yet on who they might be."

The excluded, Marti thought. In her own way, Lucy was excluded, too, but because of her lack of artistic ability not in spite of it. "So," she said, "we don't know anything about the victims except perhaps these two names?"

"And unless there's someone out there who gives a damn," Vik said, "we might never know anything else."

The lieutenant picked up the apple-shaped hand grenade that he kept on his desk. She thought of the ravaged streets of the hurricane-devastated islands and what Ben had said about it being like 'Nam. *War,* she thought. *That's what it must have been like for Lisa and Sharon. "Never again war."* She wasn't sure who had said that. She thought it might have been a pope, but she didn't know which one. *"Never again war."* Whoever said it was right. Too bad that might never happen.

As soon as they finished talking with the lieutenant, they drove into Chicago. Traffic was light, and Marti was surprised at how fast they got there. Chicago was a city of neighborhoods. Nan was staying in a house in Lincoln Park. Black metal grills covered the first-floor windows and the front door. The space between the house and those on either side of it couldn't be more than five feet at the most. A black metal fence surrounded the property, and the gate was locked. Marti pushed the button beside the lock and watched as the curtains on the second floor moved. A few minutes later Nan came out of the front door with the keys to open the gate.

"Do you know how worried I was?" Marti said.

"And afraid that I was a killer," Nan answered, as they followed her inside.

"That, too."

The inside of the house was still being worked on. The downstairs rooms were bare and the walls in the process of being stripped. Upstairs, they sat in a small sitting room that looked out on the street. The wainscotting had been sanded. The chairs were comfortable, but old.

"I drove into the city to go to the Goodman Theater with a friend who's rehabbing this place," Nan said.

"And?" Marti asked.

"And we ate afterward, and it got late, so I stayed the night. Then I heard about Arlene on the news and got scared and stayed here."

"Why did you get scared?"

"I don't know exactly. But you were asking about body parts, and I remembered something about an arm being found years ago that I don't recall was ever identified. Now there was another one. And I remembered a picture of one of the exhibits and something that I had noticed before I gave them to you. I hadn't really paid much attention at the time because I was in a hurry, and I wanted them back as soon as possible. I was breaking the rules when I let you have them."

Nan stood up, walked to the window, looked out, then returned to the chair.

"And?" Marti prompted.

"The kid in the picture. The hippy. He was with Arlene. I don't know. I got scared when I heard about Arlene. I think I was afraid that that kid—who just didn't belong there—had killed someone; and that Arlene could identify him, so she was killed, too. I met him, you see. She introduced us. Scotty. No last name. And there was that picture of him. I could identify him. I know I should have gone to you, but I wasn't in Lincoln Prairie when Arlene died; and I didn't want to go back until you found whoever did it. I was safe here."

"You don't know why he was with Arlene?"

"He was looking for Lucy Carlisle, but he didn't know her last name. I didn't tell him. He looked much too scruffy and must have belonged to that commune. Lucy's mother would have been beside herself. Lucy had enough problems trying to please her mother, and I understood that. Everyone thought

Lucy was still at the commune that summer, but she wasn't; she was in some psychiatric place, for a while at least. There was a lot that went on then that nobody was supposed to know about, the commune, the stolen art. . . ."

"Stolen art?" Marti asked.

"Yes. I'm not sure Lucy could draw a stick figure and get the proportions right, but she was obsessed with being an artist, like her mother. I think they put her in this private psych place to get her off the hook for stealing art from the people at the commune."

"How do you know about all of this?"

"As an outsider, you mean?"

"Yes."

"How do you think I got to be a member of the art guild? Mrs. Carlisle thought that was a cheap way to buy me off once she'd had a few days to think about it. Not that I wanted to belong to that bunch of . . . I just wanted to show them that they weren't quite as exclusive as they thought they were."

"How did you find out about Lucy?"

"Oh, I eavesdropped on her mother when she came to the historic society. I was working there then as a volunteer, just as I do now."

"Did Arlene give Scotty Lucy's last name?" That could account for the pleased expression on Arlene's face in that photo.

"I don't know, maybe. Lucy and Arlene were not friends."

"Are you sure Lucy was institutionalized that summer, not perhaps the summer before or after the young man was here?"

"Yes, but it was a private place, and I don't think there was much wrong with Lucy because she came home on weekends."

"Was her mother there when she came home?"

"Maybe, maybe not. Mrs. Carlisle was a busy lady, spent time in the city, spent time with friends in Wisconsin. She was a real social butterfly, flitting from one place to another."

Which meant that Lucy could have had the opportunity to meet with Scotty alone. "I see," Marti said. "Well, we have identified the killer. So it is safe for you to return home."

"You're not going to tell me who it is?"

For some reason, Marti was reluctant to say. Perhaps because Lucy Carlisle's life was already so exposed and would undergo even more scrutiny. Perhaps because Lucy was someone's daughter and couldn't live up to it, or maybe she couldn't live it down.

"Check the newscasts," Marti said, "or the newspaper. You can go home. Everything is okay now."

It was late afternoon when Marti returned to Chicago. This time the traffic was bad. Momma had called and told her to come to the hospital and bring Lisa with her. Rayveena had gone into a coma. She packed Lisa into the backseat with pillows to cushion the ride. Traffic was bumper-to-bumper at ten miles an hour from Lake Cook Road all the way in to the Loop. Joanna skipped a basketball game to come with them.

When they reached the hospital room, Joanna put her arm around Lisa's shoulders. Momma, Ben, and Sharon were there with a white minister Marti didn't recognize. She guessed he was a hospital chaplain. They gathered around the bed and said the Lord's Prayer and the Twenty-third Psalm together. Then the minister shook everyone's hand and left.

Momma sat in a chair pulled close to the bed and put her hand on Rayveena's. "Be all right, child," she said. "There is a kind and loving God calling to you. It's okay to leave now. We're all here."

Momma looked up at Sharon, who shook her head.

Marti went over to the window where Sharon stood, and said, "You will go say good-bye to your mother. Momma says so." She took Sharon by the elbow and guided her to the bed.

Rayveena had always been thin, but that did not describe the way she looked now. Her bodily functions were shutting down. Her stomach was bloated, her face puffy, her eyes closed and sunk into their sockets. The hand with the IV was swollen.

As Marti watched, tears slipped down Sharon's face. "I only wanted a mother," she said, "like all the other kids had."

Joanna brought Lisa to the bed. "Bye, Ray . . . bye, Grandmother," she said, and turned away.

They sat then, and waited. Momma kept her hand on Rayveena's. "Be all right, child, be all right," she said, over and over. Rayveena hung on for another hour. They could hardly tell when she stopped breathing.

Marti took Sharon home in her car, while Ben drove the others in the van. On the way, Sharon told her some of what had happened in Freeport. She described without emotion how she had found the handyman's body, and she didn't cry until she talked about DeVonte trying to kill Lisa. "The water," she sobbed, "the water. It was almost as if it was alive."

The way she said it made Marti wonder if DeVonte had tried to drown her, too, but Marti didn't say anything. Sharon would tell her when she was ready. The island authorities still had not found DeVonte's body.

Marti made sure that everyone was at home and with Momma. Then she returned to the precinct. Then she got on the phone to the Fort Lauderdale police and told them what she knew. They had identified a man that fit DeVonte's description during their investigation of five missing women, but they didn't have a name until she called.

Vik came in while she was on the phone. When she hung up, he said, "Too many crazies out there. I'm not even going to ask about this one."

She told him anyway.

"Know what we need?" he said. "A vacation. A long vacation."

"Not to the islands," Marti said.

"At least six months," he went on. "Door County maybe, or the Upper Peninsula. Things like this don't happen there."

"Right," Marti said, "don't subscribe to their local newspapers."

"You eat yet?" Vik asked.

When she said no, he suggested the Barrister.

"We've just about got this arms-with-hands business wrapped up," he told her on their way out.

The Barrister was crowded for a weeknight. Even though it was only September and it wasn't that cold yet, there was a fire burning low in the fireplace. A real fire, not the gas-fed logs that Marti had had installed at home. That and the dark wood and deep red upholstery and globe-shaped candles burning at the tables created a homey atmosphere that was relaxing. She ordered the shepherd's pie again. Vik ordered it, too.

"So what have we got?" she asked.

"Everyone is identified now, at least tentatively, and all of the victims lived at that commune," Vik said. "We may never know why the second two came here—looking for our Jane Doe Lily Day and John Doe, maybe. Maybe they were after their artwork. Lucy was showing it around town. We're having one hell of a time tracking down next of kin. My guess is that they were either loners or estranged from their families."

"And Arlene?" Marti was convinced that she'd died because she knew too much and had made the mistake of telling Lucy or gloating over it. She didn't think Arlene would have told her. It would have been much more satisfying to hold it over Lucy, just as Nan had held what she knew over Lucy's mother. "We knew when we began asking questions that we might smoke out the killer."

"But we didn't know that Lucy would shoot herself. I checked this morning. That's how her mother died."

The waitress brought their salads and more hot coffee.

"How was the food over there?" Vik asked.

"There's no place like home," Marti answered.

19

The special Sunday dinner was Momma's idea; but as Marti looked at everyone sitting around the table, she realized how happy she was that they were all here. Vik was so solicitous of Mildred. While Vik was helping her take off her coat, Mildred caught Marti's eye, winked, and smiled. Tony, Joanna's boyfriend—for today, at least—had helped out in the kitchen. Marti found it hard to believe, but he actually agreed with Joanna's dietary restrictions and was taking zinc, vitamin C, and drinking an herbal tea to ward off a cold.

Their next-door neighbors, Patrick and Peter, had come with their parents and brought something called Crazy Salad, multicolored chunks of Jell-O and diced fruit topped with walnuts, raisins, and whipped cream. Marti had had little time to socialize since they'd moved in and was a bit apprehensive until she found out the boys' father was a Chicago attorney.

Lisa was still moving carefully. She and Sharon were still prone to crying jags, but less frequently since Rayveena's funeral. Best of all, Momma had decided that Sharon should move into the apartment above the garage, at least temporarily. Nobody argued with Momma.

This was the first time Marti had seen Lupe out of uniform in months. She was showing Mike and Theo how to fold paper napkins into swans. When Lupe had come through the door, Ben had leaned over and whispered, "She might as well have cop written on her forehead."

"Once a cop . . . ," Marti said. They both laughed softly.

Denise had come early, taken off her hat, and gotten to work helping Momma in the kitchen. Now she came through the door into the dining room wearing one of Momma's aprons and carrying a turkey, fat and brown. Momma followed with her famous, honey-cured, brown-sugar-smoked ham, covered with pineapple slices.

When everyone was seated, Ben said the blessing.

"Dear Lord, we thank You for the fellowship of those who have joined us at this table. We ask You to watch over and protect those who could not be with us today. We ask that You receive those who have come to Your presence. We thank You for the food on this table and we ask that You help us share our blessings with others."

They all said amen.

Marti looked at Ben and gave him a thumbs-up. Their day of Thanksgiving had come early this year, and they all had so many reasons to be grateful.

OCTOBER 12

DeVonte Lutrell stood on the top deck of the cruise ship and watched as the bow cut through the Pacific Ocean. It was dark and cold. He shivered as he pulled up the collar of his jacket. As he stood there, the distant sound of ukuleles wafted toward him. He was on his way to Hawaii. It was hard giving up the cruise ships and the route to the islands that he was so familiar with. But all cruise ships must be pretty much the same. Soon he would find another place where a body could disappear. He had already found the woman who would fall silently into the ocean and sleep in the deep water forever. Smiling, he stroked his new beard. That, a mustache, a different hairstyle, and hair dye completed his new image. Still smiling, he went to the stairs, ducking his head against the wind and holding onto the railing as he climbed to the third deck.